Anthony Gilbert and The Murder Room

››› This title is part of The Murder Room, our series dedicated to making available out-of-print or hard-to-find titles by classic crime writers.

Crime fiction has always held up a mirror to society. The Victorians were fascinated by sensational murder and the emerging science of detection; now we are obsessed with the forensic detail of violent death. And no other genre has so captivated and enthralled readers.

Vast troves of classic crime writing have for a long time been unavailable to all but the most dedicated frequenters of second-hand bookshops. The advent of digital publishing means that we are now able to bring you the backlists of a huge range of titles by classic and contemporary crime writers, some of which have been out of print for decades.

From the genteel amateur private eyes of the Golden Age and the femmes fatales of pulp fiction, to the morally ambiguous hard-boiled detectives of mid twentieth-century America and their descendants who walk our twenty-first century streets, The Murder Room has it all. ›››

The Murder Room
Where Criminal Minds Meet

themurderroom.com

Anthony Gilbert (1899–1973)

Anthony Gilbert was the pen name of Lucy Beatrice Malleson. Born in London, she spent all her life there, and her affection for the city is clear from the strong sense of character and place in evidence in her work. She published 69 crime novels, 51 of which featured her best known character, Arthur Crook, a vulgar London lawyer totally (and deliberately) unlike the aristocratic detectives, such as Lord Peter Wimsey, who dominated the mystery field at the time. She also wrote more than 25 radio plays, which were broadcast in Great Britain and overseas. Her thriller *The Woman in Red* (1941) was broadcast in the United States by CBS and made into a film in 1945 under the title *My Name is Julia Ross*. She was an early member of the British Detection Club, which, along with Dorothy L. Sayers, she prevented from disintegrating during World War II. Malleson published her autobiography, *Three-a-Penny*, in 1940, and wrote numerous short stories, which were published in several anthologies and in such periodicals as *Ellery Queen's Mystery Magazine* and *The Saint*. The short story 'You Can't Hang Twice' received a Queens award in 1946. She never married, and evidence of her feminism is elegantly expressed in much of her work.

By Anthony Gilbert

Scott Egerton series

Tragedy at Freyne (1927)
The Murder of Mrs Davenport (1928)
Death at Four Corners (1929)
The Mystery of the Open Window (1929)
The Night of the Fog (1930)
The Body on the Beam (1932)
The Long Shadow (1932)
The Musical Comedy Crime (1933)
An Old Lady Dies (1934)
The Man Who Was Too Clever (1935)

Mr Crook Murder Mystery series

Murder by Experts (1936)
The Man Who Wasn't There (1937)
Murder Has No Tongue (1937)
Treason in My Breast (1938)
The Bell of Death (1939)
Dear Dead Woman (1940)
aka *Death Takes a Redhead*
The Vanishing Corpse (1941)
aka *She Vanished in the Dawn*
The Woman in Red (1941)
aka *The Mystery of the Woman in Red*
Death in the Blackout (1942)
aka *The Case of the Tea-Cosy's Aunt*
Something Nasty in the Woodshed (1942)
aka *Mystery in the Woodshed*
The Mouse Who Wouldn't Play Ball (1943)
aka *30 Days to Live*
He Came by Night (1944)
aka *Death at the Door*
The Scarlet Button (1944)
aka *Murder Is Cheap*
A Spy for Mr Crook (1944)
The Black Stage (1945)
aka *Murder Cheats the Bride*
Don't Open the Door (1945)
aka *Death Lifts the Latch*
Lift Up the Lid (1945)
aka *The Innocent Bottle*
The Spinster's Secret (1946)
aka *By Hook or by Crook*
Death in the Wrong Room (1947)
Die in the Dark (1947)
aka *The Missing Widow*
Death Knocks Three Times (1949)
Murder Comes Home (1950)
A Nice Cup of Tea (1950)
aka *The Wrong Body*

Lady-Killer (1951)
Miss Pinnegar Disappears (1952)
aka *A Case for Mr Crook*
Footsteps Behind Me (1953)
aka *Black Death*
Snake in the Grass (1954)
aka *Death Won't Wait*
Is She Dead Too? (1955)
aka *A Question of Murder*
And Death Came Too (1956)
Riddle of a Lady (1956)
Give Death a Name (1957)
Death Against the Clock (1958)
Death Takes a Wife (1959)
aka *Death Casts a Long Shadow*
Third Crime Lucky (1959)
aka *Prelude to Murder*
Out for the Kill (1960)
She Shall Die (1961)
aka *After the Verdict*
Uncertain Death (1961)
No Dust in the Attic (1962)
Ring for a Noose (1963)
The Fingerprint (1964)
The Voice (1964)
aka *Knock, Knock! Who's There?*
Passenger to Nowhere (1965)
The Looking Glass Murder (1966)
The Visitor (1967)
Night Encounter (1968)
aka *Murder Anonymous*
Missing from Her Home (1969)
Death Wears a Mask (1970)
aka *Mr Crook Lifts the Mask*
Murder is a Waiting Game (1972)
Tenant for the Tomb (1971)
A Nice Little Killing (1974)

Standalone Novels

The Case Against Andrew Fane (1931)
Death in Fancy Dress (1933)
The Man in Button Boots (1934)
Courtier to Death (1936)
aka *The Dover Train Mystery*
The Clock in the Hatbox (1939)

Tenant for the Tomb

Anthony Gilbert

An Orion book

This edition published by
The Orion Publishing Group Ltd
Orion House
5 Upper St Martin's Lane
London WC2H 9EA

An Hachette UK company
A CIP catalogue record for this book is available from the British Library

ISBN 978 1 4719 1038 8

www.orionbooks.co.uk

For Gillian Whitamore
With love

CHAPTER ONE

There were six passengers waiting for the stopping train to London that wet afternoon, sheltering in the glorified shed British Rail called a waiting-room. Penton was a small station on the Brigham-Morton line, and a train that would stop there would stop anywhere.

Dora Chester, trim and alert as a bird, surveyed her fellow-travellers with no notion that this was a day of crisis in her life. She was 29, with an apricot skin, smooth dark hair as lustrous as a horse-chestnut for all its colour, and as eager for experience as a terrier. She believed that the proper study of mankind is Man, and would pick up the evening paper before she so much as switched on the TV.

The sexes this gloomy afternoon were equally divided, though the youngest of the males, a youth with long hair and a fashionable leather jerkin, dissociated himself from the situation almost before it had turned into one. Both the others, however, would have repaid scrutiny in a much larger company. In appearance, they could hardly have presented a greater contrast. One, immaculately dressed, with a clever, clownish face, sat aloofly filling in *The Times* crossword with a gold pencil. Dora didn't need to see the trade mark to know that this was the real McCoy, not one of those got-up gilt affairs penurious friends find in little Italian gift-stores round about Christmas, packed in equally spurious gilt boxes. So far as his companions were concerned, they might have been as invisible as ghosts.

The second man was so different he might have stepped direct from a Mr Magoo cartoon. A sturdily rotund figure was clothed in a rather bright brown suit, while a checked cap to match was pulled over one bright brown eye below an eyebrow as red as a fox. He carried the sort of brief-case no school-child would be seen dead with these days, and had enormous hands and feet.

The two women were clearly travelling together, and neither looked at that moment as though she might be cast as the central figure in a *cause célèbre*. The one nearest Dora was agile and neat as a smart, slightly-outdated bird, the widow-bird who sat mourning for her love, perhaps, reflected Dora, whose father had been an unsuccessful man of letters. Her companion looked as though she'd dived into a dressing-up chest and dressed in the dark, with a preference for bright colours. She had a round pink face that should have looked silly, but somehow didn't, carried a big old-fashioned tapestry bag and wore fabric gloves. The pair made Dora think of a bear and its keeper, and she wondered if it was true that keepers could be pretty tough to their bears if they got obstreperous.

When no one had spoken for several minutes the Bear Lady said brightly that it was a nice day for the ducks.

The young man in the jerkin rose dramatically and muttering something about clichés, his God, hurled himself into the rain. The red-headed man, whose name proved to be Arthur Crook and whom they were all going to remember in due course, said in a voice that drowned the rain, which was saying something, 'And what's wrong with clichés? Don't occur to anyone that if a lot of chaps over a lot of time say the same thing there's likely to be some good sense in it.'

Dora grinned; it was the sort of come-back she appreciated. (Her brother, who was a Dean in the North, would have sided with the melodramatic young man.)

The clubman—so Dora thought of him, admitting that he might be a barrister, a doctor, (Harley Street type) or a con-man on the side—didn't look up, but she saw his pencil had remained stationary above its allotted square. And he hasn't finished writing in the clue, she discovered.

The voice of the boy came through the rain, muttering something about Zoos and their occupants.

'And he'd find some pretty healthy competition there,' opined Mr Crook.

The man with the clown's face bent it once more above his newspaper. He had thick dark hair just beginning to turn at the crest. Like a noble tufted duck, Dora decided.

The Bear Woman was chuckling. 'So comical,' she said to no one in particular. Nobody asked her what she meant, but the keeper (and Dora's instinct had led her to score a bulls-eye here) remarked in repressive tones, 'The train's almost due. Now, Imogen, wouldn't you like to make yourself comfortable before we go aboard?'

She made it sound like a journey to New Zealand, though the train's terminus was London, a distance of about seventy miles.

'I'm quite comfortable, thank you,' said the improbably-christened Imogen in a loud, clear voice.

The keeper looked slightly disconcerted. 'I think you'd better come with me to the Ladies,' she said.

'I'm surrounded by ladies practically all my life,' retorted her charge. 'A gentleman or two—' she beamed at Crook who beamed back, and at the clubman who paid no attention at all—'makes a nice change.'

The keeper caught Dora's sparkling glance. Dora, like Mr Crook, had no inhibitions about her interest in the human race. 'Perhaps,' the keeper suggested, 'you wouldn't mind staying with my friend while I . . . er . . .'

'It'll be a pleasure,' Dora assured her, meaning every word of it.

'Just see she doesn't wander out in the rain by herself, or —or stand too near the edge of the platform,' amplified the keeper, and she made a discreet retirement.

Imogen shifted a little along the bench. 'People are so

ungrateful about rain, aren't they?' she confided. 'Where would we be without it? Dying of thirst, I should think. The same with dust, I'm sure I was told as a girl that if there was no dust in the atmosphere we should all be roasted by the heat of the sun.' Carefully she abstracted her ticket from her glove and transferred it to her coat pocket. 'Miss Plum—that's what I call her, though she'd like to be called Victoria, her real name is Styles—thinks I'm a little potty. Did you notice?'

'It makes for variety,' suggested Dora resourcefully.

'The trouble is she's a conformist. I mean, she really does think that what was good enough for her father is good enough for her. No sense of progress. That's the trouble with our time—I call this the Computer Age, everyone made to look alike and think alike and act alike. I can't make Charles—that's my brother—understand that the pioneers of our day are those who won't conform. And it's necessary, I find—to express your individuality in quite definite ways. I mean, if we were all created in little bottles out of plasma or something—I don't understand much about science—then you'd expect us all to be alike, but we're *ourselves*. And nowadays to want to be yourself is called abnormal. But if anyone's crazy, who's to say if it's them or me? I mean, who's ever been able to define the norm?'

'I've always thought the norm was oneself,' said Dora, 'and the rest of the world—all those who differ from you, I mean—is ab or sub.'

Once again the clubman's pencil poised above an empty square, and yet he hadn't given the least hint of being interested in anything either of these two gossipy women had been saying. Mr Crook, on the other hand, was shamelessly absorbed.

'I couldn't have put it better myself,' he congratulated Dora. 'And why not? A world where everyone was the same would be like living in a box of tin soldiers.'

'Is she your sister?' Dora asked Imogen, shamelessly inquisitive.

The Bear Woman chuckled again. 'You ask her that, only make sure there's no milk standing about at the time,' she said.

'Meaning it might turn sour?' suggested Dora.

'I can see you've suffered too. As a matter of fact, I think she's hired to get me out of the way.'

The clubman, whose name was Ambrose Martin and who was actually a doctor, groaned—another persecution complex and no skin off his nose, he decided—and went back to his crossword. Mr Crook leaned forward to ask with every appearance of interest, 'Any special reason, Sugar, or just a homicidal turn of mind?'

'Oh, I don't mean out of the way into the *churchyard*,' cried Imogen. 'Nothing so melodramatic as that. Anyway, it would be much too risky and Charles—that's Charles Garland, my brother, he's a Member of Parliament, has his Position to Consider.' Her voice, which was unexpectedly deep and melodious, conveyed her meaning better than the actual words. 'That's why he gets so—so exasperated if I do anything in the least original. Undesirable publicity, he calls it—for him, I mean.'

'I'm still not quite sure where Miss Prim comes in,' hinted Dora, not seeing why the Gingerbread Man should have it all his own way.

'Not Prim—Plum,' corrected Imogen. 'Because of her christened name—Victoria, you see. She's supposed to Keep An Eye on me to make sure I Toe The Line. It was Flora's idea—Flora's my sister-in-law, and she and Miss Plum met at school or somewhere, at least that's what Flora says. But it would never surprise me to find that Miss Plum's a witch. One of these days she'll snap her fingers and I shall turn into a puff of dust—at least, I think that's what Flora hopes.'

'Always a mistake to hurry Nature,' suggested Mr Crook.

'I mean, that's what we're all going to turn into eventually. Still—' he sounded puzzled—'if you really believe she's a danger to you, shouldn't you be doing something about it? Speaking as the law . . .'

The doctor uttered for the first time. 'I'd no idea the law was so comprehensive,' he said.

'Most chaps don't,' agreed Mr Crook. 'That's the law's main defence.'

'I don't think I've seen you before,' continued Imogen, addressing Dora.

'I don't actually live here yet. I've just bought a rather ramshackle cottage at Ditcham. Do you know . . .?'

'The haunted one near the church?' Imogen clapped her hands. 'We heard it had been sold and naturally we wondered—they say a ghost haunts around there. Perhaps he'll come to call.'

'Why should he be interested in me?'

Mr Crook, watching and listening, was fascinated, not in the least aggrieved at being bored. You'd have said only two zanies could have carried on such a conversation, but both women were as earnest as missionaries.

'You haven't lived in the country?' suggested Imogen. 'In the country everybody calls on new-comers.'

'I can see I'm never likely to be lonely,' agreed Dora. But then she'd never been lonely in London, and didn't understand how anyone could be, unless they made a fetish of solitude. 'You must come and see me when I'm settled in,' she went on enthusiastically.

'That would be nice,' Imogen agreed. 'Perhaps the ghost would drop in that afternoon, too.'

Mr Crook wasn't surprised to realize that most women, even when they're past their first youth and live lives that would be intolerable to his sex, find mere existence enthralling. The way they accepted challenges tossed out in the dark with no hesitation at all made his hair curl.

'*She* thinks I know too much,' Imogen confided in a thrilling whisper, 'It's like that quotation about a little knowledge being a dangerous thing—though of course the real word is learning. And I told them, the 3.22 to London is a stopping train, it doesn't only stop at all the stations, it stops between most of them.' She had passed from a confederate's whisper into an afternoon tea tone of voice with no hesitation whatsoever. Another example of feminine guile, reflected Mr Crook. 'Are you ready, Miss Plum?' The little bear-leader had come snaking back unobserved by any of them, and only heard, apparently, by her charge. Must have better hearing than a bat, Mr Crook thought. Wonder what made her so sharp. 'We've been having such an interesting conversation about the norm,' Imogen continued.

The roar of the approaching train could now be heard. The doctor folded his newspaper and hung a gold-mounted umbrella over his arm. He set a hat that would have kept a dog in dinners for a month on his fine head and strolled out to the platform.

'Come along, Imogen,' fussed Miss Plum, 'you know you don't want to miss the train.'

'I don't mind whether we miss it or not,' returned Imogen placidly. 'We're only going to London so that you can go to Madame Tussaud's. Of course, the Chamber of Horrors, that's interesting. Everyone looking so ordinary you can't help wondering if they ever dreamed they'd achieve greatness in that particular way.'

'Greatness!' snorted Miss Plum, hooking her arm into her companion's.

'Well, publicity anyhow. Wouldn't you rather be famous in the Chamber of Horrors than be one of the people no one's ever heard of?'

'Don't suppose they'd any more notion they'd end up there than you or me,' said Mr Crook kindly. 'Well, stands to reason—if murderers thought they were going to be caught they wouldn't commit murder.'

'But don't they ever suppose anyone's going to be cleverer than them?' demanded Imogen ungrammatically.

'Now, Imogen . . .'

Imogen pulled back. 'No, do let him tell me. If I planned to put a knife into you, Vicky, I'm sure everyone would guess within the first five minutes.'

'Your true murderer doesn't believe anyone exists cuter than himself,' Crook assured her. 'Vanity's the first weapon you need.'

'So you'd be better at it than me,' observed Imogen simply to her companion.

Miss Plum, paying no attention to all this folderol, pinched Imogen's arm more tightly in her own and began to drag her charge up the platform.

'Aren't you coming with us?' enquired Imogen over her shoulder, addressing Dora who had stood by enthralled by the interchange.

'After you,' said Mr Crook. He shoved his disreputable brief-case under one arm, and he now put out a hand not much larger than a leg of mutton and caught Dora by the elbow. 'Wet underfoot,' he explained, 'don't want you slipping about, holding up the train, maybe, with a broken leg or what-have-you.'

With a hiss that wouldn't have shamed a serpent, Miss Plum marched off with her charge. Crook came behind them so closely he almost trod on their heels.

'Right up at the front, I think,' decided Miss Plum. 'Not so far to walk the other end. Lift your feet, dear, that's how you slip.'

They trampled to the far end of the platform; the leather-coated youth had already contracted out of the situation. Soon they reached the point where there was no more shelter from the rain.

'Is there any special reason for us getting wet, too?' gasped Dora.

'Don't know about you,' said Mr Crook grimly, 'but I don't have time to come down to this misbegotten part of the world—and apologies to you if you're coming to live in it—to attend an inquest.'

Dora was so startled she came to a dead stop. 'But you can't mean . . .'

'Make with the feet,' suggested Mr Crook. 'And in any case I don't like seeing even tough old birds mangled under engines.'

'But Imogen herself said . . .'

'To the pure all things are pure, and I'd say purity was her middle name. She may think of her Miss Plum as a keeper, but it don't occur to her she'd go as far as murder.'

'And you think she might?' A frisson of excitement disturbed Dora's spine.

'There's some chances even Arthur Crook don't take. Look out.' He jerked Dora forward so sharply she nearly fell on her nose. It was a nice nose, but perhaps a shade too long for innocent grace. It twitched and assimilated and altogether took more interest in its neighbours than many of them found becoming.

The train had now come to a smooth halt. The official, who seemed to combine the offices of ticket-clerk and station-master, and probably ticket-collector when occasion demanded, was dealing with a few bags and boxes that were to be loaded for London. The doctor snapped open the door of a first-class carriage some distance down the platform. Imogen had pulled a card and pencil out of her enormous bag and was leaning forward to inspect the engine.

'It's not like the old steam ones,' she said mournfully. 'Do you remember the lovely names they had, Vicky? The Flying Queen and the Silver King—now it's all that horrid little British Lion—if I were a lion I'd bring an action for —for defamation of character. After all, lions are the kings of beasts and go around in a pride. Oh!'

It all happened so quickly that even Dora who was watching the couple couldn't have said precisely what happened. At one moment Imogen was trying to note a number, the next her feet seemed to fly from under her, her floppy hat, lightly attached to her bird's-nest of hair by a couple of pins, fell into her eyes, she grabbed wildly at the air with her free hand. (Miss Plum had tight hold of the other.) But in an effort to aid her companion Miss Plum's grip loosened. Someone screamed. Dora? Imogen? Even Dora couldn't be sure. What she did realize was that the hand grasping her elbow had shot out and caught that wildly waving arm.

'Give a hand, can't you?' yelled Mr Crook. 'We ain't in Madame Tussaud's—yet.'

Dora resourcefully caught the poor lady by the collar of her coat, Miss Plum snatched at her other arm.

'Gently does it,' warned Crook. 'No need to break any bones. The rest of us aim to get to London in one piece and we aim to do it in time.'

The ticket-man-cum-station-master, who had hitherto been occupied loading bags into the van, and who wouldn't have looked out of place in some stylish Victorian melodrama—*The Bells*, say—came marching up to the group.

'You want to be careful, lady,' he said in severe tones to Imogen, who was trying to re-pin her hat and fluff out her hair. Dora stooped and picked up the immense embroidery bag Imogen carried on her wrist.

But Miss Plum was a match for any railway official. 'My friend slipped,' she said. 'I warned you against wearing rubber soles,' she added to Imogen.

'Good thing for you there were people close by to give you a hand,' said the man, not abating his severity one jot. If he heard Mr Crook's throaty mutter, 'Which way?' he paid no heed.

'Very lucky,' agreed Imogen weakly.

'We had better get in,' announced Miss Plum. 'We've

delayed everyone long enough.' She opened a carriage door and hustled her companion inside. As Crook, his hand once more on Dora's arm, moved towards a carriage a little lower down, Miss Garland pushed her head out of the window to shout, 'The Lord looks after His Own. And thank you very much.'

Presumably Miss Plum pulled her inside before she could attract any more attention. The clubman had vanished through the door of a first-class carriage and dissociated himself from what he probably regarded as a common brawl.

'I'd like a gold sovereign for everyone I've known who put his or her faith in that saying,' observed Mr Crook vigorously, 'and look where some of them are now. Get in, sugar. Y'know, it strikes me old Miss Dot-and-Carry-One ain't the only person in need of a guardian angel. What was she saying—Dotty, I mean—before the tamasha started?'

'Nothing much,' murmured Dora vaguely. 'Well, you heard what she said about them wanting her out of the way, and something about knowing too much.'

'Could be that don't suit Miss Plum's book. And now it could be you know too much.' Disregarding Dora's protest, 'But I don't know anything,' he swept on, 'But Miss P. can't be sure of that. So you don't travel alone, see. Company of a wolf may not be your idea of the ideal traveller, but wolves have been known to keep off intruders.'

'How melodramatic can you get?' Dora murmured. 'Anyway, I'm not travelling in their carriage.'

'Nothing to prevent Miss Plum making a trip to the loo, coming in here for a word of explanation—poor lady! (he tapped his forehead suggestively)—not too well furnished in the upper story, you do understand—and somehow you fall out of a window.'

'Perhaps,' suggested Dora resourcefully, 'I have the faith that moves mountains.'

'Dames slay me,' said Mr Crook respectfully. 'Never seems

to go through their minds that the mountain might move in on them.'

'Are you sure we ought to have left them alone?' Dora enquired. 'There wasn't anyone else in the carriage.'

'Oh, there won't be a second attempt, not this afternoon,' promised Mr Crook comfortably. 'Miss Plum's got the sense to know it 'ud be in the paper and one of us would see it, if it was only three lines on the back page, and she won't want to be asked a lot of awkward questions. No, you take my word, she'll let a little while go by. I wonder—' he broke off—'why anyone should want Dotty out of the way?'

'There's something she knows,' Dora reminded him. 'Though she doesn't look the kind who'd know anything deadly . . .'

'Or keep it to herself for more than five minutes if she did.'

'Perhaps she has all the money and Charles needs it for his constituency,' continued Dora, who, like Mr Crook, liked all her pictures twopence-coloured.

'If that's so, it's a shame. All that money—and the lilies of the field doing it so much better.'

'She isn't married, so she can't be standing in anyone's way to the altar,' mused Dora enthusiastically. 'And if anything happens to her Miss Plum will be out of a job. Or do you think she wants to marry Charles—Miss Plum, I mean—no, that can't be right, because there's Flora, and she doesn't sound the sort of a person to let even a husband go.'

Mr Crook was all abeam. 'When that young hooligan bashed into my car this morning, so I had to leave it with a local mechanic for three days—three days, mark you—and travel up on the slow train, I should have known.'

'Known what?'

'That Providence had something up its sleeve for me.'

'You could have got pushed under the engine yourself,' Dora reminded him.

But Mr Crook only said blithely there had to be a first time for everything.

'You talk about women taking chances,' exploded Dora. 'How about you? Your life must be one long thrill. Not a bit like Peter Bell.'

'Come again, Sugar.'

'A primrose by a river's brim, A yellow primrose was to him, and it was nothing more. I suppose to you it would be a tiger-lily with bells on.'

Mr Crook grinned and opened his unfashionable, shabby brief-case. From this he extracted a large, fantastically-printed card that he handed to his companion.

'Just to be on the safe side,' he explained.

'I shouldn't have thought for you it existed,' Dora said. The card itself was a curiosity. It gave the owner's name —Arthur G. Crook—and two addresses, one in Bloomsbury Street and the other in Earls Court, and it said, like a plumber's advertisement, 'Your trouble our business. Nothing too large, nothing too small,' and 'Even little fish are sweet.' And wound up by promising round-the-clock service.

'What are you?' enquired Dora. 'A private detective?'

'I call myself a lawyer,' returned Mr Crook modestly, 'though that's nothing to what some chaps have called me. How about giving me a bit of pasteboard with your whereabouts on it?'

Dora fumbled in her bag and found an addressed envelope. 'Not that I shall be there much longer,' she explained. 'I'm buying a house—well, a cottage really—you must have heard me tell the dotty one—it's a sort of glorified pigsty at Ditcham. I've been down seeing it today.'

'Fond of pigs?' guessed Mr Crook, putting the envelope into his wallet.

'I'm an illustrator—flowers and shrubs. I work for a firm that produces nature books and prefers its illustrations to be done by hand, which suits me very nicely. But of course the sort of plants they want don't grow in London, and I can't keep dashing up and down—and at least at Ditcham I won't have an unmarried couple playing pop over my head till two a.m.'

'Makes a nice holiday,' agreed Mr Crook politely. 'When do you aim to go?'

'As soon as the local plumber can make the place habitable.'

'Oh, you do have plumbers? That's nice. Well, Sugar, drop me a line before you go and give me the new address. No, I'm not making a pass—as if you ever thought I would—but if something does happen to Dotty I'd like to have my witness. And, like I said before, the time could even come when you could do with a bit of help yourself. How remote is this pig-sty of yours?'

'It stands at the end of a cul-de-sac,' Dora told him proudly. 'And it's near a haunted churchyard—quite a number of people claim to have seen the ghost . . .'

But Mr Crook didn't look amused. 'Might occur to someone the ghost 'ud like a permanent companion. He your nearest neighbour? Well, don't say you weren't warned. Hallo!' He hauled a great turnip watch out of his pocket. 'What's British Rail thinking of? They've got us there on time.'

As Dora jumped down to the platform she saw the clubman emerge elegantly from his first-class carriage, his hat still slightly tilted on his distinguished head, and join the crowd passing through the barrier. She caught Mr Crook's arm.

'There's a mystery for you.' She indicated Dr Martin. 'I mean, men looking like that don't generally travel on slow trains, they go in chauffeur-driven Daimlers and probably their own charter planes for any journey of more than a hundred miles.'

'I can see you don't miss much,' said Crook cordially. 'Still, he don't appear interested in anybody else. He's like those royal dogs—King Charleses, ain't they?—that never even know any other breed exists.'

The station was crowded. At some stage a number of additional carriages had been added to the train, presumably to accommodate a tour returning from a part of the world where gypsies predominated, if their appearance was anything to go by. Dora stopped a moment, fascinated by their appearance, and when she looked up the clubman had disappeared, and Dotty and her escort were holding everyone up at the barrier.

'I know I had it,' Imogen was saying, pulling off both gloves and peering inside them.

'I told you to let me keep them both,' said Miss Plum impatiently.

'I'm not as silly as that,' retorted Dotty. 'Supposing you'd changed your mind or something and gone off, where should I be without a ticket?'

'If you haven't got a ticket, madam, you'll have to pay the fare,' said the collector impatiently. 'Then if the ticket should turn up you can put in a claim to British Rail.'

'And maybe on Christmas Day in the workhouse you'll get an acknowledgment,' chimed in Mr Crook's irrepressible voice. 'Look in your pocket, Sugar.'

So sugar looked in her pocket and there the ticket was. Dora, who had come slipping through the gypsy crowd like some agile little grass-snake, heard Dotty say, 'If at first you don't succeed—didn't I tell you, Vicky . . .'

Dora felt a shudder go through her. Even dotty people shouldn't go round sowing ideas like that in the brains of would-be murderers. Because, like Mr Crook, she didn't for one instant believe that this afternoon's mishap had been accidental. The only accident about it was that it hadn't come off.

The clubman had disappeared, Mr Crook now followed his example. Miss Plum and her companion took their places in the queue waiting for taxis, but Dora, who knew a trick worth two of this, crossed to the bus ramp and mounted a convenient No. 52 that would take her for a tenth of the fare to within three minutes of her flat. Fitting the latch-key into the lock, she found herself murmuring, 'When shall we three meet again?' meaning herself, Mr Crook and Miss Plum. Already she accepted the fact that Dotty was doomed. It would have interested her to know that Mr Crook was confident that before they reached the Grand Finale they'd all of them be involved with the police. It might well be a new experience for Miss Chester (he'd got the name off the envelope) but to him it was as normal as breathing or drinking beer.

The next morning Dora, who subscribed to a popular paper in addition to a serious and uplifted one, looked eagerly through the former for news of an unanticipated death occurring in London the previous evening, but there was nothing. The day's post brought letters from her lawyer, the furniture removers and a man in Ditcham who was going to build wardrobes in one of the rooms of the cottage, so that by 12 o'clock she had virtually forgotten Dotty's dilemma. And during the next few weeks the pig-sty, as she found, somewhat to her annoyance, she now thought of it, occupied all her attention. Imogen and her guardian faded out of her mind, ships that pass in the night and leave no track of their passing, or whatever it was the poet had actually said. What she didn't appreciate was that ships that make a one-way passage sooner or later embark on the return journey, and a second encounter may be of more significance than the first. But what with arguing with the plumber, who wanted to install a bright blue bath—like a peacock, Dora objected—and had to be coaxed into substituting a sunshine-yellow one—and deciding what pieces of furniture to keep and making sure the movers didn't bring the wrong ones, and choosing wallpapers, one way and another the happenings of that wet afternoon almost faded out of her mind.

She even, *pro tem.*, forgot the existence of Mr Crook.

CHAPTER TWO

'When hollyhocks are full of bees
And candles burn on chestnut trees,'

wrote Dora in a flood of lyrical inspiration to her sister-in-law married to the turgid Dean, 'though, in fact, I'm not sure they do actually overlap. Still, there's always poetic licence.' She let herself run on like this for about three pages. 'I have two thrushes on the lawn called Dilly and Dally . . . No sign yet of the church ghost but that will be something to look forward to. I mean to learn to drive a car, as the buses that depart from the village square, all eight feet of it, generally go out on Tuesday morning and return on Thursday night. Still, there are some splendid short-cuts and I think the local cows are beginning to recognize me.'

('Addle-pated as ever,' sighed her sister-in-law. 'No sense of true values,' boomed the Dean. 'If she ever gets herself murdered she'll make a joke even of that,' contributed Grace Chester. Dora's rare letters gave them splendid opportunities for appreciating their own balance, due, naturally, to their Faith in Providence and, even more, to Providence's faith in them.)

Having finished her letter Dora walked down the crooked street, that Grace would have dismissed as a lane, towards the village, which consisted of a general-shop-cum-post-office, a butcher, a wool shop where letters and parcels could be left for individual collection, and a telephone booth on the village green. To reach the village Dora had to cross the churchyard, which was ancient and mossy and enchanted her with its Victorian tombstones on which local talent had unleashed every vagary of man's mind. The shattered pillar, the drooping bud, even the pitcher broken at the fountain, wielded by a buxom young lady, wife of the deceased, presumably—never a dull moment, exulted Dora, leaving the churchyard and smiling at a horse that had come up to the hedge by which she was passing. Now that she was settled she must start getting acquainted with her neighbours, and a horse was as good a beginning as any.

The general shop was in charge of one Willy Masters, an ageless individual with a fair Edwardian moustache and a dreamy blue eye that could, some declared, pierce infinity and foretell the future. This afternoon there was no one but Mr Masters in the shop. It was too early for the London edition of the evening paper that private enterprise contrived to have delivered by the driver of the Great Plumstead bus when he came past at five o'clock. Dora wandered round buying rice and coffee and Bath Oliver biscuits, and then recalled that she was running short of writing paper, another commodity stocked by the enterprising Willy.

'I seem to get through such a lot,' she explained, remembering the letter in her hand and popping it into the sack that hung beside the Post Office counter.

Willy smiled his all-comprehending smile. 'Ah, but you're from London, Miss Chester. Country folk born and bred have too much to do to bother themselves with paper and ink.' (Which was true: the extraordinary thing was that, though few of the villagers had telephones or even made use of the one on the green, news circulated at an amazing rate. Crook could have told her the local grapevine could outdo the telephone any day, as the famous Aesopian tortoise had once outdone the speedier hare.) 'But you'll get used to us in time,' Willy assured her, in the voice of one to whom Time has no meaning and no limit.

Dora had just remembered she'd like another tin of bullseyes when the shop-door was pushed open vigorously and a little round rabbit of a man bounced in. This was the rector, whose acquaintance she had yet to make. His name was Bunyan, he was in charge of four parishes in plurality, and he now gave Dora the benevolent smile of the man who knows that all creatures, no matter what their appearance, colour or creed, are the works of a mysterious Creator.

'What charming graves you have in your churchyard,' observed Dora chattily after Willy had made grave introductions. 'They look so lived in. Oh, Mr Masters,' she ran on, observing Willy pull out a short pair of steps and climb to a top shelf to find the tin of bullseyes, 'I didn't mean to give you all that trouble.'

'Trouble is what man is born to,' retorted the rector briskly. 'It's as well to get used to the idea as early as possible. I'm glad you like our graves, Miss Chester. They were built for long tenancies, and the old families didn't believe in hotch-potch jobs. Willy, you didn't hear anything of my cockerel, I suppose? He's gone AWOL again.'

'I did not, Mr Bunyan,' said Willy, coming down the steps with the tin in his hand. 'It's my belief he'll turn up in someone's pot one of these days and no one's fault but his own. I know it's in the Book about forgiving trespasses, but there's nothing said ever I heard about forgiving trespassers.'

'Sometimes I think Willy's missed his vocation,' the little parson confided to Dora. 'He'd be a great wag in the pulpit. Like that fellow my father 'ud be telling of—take for his text "Are not four sparrows sold for a farthing?" and go on, "Maybe if you was to haggle a bit you'd get the chap to throw in a fifth for luck".' He turned to Willy. 'When you've a minute, Willy, I'll have my ounce of Old-and-Mild, and the church cleaner's asking for more polish for the pews. Tell me, Willy, does it contain anything alcoholic, the way the good lady gets through it you'd say she drank it. I'm sure she looks a deal shinier than the pews.'

'I hear you have a ghost,' said Dora respectfully. 'He haunts the church.'

'Not the church,' said Mr Bunyan. 'Is it a fact you've got Pieman's Cottage? Well, that's his port of call. By all accounts, he didn't trouble the Lord much in his lifetime and he was a consistent sort of a fellow, he'd not be trespassing on the church now. I hear you've made great changes in the cottage, it's to be hoped he'll feel at home if he comes to call.'

Dora felt slightly shaken. 'Does he often? Call, I mean?'

'They say he has a habit of dropping in now and again, but very companionable, makes no demands, just settles in a chair with some paper or other. A great reader in his day, and you don't hear him come or go. After a while, I'm assured you don't even notice him, and he's very tactful about taking himself off when you have company. Well, goodbye for the moment, Mrs—no, it's Miss Chester, isn't it? Ah!' For the door was once again flung open and the driver of the local bus slammed down a parcel of the early afternoon edition on the counter. Mr Bunyan took his small parcel over the counter and proffered some change. 'Willy, is there anything in that paper ye're selling for sixpence that's worth its price?'

Willy took up the top copy and gravely surveyed the headlines.

'There's trouble in middle Europe, the Far East, the Middle East and South Africa. Busmen threatening to come out over a pay claim, two more countries sending men to the moon and Britain's out of the Davis Cup.'

'Well, you'd not say any of that was news,' said the rector comfortably. 'So I'll add a penny to that threepence which will buy a fourpenny bar of chocolate crumble. It's been grand meeting you, Miss Chester, and welcome to Ditcham. Long may you stay with us, but if your time should be up while you're here you'll get a Christian funeral and good friends hereafter.'

'Never a dull moment,' murmured Dora, putting down a pound note as the shopdoor closed.

'Now there's a man in the right place,' Willy assured her in his tranquil way. 'I've no ten shilling piece, so it'll all have to be silver, but I daresay it'll make no odds, the money'll be out of your purse just as quick. And you don't have to worry about any old ghost, Miss Chester,' he went on gently. 'According to my dad, who lived all his life here, Mr Preston was as nice a body as you could look for, he'd never do aught to inconvenience a lady, particularly under her own roof. Rector only mentioned him, because—well, we wouldn't like to think the old gentleman couldn't pay his occasional visit, it's not for us to say, but I dare say it gets a bit monotonous in the grave for one who was everybody's friend . . .' He stopped abruptly, aware that he had lost Dora's interest. Dora was staring at the copy of the evening paper, that lay face uppermost on the counter. Staring at the rather blotched photograph of a woman who could be none other than Imogen Garland, the Bear Woman of Penton Station, Mr Crook's Dotty. Above the picture, in small leaded type, ran the inscription

MP'S SISTER IN HOTEL DEATH DRAMA

Blindly Dora picked up the paper, fished sixpence out of her purse and, like one in a dream, turned towards the door and more or less walked through Mr Roberts of the Three Pigeons, who had come in for his copy of the *Argus*.

'Must ha' mistook me for the ghost,' suggested Mr Roberts.

'News to me ghosts weigh sixteen stone,' returned Willy courteously. He also helped himself to a copy of the evening paper. 'Proper scared she seemed.' He saw the picture of Dotty. 'Maybe she knew the lady. Ah well, comes of living in London, I dare say. We don't get that kind of mystery here.'

Only, as Mr Crook could have told him, there's a first time for everything.

Walking back through the churchyard, Dora paused to watch two tortoiseshell butterflies darting in and out of the fat hen and loosestrife that flourished around the untended graves. No one was going to risk his scythe cutting through that wilderness, with the chance of chipping the blade against some concealed stone or granite memorial. The life of a butterfly, Dora had heard, is only 24 hours; doubtless in the Eye of Eternity this measured up to the life of man. Which philosophy should have consoled her for the news she had just received. 'But clearly I'm not of a philosophic bent,' she decided. It still seemed a terrible thing.

Putting her key into the lock of the cottage she hesitated for a moment, thinking that perhaps this was one of the afternoons when the late Mr Preston would feel like alleviating her solitude, but there wasn't even the whiff of a ghost in the little hall, nor a breath of charnel air. She dumped her parcel and ran to put on the kettle. Gin is cheering and wine maketh glad the heart of man, but when you're in a real turmoil there's nothing like a good strong cup of tea.

At last she picked up the paper. You can postpone evil moments, but you can't put them off for ever, not even the instant of death, your own or anyone else's. And then she got her second shock. Because the victim, as the press discreetly called her, wasn't Imogen Garland, but her prim companion, Miss Victoria Styles. It was clear from reading the latest news that there had been some reference to the affair in an earlier edition, it was just chance, Dora supposed, that that morning she had felt, like the rector, the news could wait. She opened the unfolded morning *Argus* and set herself to read the whole story, in so far as the press had it. The sting of the second instalment was in the tail. Miss Garland had left the Montblanc Hotel unperceived the night before, some time after the tragedy, and had not returned to her brother's house. The police were asking that anyone who could give information as to her whereabouts would communicate with the authorities at once. Her luggage, the report added, was still at the Montblanc Private Hotel. She was believed to be wearing a blue coat and dress and a small blue helmet-shaped hat—must have changed her style since a few weeks ago, was Dora's inward comment.

'I wonder what really happened,' murmured Dora to

herself. 'One thing, if Dotty did push Miss Plum out of the window, I'm sure she must have been provoked.' Crook, hearing that later, remarked that it must be the understatement of the year. 'And Miss Plum did start it,' Dora reminded herself, 'she shouldn't have tried to push Imogen under the engine. Surely there's a limit to what human nature is expected to endure.'

(It wasn't till she was undressing to go to bed that night that it occurred to her both she and Mr Crook might have been wrong about that afternoon on Penton Station. What if it hadn't been Miss Plum trying to get rid of Dotty, but vice-versa? And she recalled her first conviction that, though the missing woman might look a bit silly, she had, in fact, been very much all there.)

She shook out the morning paper and settled down to read.

Up in London all was gas and gaiters. The actual fall had been reported in the morning editions, but the press hadn't been very enlightening. A middle-aged woman, whose name was being withheld until the relatives could be contacted, had fallen from the fourth floor of a London hotel shortly after 6.0 p.m. the previous night. She had been taken by ambulance to the nearest hospital, where she was found to be dead. Her companion was remaining in London, assisting the police.

Poor Miss Styles! She missed getting star billing because there had been a truly horrific air disaster that night, that occupied all the front page, so at first go off she only rated a couple of paragraphs. But when the press was able to reveal the companion's identity, in addition to the fact that, far from assisting the police, she had disappeared, the news rated front-page headlines. In fact, if the dead woman really had achieved the distinction of appearing in the Chamber of Horrors, she could scarcely have had more posthumous publicity.

The facts, so far as the police had been able to ascertain, were as follows.

The deceased (whose name was now revealed) had written from Sir Charles Garland's house in Upper Marston, for which district he was Member of Parliament, engaging a twin-bedded room for the Friday night in question. Some stress had been laid on the necessity for a private bathroom, though, as the deceased hadn't been found drowned, this seemed superfluous. Only when she was being questioned, Flora Garland, poor Dotty's sister-in-law, explained that on a previous occasion Imogen had opened the wrong door, on her return from the communal bathroom, and actually entered a room at a most inauspicious moment. (Later Imogen had said, 'If they were going to do anything so private they should have locked the door first. And if the hotel had been less mean with the lights I shouldn't have confused a 3 with an 8.') Anyway, there had been some unpleasantness and it had been agreed that, on subsequent visits to town, a private bathroom should always be stipulated. The couple had reached the hotel in a taxi shortly after 5 o'clock, and Miss Styles had ordered tea to be sent to their room, since final orders in the lounge were taken at 4.45. The chambermaid who took the tray up said she noticed nothing in particular about the couple, they seemed to be perfectly amicable. At 5.45 she found the tray of used crockery put outside the door. She did not again see Miss Styles alive.

The last person to do so, in the strictly academic sense of the word, was a suburban matron called Mrs Huth. This witness, an inveterate bargain-hunter, had parked her car in Portman Way, a narrow street running up by the side of the hotel. By 6.30 when she came back to retrieve it, there were no other cars to be seen. The Way was flanked by the hotel on one side and a high wall, enclosing the gardens of a block of flats, on the other. Miss Huth was inconveniently laden with parcels, knew she was going to be late home, and was rehearsing a speech that might convince the unsympathetic Percy Huth that the fault was due to the state of the roads, when, glancing up as an aeroplane went over, she was suddenly aware of something rapidly descending, apparently fallen from the sky. A dullish afternoon had collapsed into a drizzly twilight, and there was nothing to show that, with the mercurial spirits of London weather, it was going to be a clear, even a memorable evening.

'It was like some great bird,' insisted a shaken and ashy-faced Mrs Huth to the insistent police. 'No, of course I didn't see what happened. I was hurrying to my car, there weren't any others left so at least I knew I shouldn't be hemmed in, and I was worried about Percy, my husband, because he expects his dinner on the table at seven-thirty sharp, I mean he's not the sort of man who can so much as light a gas burner left on his own and I've always told him Surbiton's too far out—well, as I was telling you I heard this plane going by and I looked up because I liked to see the lights, so pretty, and there she was, this woman, I mean. And it's no use asking me what happened because I don't know. At first I didn't even realize it was a woman, just—just something dark like a great black bird. I mean, it's true, isn't it, that you generally see what you expect to see, and no one expects to see a body falling through space from—well, from nowhere.'

Asked if she'd noticed an open window, she stared. 'I didn't see anything, I keep telling you, she might have fallen off the roof, well, of course I don't know what she'd be doing on the roof, what I'm saying is I don't know anything about a window. If she fell out it would be open, wouldn't it?'

'Unless someone else had shut it.'

'Well, I don't know, do I?' protested Mrs Huth again.

'What made you come in here?' she was asked.

'I looked round but like always when you want somebody they're not there. There's a phone box across the square but someone was in that, and anyway I thought she must have fallen from the hotel, so I came along here.'

The manager, who bore the improbable name of Mr Harlequin, took up the story. This fair, plump, tousled lady, with a face the colour of a dingy white sheet, her short arms full of parcels, had stumbled over the threshold crying to all and sundry, 'There's a woman on the pavement, she fell from above, somebody call the police.' Mr Harlequin, the reputation of his hotel at stake, said quickly to the hotel porter, 'Better go and see what it's all about, Ted. And if there's been an accident and anyone's hurt, ring for an ambulance.' At which Mrs Huth lifted her head and howled, 'IF anyone's hurt! You try falling from a height on to a pavement and see if you get off with a broken ankle or something.'

There was a number of guests in the foyer, and one of the men said sharply that the lady better have some brandy, but Mrs Huth was sufficiently mistress of herself, or nervous of Percy, to refuse. Not brandy, she insisted, she'd got to drive back to Surbiton.

'Someone better telephone the husband and tell him what's happened,' the man insisted. He was a doctor, secretly as sick as mud that a thing like this should happen on one of his rare free evenings. 'He can come up and fetch the car and the lady.' When Mrs Huth began to babble something about Percy not liking driving the doctor said in curt tones that if she couldn't think of herself she might think of her fellow-drivers. In the condition she was in now she'd be all over the road, and one fatal accident in an evening was quite sufficient. For while all this parleying was going on Ted had taken a peek at the victim, and come back, looking nearly as white as Mrs Huth, to say this one had bought it and in God's name hadn't anyone got a rug. So Mr Harlequin and Ted went out and someone rang up Mr Huth, and Mrs Harlequin, who'd kept discreetly in the background, called an ambulance, and Mrs Huth found herself sipping brandy, after all. A crowd of idlers, the sort that seem to spring up whenever anything dramatic occurs, were gathering round the hotel entrance like a band of supers waiting for their call. 'Haven't you people got homes to go to?' demanded the doctor furiously. 'Even vultures have their nests, I'm told.' Then the police car, hooting its siren like a bird of ill-omen, came dashing up, followed by an ambulance whose driver remarked, *sotto voce*, that you didn't have to pass any bleeding exams to see this one had bought it. The chambermaid identified the clothing, good quality country gear, last year's style, you could always tell, she said and asked the relevant question, 'What happened?'

'We don't know yet,' said the police repressively. They'd caught some of the stragglers whom the doctor had attempted to disperse, but no one could be of assistance. No one had seen anything, and there was Mrs Huth's word for it that there hadn't been anyone in the street she could approach.

'Why don't you ask *her*?' the chambermaid added. 'The other one.'

It was the first time authority had realized there was anyone else involved. Mr Harlequin hadn't been on view when the ladies arrived, and in any case he left all reception duties to his wife. But now, while the ambulance did what it could to collect what might faithfully be described as the remains, Mr Harlequin and the police went upstairs to interview the survivor. Somewhat to their surprise, when they reached the door of No. 39, they found it fastened from the inside. Poor Mr Harlequin instantly wondered if he had a double tragedy on his hands, but his smart rap on the panel was acknowledged by a swift 'Who's there?'

'Kindly unlock the door,' said Mr Harlequin, aware that all the doors he'd have preferred to remain shut were opening right along the corridor.

'That's not Miss Plum,' declared the voice. 'She said she'd knock three times—like a witch or a wicked fairy.'

'This is the manager,' declared Mr Harlequin in a voice that sounded as if it had just been taken out of the deep freeze. Then they heard the slightly lurching, uninhibited step come blundering across the floor and found themselves confronted by a big woman in oatmeal-coloured jersey with a not quite matching coat and the shoes not matching either. You could say the same about her features, which were good of their kind, but somehow didn't build up into a right pattern, as though they'd been picked out of a box and hastily thrown together.

'If it's Miss Plum you want,' said the personage simply, as though it was incredible that anyone should be here on *her* account, 'she's gone out, she didn't say where. But if you don't believe me, you can look for yourself.' She stepped back with an expansive gesture. 'Nobody in the bathroom, not now, I did have a bath myself, Miss Plum suggested it would save time in the morning, and I can promise you she isn't under either of the beds. Well, even a skeleton couldn't hide so close to the ground.' She smiled at them, still pink and a little moist from her bath, with her fair hair wispy round her ears.

'Why did you lock the door, miss?' asked the policeman, and Dotty answered readily, 'Oh, she told me to—Miss Plum, I mean.'

'Why should she do that, miss?'

Imogen suddenly became aware of the Peeping Toms all down the corridor. 'Why don't you come in?' she invited. 'I'm sure Miss Plum wouldn't mind. Oh, you were asking me about the door. It wasn't, as you might think, to keep me in, but to keep everybody else out. She said so long as I was in her charge she felt responsible . . .' She seemed to realize for the first time that one of her visitors wore a uniform. 'What's happened to Miss Plum?' she demanded in a different voice. 'You didn't say she'd got into trouble. Not MISS PLUM?'

'There's been an accident,' the officer said stolidly.

'But—I don't understand,' protested Imogen. 'Accidents never happen to Miss Plum. I'm the one who's accident-prone. Like that day I nearly fell under the train at Penton, only that extraordinary-looking man saved me.' She paused, staring from one face to the other. 'What happened?' she repeated in a voice that for her was muted and apprehensive.

'She—had a fall,' the officer said.

'In the street?'

The policeman was looking round the room. 'Is that your bag, madam?' He indicated a squat brown bag looking rather like a captive toad, that stood on a side table.

'No. No, of course that's not mine, that's hers.' She waved a hand at her own tapestry affair. 'That's funny. Why should Miss Plum leave her bag behind? Or did she just come down to arrange something with the manager? Even then I don't believe she'd go without her bag. It accompanies her everywhere. I tell her it's like a third hand. Still shaking hands with yourself, Miss Plum? I say. Well.' She stared defiantly at the unmoved faces. 'When two people spend so much time together you have to have the occasional joke. Don't you ever have a joke with your inspector?'

But the man only said, 'We don't think Miss—Plum?'

'Oh, that's not her real name. Her real name's Miss Victoria Styles.' She looked as though she were going to explain the association between Victoria and Plum, but thought better of it. If people hadn't got a sense of humour, it was no use trying to appeal to it.

'We don't think the lady went down to see the manager.'

'Well,' said Imogen decidedly, 'it's no use asking where she went, only it's not like her to go out of the hotel without her bag. I don't really know much about her, you should ask my sister-in-law, she engaged her—to look after me, I mean. She said she'd taken a very good degree—of course they didn't have A-levels in those days—I don't really see why she wants it just to be my companion, but there it is.'

'You've been ill, Miss Garland?'

'No, not ill, I'm very healthy really, but I get a bit absent-minded, and Charles, that's my brother, says he has his reputation to consider, he's in the House—the House of Commons, you know—and they don't like publicity. That's what he says, but he could have fooled me. Couldn't he you?'

'Did Miss Styles say anything to you about her plans?' The police officer felt like a man battling against a strong wind, one step forward and two steps back.

'I was having my bath—I thought I heard her talking to someone, I thought it must be the chambermaid, I mean, we haven't got a telephone, but of course she must have been talking to herself.'

'Did she often do that?'

'Well, sometimes. She used to say she liked to hear a clever chap talk and a clever chap reply, if I teased her, I mean. But of course I can't be certain. There were the taps, and I had my little transistor playing . . .'

'What programme would that be?'

Imogen stared. 'I wasn't listening, of course, I had too many other things to think about. It was just a background noise.'

'And you didn't hear anything while you were in the bathroom?'

'Well, just the water, it's very *assertive* plumbing in this hotel—and I tried the shower, I'm not very used to them, I found this one rather difficult to control.' She looked guiltily down to where a dark snake of water crept under the bathroom door.

'Now the window,' the police officer bore on, while Mr Harlequin openly fidgeted. All this subtlety, when in the end the fellow would have to come out with the facts, if indeed this rumty-too old girl didn't know them already. 'Did you notice if the window was open when you came from the bathroom?'

'I supposed Miss Plum had opened it because of the steam or something, but I thought the room was rather cold, so I shut it.'

And then at long last they told her. She looked at them with complete unbelief.

'You mean, Miss Plum left the room by the window? What do you think she is—a witch? All I can tell you is I've never seen any broomsticks standing about.' She laughed.

'It's no joking matter, miss,' the policeman said in sharp tones. 'All the evidence points to Miss Styles having fallen from the window of this room.'

Dotty's vague and humorous manner disappeared like figures rubbed by a duster from a blackboard.

'You mean—*she fell out of a window*! She wouldn't be so careless. I mean, Charles was paying her—or anyway Flora was—to look after me, not to go round breaking her leg or something. Is that what she's done?'

'She's been taken to the hospital,' the officer said. 'We haven't had their report yet.'

Mr Harlequin broke in uncontrollably. 'Her injuries are severe . . .' But the officer overbore him. 'You told us just now, Miss Garland, that Miss Styles isn't the kind of person to whom accidents normally happen?'

'I shouldn't think they'd dare,' said Dotty, so solemnly that nobody even smiled.

'But you did hear voices?'

'I thought so—but it might have been the radio breaking through or someone in the street below.'

'You heard nothing else—not the sound of a door opening or shutting?'

'If she didn't go out of the room why should a door open or shut?'

'If she was talking to someone that person must have come in.'

'Oh yes—I suppose so. But—' she shook her head—'you don't know Miss Plum, she's not the kind of person to let herself be *threatened.* If any threatening was going on I'd expect her to be the one to do it. If it wasn't that I can't see what there was in it for Miss Plum, I'd say she stayed at Upper Marston because she wanted to. Not even Flora—and she's rich enough to make most people do what she wants, she could make Charles do it if only she knew how to make him listen to anything she says—not even she could make Miss Plum stay unless she wanted to. Once or twice I've said to her, "You don't have to stay unless you want to, anyone as clever as you could get a much better job"—of course, if this was a story-book she'd be in love with Charles, but I'm sure it's not that, I don't believe he's ever really seen her, I mean he knows she's there, but that isn't the same thing, is it?' (It was too bad that Mr Crook couldn't have listened in from behind a curtain, he'd have relished hearing Dotty confounding a rozzer.)

'Has she been with you long?'

'Well, it seems ages,' confessed Imogen frankly, 'but I suppose it isn't really as long as that. She tells me sometimes I'm lucky not to have to earn a living, but I don't agree. People talk sometimes as if they were—oh, penalized by life because they earn their own bread-and-butter, but nothing is for free, as my brother's always saying, and it's worth a lot to be independent. I think—you did say she's in hospital?—I think I should go and see her. It seems so unsympathetic.' She turned an unexpectedly bright eye on Mr Harlequin. 'I expect you could get me a taxi.'

'Miss Styles won't be receiving visitors tonight,' said the manager harshly.

'I'm not a visitor . . .' Her face changed. 'What is it you mean? You're not telling me she's—she can't be dead. Not Miss Plum.'

'We haven't had the hospital's report yet,' repeated the policeman heavily.

'But you know just the same.' She turned to Mr Harlequin. 'You do know, don't you?'

Mr Harlequin looked away. 'It's a high window,' he muttered.

There was a moment's silence. Then Imogen made the remark that was going to be quoted in all the organs of the popular press. 'Poor Miss Plum! Now she'll never get into Madam Tussaud's.'

CHAPTER THREE

She supposed in her ignorance that that would be the end of it, at all events for the time being.

'I've told you everything I can,' she insisted. 'Now I should like to go back. I'll have to telephone Flora—if she's back, that is, she's been doing a round of exhibitions, Church embroidery, you know, it's one of her fortes, but I should think she'd be back by this time because of tomorrow's being Charles's constituency day. She always likes to be there then, she's a great help to him. Mr Phelps, that's the agent, says some of the constituents aren't sure which of them is the Member—where can I find a telephone?'

She was told she could telephone from the box in the hall, but she couldn't go home that night. 'There will naturally be a full enquiry into the—the disaster, and we should like you to be on the spot. There may be further questions we should like . . .'

'I shouldn't have thought even the police could have thought up any more of those,' said Dotty candidly. 'I wasn't here, I mean I was in the bathroom, and I can't see through a wooden door, so even if Miss Plum had someone in here, and I can't actually swear to that, I couldn't tell you who it was.'

'You could perhaps tell us if it was a man or a woman. You spoke of a possible chambermaid.'

'Only because I couldn't think of anyone else Miss Plum would be likely to be entertaining in a bedroom. She's very conventional. Anyway, some women have very deep voices and some men squeak like mice. Flora always says there's a reason for that but she never tells me what it is. Anyway, I couldn't sleep alone here after what's happened. The ghost or whatever it was that pushed Miss Plum through a window might come back for me.'

The officer looked at Mr Harlequin. 'I dare say some alternative arrangement could be made,' he hazarded, but the manager saw no reason why he should be further penalized for something that was no fault of his. In a well-balanced society he'd be able to claim damages—he wasn't sure from whom—for loss of prestige, since no one likes the idea of putting up at an hotel where there's been a fatality—whether accident, in which case they might question his safety precautions—or deliberate malice, which could well involve a coming and going of policemen which even honest citizens don't appreciate. So he said he regretted that no other room was available, but he would be glad to assist Miss Garland in any way he could, she had had a shock, and he suggested that a lady of his acquaintance, his wife's sister, in fact, a trained nurse, but extremely discreet and naturally not in uniform, would be available to act as Miss Garland's companion until such time as she could return to her own roof.

'Charles's roof,' amended Imogen. 'And really I don't need a nurse. Anyone would think I was going to rush round the hotel like a demented cockatoo.'

Which, of course, was precisely what Mr Harlequin feared.

The officer said that perhaps Sir Charles would come up, but Imogen interrupted him, speaking in a scandalized tone. 'With his Constituency Day tomorrow? Of course he won't. And anyway he couldn't sleep in the same room. He'd be asked to resign at once.'

Still, she was persuaded to accept the nurse, who preferred to be called Miss Holmes, and she said she was sorry she didn't know anything about Miss Styles's relations.

'She never talked about them, except to say that God thought of hell and gave us relations and thought of Heaven and gave us friends. and she usually knew what she was talking about, Miss Plum. But nobody ever came to see her or rang her up on the phone so far as I know, Charles used to say she must have lived in limbo before she came to us, only of course she didn't, because Flora met her somewhere. Perhaps,' she added, helpfully, 'Flora would know.'

'Letters?' murmured the police officer, and Imogen looked shocked and said how could you read other people's letters? Adding, 'Even if she'd ever left any lying about, and she was much too tidy for that.'

'References?' The officer was hard to discourage. 'Wouldn't Sir Charles . . .?'

'I shouldn't think so,' said Dotty frankly. 'I shouldn't think he'd dare, not if Flora vouched for her. The soul of rectitude, upright as a coffin-nail, that's Miss Plum. But I suppose,' she relented, 'you could ask.'

She wouldn't talk to her brother on the telephone. 'You'll explain so much better than I could,' she demurred, 'besides he'd listen to you. I mean, it's not my fault Miss Plum fell out of a window, she was supposed to be looking after me, but he's sure to think it is, my fault, I mean.'

'On the hysterical side,' Mr Harlequin warned his sister-in-law guiding her up to No. 39. 'A bit—you know,' and he tapped his forehead.

'I should get danger money,' said Miss Holmes humorously. She was a well-built figure of a woman not far off fifty, wearing a well-cut dark blue dress with matching coat. You'd never call her fashionable, but in her own way she wasn't negligible.

'I do hope they haven't misled you,' said Imogen chattily. 'I'm not ill, and I've no suicidal tendencies. I'm perfectly capable—it's just that I didn't exactly fancy staying in the room that, as you might say, had already rejected Miss Plum.'

Oh, brother! thought Miss Holmes, you didn't tell me the half.

'Are you sure,' Imogen continued, 'that I'm not interrupting something much more important? Shouldn't you be delivering a baby?'

'I don't undertake midwifery now, only in exceptional cases,' Miss Holmes explained. She didn't think it necessary to inform Imogen that she'd once had to act in the capacity of a midwife at a premature birth in this very room.

'I suppose you're like the police,' mused Imogen. 'When they get high up they don't have to wear uniform, do they?' She cocked an untidy eyebrow. Flora was always on at her to have them neatened, but Imogen declared sturdily that the Lord had given and only the Lord should take away.

'The management,' continued Miss Holmes in the tone of one employing words of one syllable, 'prefers no advertisement.'

'Like Charles,' approved Imogen. 'One sees their point. People might think this was a sort of hospital for the weak-minded.'

'There's no call to talk like that,' said Miss Holmes in a chilly voice. 'People might get the wrong idea.'

'I wonder how many of them have that anyway,' Imogen brooded. She watched her companion put her handsome blue coat on a hanger. 'Birds of a feather,' she commented.

'I wasn't aware you had had nursing experience, Miss Garland.'

'I didn't mean that. I meant—well, you've got a forty-two waist—no, I mean, you take a forty-two fitting, don't you? So do I. Though it doesn't show on you like it does on me.' She nodded approvingly. 'What the Victorians would have called a fine figure of a woman.'

'Believe it or not,' offered Miss Holmes, 'I was once followed from Liverpool to London by a gentleman who admired my figure.'

'He must have had a lot of time on his hands,' offered Imogen innocently. 'Well, if you're sure it's all right for you to stay . . .'

'The doctor considers it unwise for you to be alone.'

Imogen stared. 'I haven't seen a doctor.'

'You may not have seen him, he's seen you. And Mr Harlequin had a word . . . That poor Miss Styles! It must have been a great shock.'

'Except that I don't suppose she had much time to realize it. The law of gravity would prevent that.'

'Between the saddle and the ground,' quoted Miss Holmes fluently.

'He mercy sought and mercy found. But Miss Plum wouldn't think she needed mercy. And I'm sure she didn't do it on purpose. Though if you had got suicide in mind,' she continued thoughtfully, 'I can't think of a more appropriate setting. Whoever decorated this room must have been colour-blind. That awful shrimp-pink distemper and lettuce-green paint—like an eternal shrimp cocktail. Do you think this is the sort of hotel where one changes for dinner?'

'Mr Harlequin has arranged for us to have dinner privately up here.'

Imogen looked as shocked and disappointed as a child. 'But he can't—I mean, it isn't fair to the others.'

'I don't know what you're talking about, Miss Garland.'

'They'll only think the worst—about me and Miss Styles, I mean. Besides, won't they feel cheated? They can't have people falling out of windows every day of the week.'

'You mustn't get hysterical, Miss Garland. And perhaps we should tidy the room a little.'

'You mean tidy away all references to Miss Plum? It's obvious you never knew her or you wouldn't dare.'

Miss Holmes was still obliterating all traces of the deceased when the waiter knocked and brought in a table, which he covered with a cloth.

'I hope it's steak,' said Imogen greedily. Flora practically never ordered steak.

'I thought casserole of chicken would be most suitable in the circumstances.'

'Charles calls that under-carriage of chicken. Like charity, he says, it covers a multitude of misdemeanours. I think I ought to have a little brandy. Oh, poor Miss Plum, it's such a shame she should be missing this. It's just the kind of emergency she could cope with so well.'

After dinner Miss Holmes produced a set of patience cards and proposed a game of racing demon.

'Were you ever a professional co-respondent?' asked Imogen, as they laid out the cards. 'It's perfectly respectable, nothing *happens*, and so long as the law's an ass people have to find their own way round it. I knew someone once who had to get that kind of divorce, he said by morning he never wanted to see a card again, and he thought murder must be less exhausting.'

At 9.30 a near-exhausted Miss Holmes suggested early bed. 'You've had a very emotional day, you're bound to get the reaction sooner or later. A good night's sleep will help you to face it.'

'I've had my bath,' said the accommodating Miss Garland. 'Miss Plum suggested it; I did think it rather odd, seeing I always have mine in the morning—what I'm trying to say is that the bathroom's all yours. Only I could just undress in there first . . .'

Miss Holmes looked suspiciously into the bathroom. There was no window—it had been sliced out of the bedroom proper—and she assured herself that the door opening to the corridor was locked. So she made no demur when Imogen took her flowered nightdress and the dressing-gown with its pattern of humming-birds that Flora had bought at a Conservative Party Sale, and disappeared. It wasn't long before she returned, her clothes bunched anyhow under her arm. She threw them unceremoniously on to a chair and the dress slipped to the floor.

'Dear me!' said Miss Holmes, 'that's no way to treat a good dress. Look, you've got a stain on it, I'll just sponge that off for you. I have a tube of the most wonderful stuff for stains . . .'

'I expect it removes the surface as well as the stain,' said Imogen composedly.

'Nonsense!' Miss Holmes's voice was severe. 'It gets out absolutely anything.'

Imogen's face changed. 'You're not suggesting it's BLOOD?'

'Of course not, Miss Garland, how should it be blood? While I'm about it,' she added casually, 'I'll just brush your coat as well. They seem to pick up so much dust—these railway carriages . . .'

Imogen sighed her agreement. 'Seeing we shall be dust ourselves one of these days . . . Oh well, I expect Flora would approve.'

She pulled off her dressing-gown and climbed into bed, a rather bulky figure, and started to plait her abundant and still light brown hair. Then she rolled up the plaits under what she described as a slumber cap, an affair of bright blue silk and lace and a ribbon bow. 'At least my hair won't get dusty while I'm asleep,' she promised.

'Do you generally take anything?' Miss Holmes asked, prepared to immure herself in the bathroom. A nice hot bath was just what she wanted to send her cosily into the Land of Nod.

'You mean a pill?'

'A sleeping tablet.'

'I never need those. I'll have my light off by the time you come back, and it won't be any use your talking to me because I shan't be there to answer.'

'Sleep tight,' said Miss Holmes indulgently, 'and remember if it wasn't your fault about poor Miss Styles, you've nothing to blame yourself for.'

And into the bathroom she went, laden with Imogen's dress and coat, and locked the door firmly. Even Imogen wouldn't think of trying to go out in her night-clothes, and if she did Mr Harlequin or whoever was on duty would alert the staff.

'I don't say she did push that friend of hers out of the window,' Miss Holmes said aloud—like that other managing female, Miss Styles, she often talked to herself for want of a better audience. 'But no harm playing safe.'

She turned on the water and it flowed through the taps with a whoosh that made her think of Niagara Falls. Or perhaps something nearer home.

'That's how the waters come down at Lodore,' she quoted, unzipping her ample girdle and stepping into the bath.

When she came back the only light in the room was the bedside lamp, its beam turned on her own pillow. She looked across to the other bed, but the slumber cap was all she saw of that plump adolescent face (that's what she is, discovered Miss Holmes, a middle-aged adolescent). Imogen's dressing-gown was drawn closely round her neck, she lay as still as a log.

Worn out and no wonder, reflected Miss Holmes, wondering if she should draw down the dressing-gown a little in case the creature smothered herself. But once wake her, decided the nurse shrewdly, and she'll be yak-yakking half the night. The creature's sturdy tan brogues stood under the bed. Shan't risk opening the door, Miss Holmes decided. The chambermaid can take them when she brings the morning cuppa. Softly she turned the key in the lock.

'Cheery-bye,' she said, but nobody answered.

Which wasn't surprising, seeing there was nobody there.

Sir Charles Garland was the Tory Member for a south-east constituency and had had the good sense to set up his headquarters in a market town that hadn't yet been enveloped in the general southern sprawl. His wife in her own way was as distinguished as he, being an authority on Tudor architecture, about which she was in some demand as a lecturer —such a clear ringing voice, people said. Like the Angel of Death calling in the damned, was Imogen's way of putting it. And then there was her ecclesiastical embroidery, a lot of fiddle-faddle, said her husband, but it could have been worse. She might have wanted to breed snappy little toy dogs who bit his constituents when they called, and changed them between one minute and the next from respectable Tories to unmentionable Reds. Charles knew, like all politicians, that that's the kind of thing that makes up the mind of the Floating Voter, who could read either party's election address and not know t'other from which. What with Flora's cultured activities—she'd been lecturing to a snob-school on needlework that night poor Miss Plum bought hers—and Charles's predilection for chaps like Sam Gore and the village idiot, who mightn't know a hawk from a handsaw but always knew where the fish were to be found on an angling expedition, the Garlands had the constituency taped from A to Z. Locally the pair were known as Luck and Lucre. Charles had the luck and Flora the lucre. Some time during the war she'd contracted one of those lightning alliances that couldn't have happened in the piping days of peace, marrying a man with great expectations. He'd been killed one morning soon after D-Day, when the enemy made a dead set at the secret service station in which husband and wife worked. The sceptics said no doubt the money, which she subsequently inherited, must be oil on the wound. A few years after the war she met Charles, a widower with a very young son, a bossy housekeeper, and Imogen, as odd a household as you could look for this side the moon. Charles, with his Army pension and a bit his old man had left him, was, said the uncharitable, an easy prey. But the small boy, Tim, who didn't recall his mother, took to her at once, the bossy housekeeper departed, and Imogen accepted her brother's new wife as tranquilly as she'd have accepted anything else.

On that Friday evening the Garlands were occupied, the one with correspondence, the other with what her husband called a Romish neckpiece she was embroidering, when Sam Gore, their only regular staff, trudged in. Flora's mother, reminder of a world where young women were presented at Court, complete with ostrich-plumes, would have called Sam a factotum. Flora called him 'That man of yours', while to Charles he was 'my chap'.

'There's two men asking to see you, sir,' he announced, taking no notice of Flora.

'Do they look like constituents?' demanded Charles.

'They looked more like policemen to me,' retorted Sam.

'If they're bobbies you'd recognize 'em, wouldn't you?'

'They're neither of them Sam Higgs (he was the local constable), nor that jumped-up sergeant down at the station. One of them says he's a detective-inspector.'

'Oh no,' murmured Flora. 'Even Dotty (they all called her Dotty) has never rated a detective-inspector before. What on earth can she have been up to?'

'Is he on a stretcher, Sam?—the inspector, I mean?' enquired Charles blandly.

'He's on two of the biggest feet you ever set eyes on,' Sam assured him.

'Top brass, then. Well, Sam, what are you waiting for? Wheel him in.'

And when Sam had disappeared, he added to his wife, 'You stay, Flo, I don't trust these foreigners,' by which he meant anyone who lived outside his village.

'Perhaps they're collecting for something,' Flora murmured.

'In my constituency I don't expect the police to go touting for subscriptions,' said Charles in a scandalized voice. 'Come in—Inspector, is it?'

'Detective-Inspector Currie, sir. This is Detective-Constable Morton.'

'Crime squad, eh? What's up?' For the first time he looked apprehensive.

'I'm sorry to take you by surprise, sir. We tried to telephone earlier, but . . .'

'I didn't get back till latish,' Charles conceded, 'and my wife was giving one of her talks to a sixth form somewhere. Sam—my chap—should have been around, though.'

Like most people in the country, the Garlands had no servants living in. Miss Styles could be relied on to take messages or deal with emergencies in the ordinary way, but Miss Styles also had been unavailable.

'Gone to London with my sister,' Charles explained. He didn't think it necessary to add that he generally tried to arrange for Dotty to be out of the way when he had constituents to interview. Not that she wasn't a dear good girl, but she did tend to make chaps think of All-Hallowe'en, and they got fun enough out of their wretched Member as it was.

'We know, sir. It's in that connection we're here.'

'What did I tell you?' murmured Flora, threading another ecclesiastical needle with a strand of rainbow silk.

'Well, come on,' said Charles impatiently. 'Let's have the bad news.'

'You were anticipating bad news, sir?'

'You're as bad as those chaps on the telly. What's my sister been up to this time? And why didn't Miss Styles stop her? It's what she's there for.' Long mooing voice this inspector chap had, he reflected. Made a man of his, Charles's age, remember the air raid sirens. Never get into the House with a voice like that, he reflected.

'Whatever it is,' said Flora, who would scarcely have been disconcerted by the appearance of the Recording Angel, let alone a couple of rozzers in undress uniform, 'you can rest assured there was no malice behind it. My sister-in-law may be a shade—unconventional . . .'

'Mad as a hatter,' contributed Charles, 'but seeing it's a hatters' world she shouldn't be specially noticeable. Still, she can't have got into much trouble with that Styles woman at her elbow. Speaking for myself, I'd as soon go around with a dagger tipped with curare. Only she and my wife—' he waved a hand in Flora's direction—'war-time buddies. More like an unexploded bomb, if you ask me. It says a lot for my sister that she can cope.'

'You haven't heard the news, then?' Though, come to think of it, it wasn't likely they would. The police hadn't been alerted till seven o'clock.

'What do you think this place is?' demanded Charles. 'A radio receiving station? You know, you're wasted in your present job. You should be in the House. Be a match for old Waldron, I shouldn't wonder. Takes so long to get round to a point the Chamber's emptied and he has to sit down—pity he can't sit on it, the point, I mean. Let me ask the questions. What's my sister been up to?'

'It's the other lady, Miss Styles. There seems to have been an accident . . .'

'And Dotty's given her the slip. I hope you'll dock this out of her pay, Flo.'

'The accident concerns the other lady, Miss Styles. She appears to have fallen from a fourth-floor window.'

Disregarding his wife's exclamation of 'Oh no!' Charles said testily, 'What do you mean—appears? Either she fell or she didn't.'

'She fell,' the officer agreed.

'Well, you're not suggesting my sister pushed her out, I suppose? Good God, man, you must be out of your mind! Got it by phone, I suppose. Well, there you are. I'm always complaining to Ronnie (Ronnie was the Post-master-General) what a shocking line we have from town. Help yourself to my instrument and try again.'

Realizing that all three men were momentarily speechless, Flora came in smoothly. 'My husband's right, Inspector. Miss Garland hasn't got a malicious bone in her body. Any—inconvenience—she may cause comes from sheer high spirits. If she had wanted to get away from Miss Styles she would have contrived it with very little difficulty—she is a most ingenious woman, though you mightn't think so to look at her—there would have been no need for violence.'

'And how about a motive?' demanded Charles. 'I mean, pushing someone out of a window isn't something you do without a motive.'

'Perhaps Miss Styles recognized someone in the street,' hazarded Flora, 'and leaned out to wave and perhaps leaned too far.'

'We don't think it happened that way, madam. That is, London doesn't. We are trying to trace any relatives she may have had.'

'I don't believe she's got any,' said Flora. 'We met during the war, we were both in the Hush-Hush Brigade. (So Imogen had got it wrong about their being old schoolmates.) I do recall her saying once that if she became a casualty no one would have to buy black on her account. And I've never heard her mention a living relation all the time she's been here, which is rather more than a year.'

'No visitors? Telephone calls?'

'Well, not here. Of course, she could have telephoned from a call-box, there's one on the Green—but why should she, when we have two in the house?'

'If she'd got any family she wouldn't be eking out a bare living acting as companion to my sister,' suggested Charles, disregarding Flora's deprecatory, 'Hardly a bare living.' 'No woman lives in another woman's house, if she can help it,' Charles continued, 'and I wouldn't say she was exactly meek in spirit. All the same, now you raise the point, she is a bit of a mystery. I mean, I could quite easily believe in the hooded man who followed her to the hotel and tipped her overboard while—that's a point. What was Dotty—my sister—doing at the time?'

'Having a bath,' said the inspector, deadpan.

'How inconvenient. I wonder who suggested that. Still, it lets her out. You're not suggesting she was having a bath in the bedroom?'

'My husband doesn't mean to suggest that Miss Styles could have taken her own life,' Flora said quickly. 'She was a woman with a considerable possessive sense, she certainly wouldn't have thrown her whole life away, whatever the circumstances.'

'Might have been in a jam,' said Charles glumly. 'You can't say she was exactly the confiding type.'

'Even if she was she'd never have chosen this way—so messy. She's as neat as a new pin—well, was.'

'And if she was in a jam, m'wife's right, she'd never have taken this way out. If it came to a set-up between her and the boys in blue my sympathy 'ud be with the boys in blue. Incidentally, where is she—my sister, I mean?'

'The management arranged for a private nurse . . .'

'You didn't say she'd fallen out of the window, too.'

'She's naturally suffering from shock. She didn't wish you to be sent for or even disturbed tonight, urgent public business, I understand . . .'

'It's too late tonight,' Flora agreed, 'particularly if she's got this nurse with her. But you'd better go up in the morning, Charles, yes, of course you can. I'll take your constituents for you.'

'You'll have 'em thinking you're the Member by the time I get back,' complained Charles. 'Any reason why this nurse person shouldn't bring my sister down here? All expenses paid, of course.'

'London would like Miss Garland to stay put for the moment,' said the inspector. 'There may be further questions.'

'You make it sound like the Inquisition. Well, as my wife says, it's too late to do anything tonight, so unless in some mysterious way she's escaped your clutches, I'll go up and collect her first thing tomorrow. Then we'll be able to see whether the police want her more than we do.'

'If this is going to be in the paper,' said Flora bluntly, 'and if this nurse person can stay on for a day or two, it might be as well to postpone Imogen's return until after your Constituency Day. Once the story gets about you'll have people like that mad Miss Marker coming to importune for birth control for poodles.'

'They don't need to importune,' said Charles sunnily. 'All the with-it ones are on the pill already.'

'And you're sure you can't help us about Miss Styles's relations?'

'I thought we'd made it clear that so far as we know, she had none, none living anyway.'

'Well, sir, it stands to reason there must have been someone. A woman of her age.'

'Oh, I don't know,' said Charles. 'History records a number of instances of people—individuals—suddenly appearing in a community, literally from Nowhere. No past history, no ties, as though they'd sprung into existence at their present age. Interesting stuff, history. And, of course, there was that goddess—Athene, wasn't it?—who sprang fully grown from the head of her father. Save a lot of trouble if we could learn some of those old fellows' tricks. No diapers, no plastic pants—OK, Inspector, I'm only thinking aloud. Have you tried Somerset House? If she did have normal parents and isn't a witch's byblow or anything, wouldn't they have a record?'

It was Flora who asked about identifying the body. 'Or has my sister-in-law done that?'

'It wasn't thought advisable for Miss Garland to see the body.'

'If you haven't unearthed any next-of-kin by morning I suppose I could do that chore, too,' agreed Charles, rather grudgingly. 'Oh come, man, don't look so glum. The corpse can't run away.'

But in the end he didn't go to London, because soon after 7 o'clock the next morning he was called by the police to say that, although Miss Styles had stayed put as any decorous corpse would, Miss Garland had disappeared.

CHAPTER FOUR

Up in London the feathers were flying as if someone had shaken a gigantic pillow out of the skies. The person least concerned by all the tamasha was Imogen herself.

When she heard the key turn in the lock of the bathroom door she pushed back the bedclothes, saying *sotto voce*, 'Silly old moo! Does she suppose I don't realize why she's removed my coat and dress? If she'd had any sense she'd have taken my handbag but I suppose she couldn't think of a good excuse on the spur of the minute.' She pulled her nightdress over her head to reveal a conglomeration of underclothes that would have delighted a dealer in Victoriana, and coolly opening the wardrobe, took Miss Holmes's admirably-cut dress and coat from their hanger. The dress, as she had suspected, was a reasonably good fit, considerably better than her own, and the coat was positively stylish. Over her bird's-nest hair she pulled the bathing nurse's neat blue felt helmet, and squeezed her feet into the low-heeled laced walking-shoes. They pinched a bit, but if it's necessary to suffer for beauty's sake, surely it's still more necessary when you're making a bid for freedom. She arranged the pillows quite adeptly—you'd think I'd been doing this all my life, she congratulated herself smugly—perched the silk-and-lace cap atop, pulled up the dressing-gown and stuffed some underwear beneath the blankets to give the impression of feet. Her shoes she was careful to leave very much *en évidence*, likewise her washing apparatus. She was fortunately adequately supplied with funds, and even in super loos, like the one at Victoria, it only cost sixpence or so to have a wash and brush up, or so she'd been told. Miss Styles would have discouraged the expenditure, they were coming to an hotel, weren't they, with a private bath, and for an emergency there were the lavatories on the train. Every sixpence you spend someone has had to earn, she would remind Imogen. Miss Holmes was splashing away like a lady walrus as Imogen, with a final glance round, stole out of the room, closing the door with exaggerated care. There was no one to be seen in the corridors, except a doleful lady pressing the button for the lift.

'It's stuck,' she told Imogen in a voice that matched her appearance. 'It was just the same when I came up. Of course, somebody leaves the door open.'

'So we'll have to walk, won't we?' said Imogen, catching at the doleful traveller's arm. A bit of luck, she reflected. No doubt Mr Harlequin (and where had his mum been to saddle him with a name like that?) had been told to keep an eye open in case she foiled his marvellous Miss Holmes, but he wouldn't be looking for two ladies. And really, Imogen reflected, we all look so much alike he's not going to notice me. There was quite a gaggle of guests in the hall—the word having gone round that one old girl had shoved another out of the window.

'The menopause,' said a voice clearly, as Imogen and her companion battering-rammed their way through the crowd.

'Were you going out?' Imogen enquired, and the doleful one said Yes, she was meeting a bosom friend . . . 'Make sure she doesn't turn out to be a viper,' counselled Imogen. 'They're what's specially known for residing in bosoms,' and seeing the doleful one turn in the direction of what she called the bright lights, Imogen walked the other way, through a side-street, ironically past the police-station until she came into the main road where she caught a bus for Piccadilly. Even at this hour—it was past 10 o'clock—Eros was surrounded by a horde who all looked, she thought, as if they'd been cast in the same mould as Doleful. Mostly they were young and had enough hair to arouse envy in the breasts of an army of chimps. Eros himself was enclosed in a gilt contraption, presumably to protect him from the assaults of the masses. Only an Englishman, a Frenchman had observed, would try to keep love in a cage. There was no riotousness about this crowd, they stood or sat dejectedly —Love's Victims, thought Imogen, and smiling at her own wit she crossed the street and joined a queue of more conventionally attired citizens waiting to get into the underground floor of a large restaurant with a different kind of eatery (that was what the management called it) on every floor. She had, of course, had the chicken casserole at the Montblanc but there still seemed a number of corners that required filling.

'One?' asked a harassed waiter, when it came to her turn.

'If you see more than one you should take an aspirin and lie down,' Imogen told him briskly.

They didn't like singletons at this hour. Mostly these objected to sharing tables with strangers and on this floor they could fill every table twice over between now and midnight. But he found her an inconvenient little one beside a pillar and almost on top of the band.

'A band,' said Imogen approvingly. 'Most entertaining. At home it's always talk about the House . . .' It wasn't the waiter's fault that he didn't realize she meant House with a capital H. When presently a younger waiter brought her half a neatly sliced roll, she looked at it in surprise.

'Where's the other half?'

'It's the experience of the management that most ladies don't require a whole roll . . .'

'Do you only charge for half? I quite appreciate your wanting to keep down expenses, I daresay the Bandleaders' Union charges twice as much as it used to and there's that thing called S.E.T. isn't there?—but you mustn't economize at the expense of clients. What's a buck rarebit elegante? I know what a buck rarebit is, of course. Just a slice of bacon added? It ought to be a big slice for the extra shilling. And a glass of stout.'

'Stout isn't served in this part of the restaurant.'

'You mean, you're not licensed?'

'Stout can be had in the Happy Warrior bar on the next floor.'

'Would they give me an elegant buck rarebit there? No? It's what the poet says. Never the time and the place and the loved one all together. All the same, you might consider serving stout. Representations are always being made in the House of Commons about eating facilities for tourists, and I daresay they'd be prepared to consider similar facilities for British citizens.'

'You've got a right nutter there,' the waited murmured to the Master of Ceremonies, as the head waiter liked to be called. 'Member of Parliament if you can believe her.'

'Oh, I can believe it,' retorted the MC bitterly. 'Anything to make our job a bit harder. That's politicians for you. Take her a glass of wine with the compliments of the management. Member of Parliament, you say?' he added, staring at the plump blue-clad figure. 'Four thousand a year and she buys a hat like that!'

Imogen received the wine graciously, but 'B and C' she noted inwardly. Even if she'd said the letters aloud the waiter wouldn't have realized they stood for Bribery and Corruption. It wasn't till she came back to ground level that she realized she'd nowhere to go that night. Well, she had her return ticket to Penton, of course, but she couldn't very well go home, not with Charles's Constituency Day in the offing. A case of touching pitch and being defiled, she reflected, besides, Charles is sure to think it's my fault about Miss Plum, and if he doesn't Flora will. In the entrance hall someone had dropped a newspaper and she picked it up and sank into a chair as if she were waiting for a friend. From her voluminous bag she produced a pair of glasses with plain lenses—an emergency measure only, she had assured Miss Plum. In case we get separated. You know what they say—

Men seldom make passes
At girls who wear glasses.

She put them on now and shook the paper open. There was a picture on the inside sheet of a number of young people camping out in Green Park. They looked rather like the crowd she'd seen round Eros earlier, who had now completely melted away, except that this lot looked more cheerful. And there was a second picture showing a perfectly-respectable looking woman lying full stretch on a Park bench. Park squatters, they were called collectively. But what a good idea, though Imogen. She hadn't a hope of getting into an hotel, not enough money for one thing, and no luggage, and for all she knew Miss Holmes had discovered the impersonation and the alarm was out. This day a stag must die, thought addle-pated Imogen. She dropped the paper and walked quietly out of the restaurant. Wearing glasses and Miss Holmes's clothes she looked quite different.

The lovely night sky, sapphire blue and silver, was darkening as she reached the still-open gates of the Park. Moving carefully, she saw that small encampments were already set up under overhanging trees, quite like something out of the Old Testament, she reflected, if only there'd been a camel or so standing about. Some of the couples under the trees lay in remarkably affectionate poses, but she wasn't shocked. Nothing so frank could be evil. A number of other people had already had the same idea as herself and she had passed a number of benches before she noticed one that was still unoccupied. She wrapped Miss Holmes's coat closely round her, bunched up the neat felt hat to serve as a pillow and remembered, too late, that experienced sleepers-out, like tramps, always supplied themselves with layers of newspapers for keeping out the cold. She looked round hopefully, but here were no papers blowing across the grass, so she lay scrunched up, fascinated by the slight movement of the leaves against that marvellous sky. This, she supposed, was how abstract painters got their inspirations, only when the idea was on paper it seemed to lose its charm. The tree under which she lay was, she thought vaguely, a fig tree. There was a very fine specimen near Pelican Island in St James's Park, and hadn't there been a prophet who crouched for forty days under a similar tree, being fed by a divinely-appointed raven? But in England in this year of grace the only ravens one knew about lived in the Tower of London, and it wasn't likely you'd care for a portion of their carrion, even if they were prepared to part.

Suddenly she became aware that someone was standing beside the bench. She shut her eyes tight, hoping that whoever it was would go away. She'd not got much money and surely the police had better things to do than try to deprive not-so-young women of their single sleep.

'I know you're faking,' said a confident voice. 'But not to worry. I'm not the fuzz.'

'The fuzz?' She opened her eyes wide in astonishment.

'The police. Matter of fact, they tend to leave us alone until morning. Shows their good sense. If they routed us all out they'd have to find some place to put us for the night, and according to the force, the cells are bursting at the seams as it is. You stay quiet and you'll be all right till morning. In the meantime, I brought you this.' She saw he had a rug draped over his arm. 'It gets cold in the small hours.'

'I didn't expect to be sleeping here,' she acknowledged. 'Won't you want it for yourself?'

He grinned. 'Thy need is greater, friend.' He was wearing what looked like his Mum's discarded fur jacket over chestnut-coloured velvet trousers. 'Just leave it when you go. There's no lying late here, you know. They move you on at an absurdly early hour.'

'I dare say I'll have moved myself on by then,' said Imogen. 'Do tell me, why do you take so much trouble for a stranger?'

'Self-preservation for one thing,' said the young man

frankly. 'Say you get pneumonia, there'll be an outcry from the general public, who all have beds to sleep in, to say nothing of the hospitals who're always belly-aching about shortage of accommodation. That 'ud put the kybosh on all of us, and we'd find the gates locked when we turned up.'

'And, of course,' contributed Imogen dramatically, 'if I died, you might be called as witnesses.'

'If you were thinking of taking an overdose of LSD we weren't to know, were we? What is it, love? I mean, mostly when you've got your far along the road you prefer your own bed. Couldn't be the fuzz are after you, I suppose?'

'In a way,' Imogen acknowledged. 'You see . . .'

He shut his eyes. 'I don't want to see. Your troubles are your affair and we're not nosey. But I'll give you one tip. Remember, the fuzz always has the last laugh. Well, pleasant dreams and make the most of 'em. It's like I said, you'd think the fuzz owned the whole bloody park.'

He nodded casually and went back to tell his mob they'd best be on the move bright and early, the old girl had got away from some place, could be the bin, anyway the fuzz had been alerted. 'We like things nice and easy,' he reminded them. 'These old girls believe in the flag and John Bull and I don't want to be a witness if she sticks a hatpin into some scoffer's heart.'

When Imogen woke day was breaking and she lay speechless and motionless in sheer delight at the slow coming of colour and the sharp stirring of birds. She must have drifted off again for the next time she opened her eyes the day was growing bright about her and she realized she was as stiff as a whalebone corset. All the same, she reflected, I wouldn't have slept so well with Miss Plum, and that started a fresh train of thought, so that she wondered just where Miss Plum had slept—in the eternal dark? or bunked down in some celestial corridor? She was still wondering about this when a policewoman came marching up to the bench, telling her, 'Upsadaisy, your folk won't like it if you're picked up for loitering.' She looked with some curiosity but no particular surprise at the rosy face and light brown hair. This was a new one, you got to know them, the regulars, that is. But she didn't spend much time pondering, it was a new day and there was work to be done, and part of hers was to see these old tramps were off their benches before the general public started coming in. This Park was used as a sort of thoroughfare by office workers, a short cut to Whitehall or St James's. 'Now come on, you don't want to catch cold . . .'

'I have my rug,' began Imogen, and then glanced down and realized this was no longer true. 'They must have taken it away while I napped,' she said.

'They?'

'Some very nice young people (better not to generalize) who were afraid I should catch pneumonia. It seems dreadful that in the Welfare State they should have to camp out on the grass, while the bigwigs' salaries go up and up . . .'

'You don't want to worry about them,' said the policewoman comfortably. 'They've mostly got homes if they choose to go to them. If you were to meet most of them five or six years hence you wouldn't recognize them.'

'I do remember I always wished I could camp out and sleep in the fields when I was young,' Imogen confessed. 'You can sleep in beds when you're old . . .'

'And for the most part sleep alone,' agreed the policewoman. 'Do your family know where you are?'

'Oh, I've got a bed, too,' Imogen assured her. 'It's just that I missed the last train, and I hadn't enough money left for an hotel, and anyway if you haven't any luggage nobody wants you, and this seemed better than a railway station where people think you're on meth and want to save you—one thing, it's a lovely fine morning and I'm nice and near Charing Cross.'

She shook out the felt hat that looked as though it had been nested in by a too-large bird and jammed it on to her hair. 'I shall just have time for a nice wash and brush up,' she announced gaily, 'before I get the first train home.'

'Got enough money?' This was a queer bird and no mistake.

'Oh, I have a return ticket. Anyway, they know me the other end, if I hadn't got a ticket at all they'd let me through.'

The policewoman let her go. Well, she hadn't any choice, a sober and obviously respectable party who moved on when requested. It was nearly an hour before the chambermaid at the Montblanc was to take early morning tea to Room 39, and discover the cruel hoax Miss Garland had perpetrated on a woman who'd only come to do her good. It wasn't till she returned to the station and heard about the runaway that WPC Williams recalled the woman on the bench.

'She was going to Charing Cross,' she said. But nobody at Charing Cross remembered seeing her, and they drew an equal blank at Victoria. Which wasn't surprising, as Imogen had been to neither.

At Ditcham Dora was still knocked-out by the news. She wished she could talk to someone. She'd put on the radio at 6 o'clock, but there was nothing fresh, nothing tangible, that is. A policewoman had seen someone answering to Dotty's description in a London park but hadn't detained her, because at that time the news of her disappearance wasn't public property. Miss Holmes had been interviewed and said she'd never heard of anything so ungrateful. The woman was clearly a mental case, and for everyone's sake should be apprehended without delay. Mr Harlequin was outraged—that such a thing should happen in HIS hotel. The missing woman's family had no statement to make. Various people had believed they saw her, though no two in the same place, but no one could really assist the police. There was a murmur of amnesia.

Not that one, decided Dora scornfully. She knows how many beans make five, and it wouldn't surprise me if she made them six but never four.

She noticed there was no reference to an odd little occurrence at Penton Station some weeks before, but really why should there be? The station-master wouldn't want to court the limelight in case someone suggested it was his fault—quite unfair, of course, but only mugs and the very young expected life to be fair. The boy had dissociated himself from the pack of them before the drama began, the clubman wouldn't consider the affairs of two not very striking spinsters much in *his* line—which only left Mr Crook. She got his card out, and sat with it in her hand, looking from it to the telephone for quite a while. At last she picked up the instrument, but though she dialled both numbers there was no reply. (Mr Crook had closed down the Bloomsbury Office for the day and was having a jar at the Two Chairmen before resuming work at his Blandford Street flat.)

After that the evening seemed to stretch out into infinity. Dora felt she'd even welcome the phantom Mr Preston, who must at least have been a person with experience, and might be able to reassure her in her present perplexity. It didn't occur to her to contact the police herself direct. There was nothing on the television to hold the interest, no one telephoned. Mr Preston was presumably sleeping snugly underground, oblivious of the troubled world he had left behind.

'Wanted—one friendly ghost,' said Dora, restlessly.

It was less than five minutes later that a tap sounded on the door.

Imogen had had a gorgeous day, she told Dora. Beetling out of the Park, she walked with a rather swaying step to Victoria Coach Station, where she mingled with an exhausted-looking crowd who had just got off an overnight bus, and had her promised wash and brush up. Then she walked down Buckingham Palace Road and found a working-man's café, where she got eggs and bacon and good strong tea, and no one took any notice of her at all. There was a number of women here, all very cheerful and loud-voiced—cleaners at local offices—what fun they seem to be having, Imogen thought, I've always believed Flora was wrong thinking gentility's the thing. It might have been once, but now it's the faded flower of a blameless life. She walked cheerfully along Victoria Street, then mounted a city-going bus and arrived at the Tower of London. Her high spirits were daunted for a little at sight of the little stone memorial square that marks the spot where so much blood was shed. We're a very bloodthirsty race, she decided. Tyburn Tree, whose site is now a religious chapel, and now this—you'd expect people to want to forget. But this was a holiday and no time for mourning. When a boat docked just below the Tower she went on board and travelled down to Greenwich in the company of a number of Salvation Army lassies who seemed to have gone mad with a camera.

At Greenwich she went first to the church and then to the Maritime Museum, where she stood spellbound in front of the magnificent Canaletto. She thought she'd never recall Greenwich without recalling this painting. To leave that behind you when you go, she thought, what more immortality could any man desire? She had lunch at a little café where she was joined by some of the Salvation Army lasses. They were down from the north on a convention and for many of them it was their first sight of London.

'They said it was a wicked city, wasn't it?' Dotty told an entranced Dora. 'But God rules there as elsewhere and even Londoners had souls to save. Any minute I expected them to strike up a hymn. Then I came back to Westminster and suddenly I began to wonder where I should spend the night. I didn't dare go back to the Park, and I couldn't very well go home, I was sure they'd be on to Charles, and Flora's one of those people who don't like their plans to go wrong. I mean, if I'd fallen out of the window, she'd have been sorry because I'm Charles's sister and it's the same name, but the ways of the Lord are not our ways. And really I had nowhere else to go. And then suddenly I remembered you and how you'd said "You must drop in," and there was that man in Dickens who said there's no time like the present, and I thought I'd better come right away, before it occurred to anybody that I might be here.'

'Why should anybody know we'd met?' asked Dora, absorbed.

'Well, there was that club man type, he saw us, and the Gingerbread Man, and Charles always says you can't beat the man-to-man encounter, and I suppose that would cover the woman-to-woman as well. Anyhow, I came.'

'Just when I was longing for company,' beamed Dora. 'And you're much better than Mr Preston. But actually, you know, it isn't me you should be telling all this to'—because in her rather frenetic fashion Imogen had tumbled all the facts before her audience, making Dora think of a work-box that's been upset, all the reels are dangling threads, the pins and needles are inextricably mixed up, and if you aren't careful you may prick yourself on a darner or pierce yourself on an open pair of scissors. Still, as one of the Sunday papers used to advertise, all life was there, all the relevant facts anyway, and as Mr Crook was to tell them both later, it don't matter in which order you deliver them, it's the order in which the experts arrange them that matters.

'So I remembered you,' beamed Dotty. 'It seemed like a heavenly inspiration. I mean, even Charles, even Flora, couldn't think you were not respectable.'

For some reason this didn't reasssure Dora as it was intended to.

'And I thought,' continued the single-hearted Imogen, 'you'd be able to advise me what I should do next.'

'You don't need me to tell you that,' said Dora crisply.

'You're holding out on the police, I'm not sure what they can do about it, but isn't there something called impeding them in the execution of their duties?'

'Impeding them?' Imogen exclaimed. 'I'm not in their way, in fact, I've put as much space as I possibly could between them and me.'

'You know perfectly well what I mean,' said Dora. 'You can't go on hiding.'

'You mean, you'd tell the police . . .?' It was clear that she couldn't believe it.

'No, you'll do that, in due course. But at the moment you should be telling a lawyer.'

'I don't have a lawyer,' Dotty said. 'At least there's Charles's Mr Firebrace, but he's like Charles, he won't want publicity, not this sort. If that's the best suggestion you can make . . .' she looked round. 'Where did I put my things? I'd better be going.'

'Oh, don't be absurd!' Dora restrained a longing to stamp her foot. 'Of course you can't go. You'd put your head straight into a noose. At the same time, you're not an ostrich, sooner or later you'll have to take your head out of the sand. No, the person you've got to see first is a lawyer—not that stuffed shirt your brother patronizes—but someone with some knowledge of human nature, and I know exactly the man. I've got his card here, I was just wondering if I should ring him . . . only he'd probably say he doesn't poach on other people's preserves, but naturally it's different if you're invited. I did try and get him earlier, but he was out. Still, he'll probably be back by now, and it's not as though he's a stranger to you, he's saved your life once, and he doesn't look the sort of person that likes leaving things unfinished, so you see in a way you'd be doing him a favour. And don't think the police wouldn't track you down sooner or later even if you stayed here, but he'd be a match for the Director of Public Prosecutions himself.'

And picking up the telephone she once again dialled Mr Crook's number.

Mr Crook heard the bell as he came trudging up the stairs. He was a big-made chap and you'd be looking at a chicken a long time before you thought of him, but he could no more resist the phone bell than an alcoholic can resist the last glass that tips him over the edge, and he came up the remainder of the steps like a streak of light.

'You won't remember me,' bubbled Dora into the phone, but he cut her off short, saying, 'The Pig Lady. I was wondering if I might hear from you.'

'You must have a memory like a computer,' Dora said. 'Don't they say they remember everything?'

'Sure they do,' agreed Crook. 'Trouble is they so often remember it wrong. Well, Sugar, I can guess why you're ringing. It's a proper turn-up for the book, ain't it? Like that chap in the poem. (only he pronounced it 'pome') The man recovered from the bite, The dog it was that died.'

'Well, it's not really the dog I'm interested in.'

'Hold everything,' murmured Crook, in a reverential voice, 'you're not going to tell me you know where Dotty is?'

'Why else do you suppose I'm ringing you up? She's here—here—in this room—she slept on a park bench last night, and, here's the joke, it was a policewoman who moved her on.'

'What made her come to you, Sugar?'

'She hadn't much choice, said Dora scornfully. 'It was me or her relations, she couldn't sleep a second night in the Park. And I've got relations myself.' She thought of her prim churchy brother, her managing sister, Helen, who'd managed one husband out of her life already, and was setting to with splendid appetite on the second. 'So, you see, if I were in Imogen's shoes—she's asked me to call her that, I can't go on saying Miss Garland, and anyhow we shall all have our first names in Heaven—I wouldn't want to go home either. But before the police run her to earth . . .'

'I should koko,' said Mr Crook amiably. 'You'd probably pass her off as the ghost. And it wouldn't surprise me if you was to get away with it.' Mr Crook was nothing if not generous.

'So why I'm ringing you,' continued the dauntless spinster, 'is to know if you'll represent her at the enquiry or the inquest or whatever it's called. Then she'll get fair play.'

'Couldn't have come to a better shop,' said Mr Crook unblushingly.

'Oh, and I was thinking. Hasn't she got a case against the police? I always understood they had to prefer a charge or let you go completely free, not shut you up with a monster like that Miss Holmes . . .'

'That wasn't the rozzers. The lady was a nurse.'

'Imogen didn't need a nurse, she wasn't ill.'

'And if it had been the police, it 'ud have been called police protection. I mean, say someone pitched Miss Plum out of a window, Dotty might be next on the list.'

'She might have got pneumonia sleeping out in the park.'

'Sugar,' said Mr Crook, 'nobody made her sleep out in the Park. And she's the only one can help them, if she's a mind.'

'How can she help them? She was in the bath.'

'They need a witness.'

'People having baths don't expect to be asked to act as witnesses.'

'And she swiped the lady's clobber—remember.'

'Only because the nurse had already swiped hers.'

'I can see you're just the kind of witness I'd like to have on my side when I'm up in front of the beak,' said Crook gracefully. 'But just remember, it ain't always a good idea to know all the answers. The police do like to be allowed to score a few points.'

'We only want justice,' said Dora gently, and the sigh that came over the line nearly broke it.

'Now,' said Mr Crook, 'I've heard everything. And remember, quite a lot of chaps who've temporarily diverted other chaps' funds into their pockets have used just the same argument Dotty's going to use about borrowing Miss Whosit's gear without permission. So don't push your luck, Sugar. You may sound as logical as an angel of light to yourself, but it don't follow the old bird on the box—judge to you—is wearin' the same rose-coloured glasses. Do they run to a pub in your part of the world?'

'Of course they do,' cried Dora, delighted. 'And I'll book you a room in it. How soon will you be here? And suppose the police do arrive before you do, aren't I entitled to refuse to let them in without a search warrant or something? It's not as though they've really got anything against Imogen. And don't tell me about Miss Holmes's dress again. She couldn't get at her own because Miss Holmes had got it in the bathroom, and if she'd gone out without any clothes she'd have been had up for indecent exposure. You can't win, can't you?'

And without giving him a chance to have the last word, she rang off.

CHAPTER FIVE

SOME TIME LATER that evening, when they were sitting *à trois* round Dora's hospitable fire, Mr Crook having arrived like the phenomenal streak of light, Imogen said thoughtfully, 'I suppose the person most likely to be able to help us would be Miss Plum's brother, only he doesn't seem to want the limelight, and I dare say you can't blame him.'

'Brother?' ejaculated Mr Crook. 'That's a new one on me. Who says she's got a brother?'

'She did, she told me. But as I don't think she told anyone else, I can't absolutely prove it, unless he chooses to come forward.'

'Any reason why he shouldn't—unless someone's pushed him out of a window, too?'

'I suppose if there wasn't a reason he'd have—what's the word?—surfaced before this. But if he wasn't some sort of Man of Mystery why should Miss Plum have been so secretive about him? I never heard him mentioned at home. I don't believe even Flora knew.'

'But you winkled it out of her—Miss Plum, I mean?'

'Not exactly. I found out by accident. I mean, I guessed she was trying to hide something, because of all those walks to Oakhill, and if she wasn't trying to keep it from Flora and Charles, why did she have to go so far afield?'

'I don't follow you, Sugar,' said Mr Crook, patiently. 'Where is this place, Oakhill?'

'Oh, it's only about two miles. Miss Plum used to say it was such a nice walk, but she didn't really enjoy walking and if she had there are much pleasanter places to go than Oakhill. But it was because of the Post Office. She used to get letters there.'

'Have you told the police any of this?' asked Crook suspiciously.

She looked at him wide-eyed. 'How could I? I promised Miss Plum and you can't break a promise because someone has died.'

'You're telling me,' Crook pointed out.

'That's different. You're my man of affairs. I've often heard my father say you must never hide anything from your man of affairs. And I couldn't have told you any sooner because I haven't seen you since that afternoon at Penton.'

'When Miss Plum tried to introduce you to the wrong side of a railway track?'

Imogen stared. 'You must be joking. You can't really believe she was trying to push me under the engine?'

'I trust I'm always ready to learn,' said Crook meekly. 'But that was my impression.'

'That only shows you didn't know Miss Plum. If she'd wanted me under the engine under the engine I'd have gone. No one could have stopped her. But how could me being dead, even if she could make it look like an accident, and being Miss Plum she probably could, how could it help her? One of the things Flora was paying her for was to look after me, I'd been a bit off colour, having little faints, nothing to worry about and so I told Charles, but he said it looked bad me falling about in all directions, as if I was drunk, and all his political opponents would be sure to put that construction on it, and Miss Plum turning up out of the blue—the Hand of Providence, Flora said, though I don't know if Charles agreed. He didn't really like her, I couldn't say why . . .'

'Ever noticed that husbands hardly ever care for their wives' friends and buddies?' asked that Man of the World, Arthur Crook. 'Don't know why . . .'

'I can tell you,' put in Dora eagerly, feeling she'd been silent too long. 'They don't like the idea that anyone's company can be preferred to theirs. I've heard my brother say it. But, dearest, he'll tell Grace, how can you possibly want A or B or C to stay when you have Me? It's not as though I were one of those nine-to-five spouses—he really does use that word, he says it's biblical—you have Me all the time. He's a Dean,' she added for her audience's mutual benefit.

'And then they call matrimony the holy estate,' marvelled Mr Crook. 'Go on, Sugar, sooner or later you're going to tell us how you found out about Brother, and even, if we're lucky, what game Miss Plum was playing when the both of us got the notion she was trying to push you under a train.'

'She had my arm in a grip of iron all the time, even if it didn't look like it,' Imogen assured him confidently. 'But she had an audience, which was unusual, not just neighbours who never notice you anyway, but you and the mysterious man and Dora here, of course, so you do see what a chance it was for her to give the impression that I was a bit *non compos*, and then if anything should happen later on one of you would probably remember. She did her best by asking Dora to see I didn't stray into the rain, or fall off the edge of the platform—if she actually didn't say that I expect you got the message—well, then no one would be likely to listen if I started to talk about Brother and the mysterious letters she used to collect at Oakhill Post Office.'

'I ain't a naturalist myself,' Crook confided, 'the human animal's sometimes too much for me, but I have heard that cats take a long time to come home because they always go the longest way round. No offence intended, Sugar, but it wouldn't surprise me to learn you'd been a pussy-cat in some earlier incarnation.'

'It's just that I want to make everything clear,' Imogen insisted. 'I know Miss Plum said we'd keep it a secret between us, but she didn't really trust me, she hadn't got a very trusting nature, and I'm sure Flora didn't know about the brother.'

'I thought you said they were wartime buddies.'

'Ah, but they didn't meet till the war. I was wrong when I said I thought they'd been at school together. If they'd been at school Flora would have known about the brother, I mean that there was one, because at school you always know about your friends' families. If somebody's father drinks or her mother carries on, nobody actually says anything, but everybody knows. And sooner or later the girls leave school because they can't stand it. But if you don't meet somebody till you're both grown-up, you don't have to start by saying I've got a brother and he's a bad hat.'

'Was he? I mean, is he?'

'Well, I don't know, do I? Only if he was all right why did there have to be so much secrecy? Why did she have to go to Oakhill to post her letters, because I noticed she always posted at least one letter when we went to Oakhill . . .'

Mr Crook looked pardonably confused. 'Are you suggesting Miss Plum had more than one brother?'

'I only said she posted more than one letter, and I thought that was her cunning, because if I noticed there was only one envelope each time, I might begin to put two and two together.'

'And make them about ninety-six. I get you, Sugar. Sure it was always to the same person?' But before she could speak he had corrected himself. 'Ask a silly question . . . You never saw the envelopes, of course.'

'I never saw the ones she picked up either. I only know about them by a sort of accident. As soon as we got to Oakhill she'd say, "Why don't you go and reserve a table for us at Aunt Charlotte's café? I've just got to telephone." Though she could easily have telephoned from the house. If she didn't know how much the calls were Flora would have told her. She's the kind of person who keeps a record of trunk calls, so she'd soon know which were hers and Charles's, and which weren't.'

'Ah!' said Crook solemnly, 'but then she'd also know the

number of Miss Plum's acquaintance, Exchange always tells you if you query the charge of a call, and that would defeat the object of the exercise.'

'Yes, of course,' agreed Imogen. 'I hadn't thought.'

Dora turned to her eagerly. 'Was that what you had in mind when you said about a little knowledge being a dangerous thing?'

'It was certainly little,' Imogen agreed. 'But big oaks from little acorns grow. And don't ask me why he had to be kept such a secret, but Charles is very fussy about his reputation, and if Brother had Criminal Connections . . .'

'You were going to tell us how you found out about him in the first place,' Crook reminded her.

'Oh yes. Well, it was this day at Oakhill, I'd gone off to do a bit of shopping because Miss Plum said she wanted to ring someone up, and then I remembered I wanted to ask about opening an investment account at the Post Office. I could have found out nearer home, of course, but in a small place people talk so . . .'

'It's what tongues were given us for,' offered Crook mildly.

'I thought it would be nice if I could have a secret, too, so I went back and there was Miss Plum at the far end of the counter looking at an envelope and asking, "Are you sure that's the only one?" '

'No attempt to make a secret of it? or didn't she see you?'

'She always said it was a mistake to whisper when you had anything private to say, it always attracted attention, whereas if you talked in an ordinary voice nobody listened.'

'Seems to have had all her marbles,' said Mr Crook.

'I asked the clerk for a leaflet about the Investment Account, and I got away before Miss Plum had finished askinq questions. When she joined me at the café I said "I'm sorry you didn't get your letter. Perhaps it'll be there tomorrow. You know what the posts are these days." She said, "I don't know what you're talking about," and I said,

"Well, I happened to be in the Post Office, and I heard you ask . . . I'm sorry, I'm not inquisitive." But, of course,' added Imogen, naively, 'I was. Anyone would be.'

'How did Miss Plum react to that?'

'She gave a funny sort of smile and said, "Can you keep a secret?" so I said, "Well, I wouldn't tell Charles or Flora, if that's what you mean," and of course that's what she did—mean, that is. She said Flora had had trouble enough and she'd been so good to her, Miss Plum, and she didn't want her bothered.'

'Why should Miss Plum's brother bother your sister-in-law?' Dora wondered.

'I thought he was probably a bit of a scapegrace, no, I thought more than that, I thought she didn't want anyone else to know about him in case Flora thought she couldn't stay with us.'

'Why should she want to?' asked Dora with an innocence Crook could envy.

'I did wonder myself. I think she must have had rather a difficult time before she came to us and after she and Flora parted—I know she went overseas and her ship was torpedoed, and for a time she was put down as lost. She never talks much about what happened afterwards—perhaps she was rescued by savages or something . . .'

'I'd have thought she'd have wanted to broadcast that, it's so unusual,' Dora suggested.

'Well, anyway, she said it was wonderful to have a home, I don't think she had any money, and unquestionably she was useful to Flora—who's a great manager but she doesn't like housework, and even people with money can't get servants these days. And then it did mean that Flora didn't have to worry about me. Not that I was really ill, but I had these dizzy spells when, according to Flora, I didn't know what I was doing. The trouble with Flora is she hasn't much sense of humour, I knew perfectly well what I was doing. Anyway, Miss Plum was terribly useful, though I did ask her if she wouldn't sometimes like to better herself. I mean, where was the use in passing all those exams if all she was going to do was cook and garden? I liked the gardening part, I wanted to help, but Miss Plum wouldn't let me, not after I pulled up the antirrhinums she'd just planted, thinking they were weeds. I'm sure they looked just like them.'

'Who decides which are weeds and which are flowers?' asked Mr Crook. 'Ain't Dame Nature responsible for them all?'

'I wish we'd had you with us when Miss Tweedsmuir-Daly came to lecture on gardens and their uses,' said Imogen wistfully. 'She talked a lot about weeds. No one had the nous to ask *that* question.'

'Might be a good idea to find out if Lady Flo does know anything about the brother,' Crook suggested. 'The clerk at the Oakhill office might remember the lady, too. If she often went, I mean.'

'I don't even know if she used her own name,' said Imogen doubtfully.

Dora broke in with unreserved enthusiasm, 'You don't think Miss Plum can have been a member of a *Gang*, do you? And her visits to the Post Office were to get instructions . . .'

'I can see you don't need any old ghost,' said Mr Crook resignedly. 'Never a dull moment. But whatever name she used the chap would recognize her picture, I suppose.'

'There wasn't any very good one of her,' Imogen confessed. 'She said she hated being photographed. She always looked like the Mother of the Wizard of Oz, though I don't know how Miss Plum knew what she looked like. As a matter of fact, photographs didn't play much of a part in our life at home. I've never seen a picture of Flora's first husband, I don't think she's got one.'

'Not a husband or a photograph? Well, sugar, you wouldn't expect her to flaunt a likeness of the dear departed under her present husband's roof. I ain't one myself, a husband, I mean, but I'm given to understand they can be sensitive about these things. Not even a snapshot—Miss Plum, I mean?'

'Nothing you could produce, I don't think. Of course, Charles is different. He has to be photographed for his constituency addresses and for the press. And there are a few of Flora, she's one of those people who photograph well. I always look like something out of Beatrix Potter.'

'The police are beginning to get my sympathy,' said Crook, in candid tones. 'Not a helpin' hand, even from the grave. Still, there may be letters among her papers, and the police are sitting on 'em, waiting to hatch.'

'I remember her saying once, Miss Plum, I mean, that only fools kept letters, you never knew when they might be used against you, and everybody has a right to change his mind. I've seen her push envelopes, I suppose with the letters inside them, into trash-bins on the way back from Oakhill.'

No one commented on that.

'Do you think the brother was blackmailing her?' continued the resourceful Miss Garland.

'Meanin' she had a past?'

'I meant that he had, and she might think it worth while to shut his mouth. And perhaps she stayed on with Flora because she knew the brother wouldn't be admitted there, and that's what she meant when she spoke of being safe.'

'But I thought if anyone was being blackmailed it was the blackmailer who died,' objected Dora. 'It doesn't make sense.'

'The goose that lays the golden eggs,' Mr Crook agreed. 'May annoy you by cackling over much, but a dead goose don't lay any eggs at all.' He turned sharply to Imogen. 'Yes, Sugar, what is it?'

'I was remembering something,' said Imogen. 'I don't know if it was important, but it was about the bills.'

'What bills 'ud those be, Sugar?'

'I don't know what they were exactly, but I suppose everyone has bills. Only mostly they pay them by cheque?'

'Well?'

'Miss Plum used to get postal orders.'

'Then maybe she didn't have a checking account.'

'But Flora paid her by cheque.'

'She could have paid it into a Post Office account.' Mr Crook caught himself up. 'That's a funny thing. I never heard any mention of a Post Office book.'

'I didn't mean she never drew a cheque,' elaborated Imogen. 'But she did get postal orders sometimes.'

'Post Office accounts are very useful,' Dora interposed. 'I always have one. Banks close at such inconvenient hours, and now they don't even open on Saturdays. And, of course,' she continued, 'you don't have to sign a postal order. You needn't even write the recipient's name if you don't want to, though I know the Post Office says you should, and you don't have to buy it in your own neighbourhood . . .'

Imogen electrified them both by exclaiming suddenly, 'Baker Street.'

'How come, Sugar?' asked Crook.

'When we went to London we always went to a Post Office in Baker Street. We didn't always stop at the same hotel, but we always went to that Post Office. Of course, it was near Madame Tussaud's.'

'Always go to Madame Tussaud's?' asked Crook.

'Miss Plum had a passion for it, especially the Chamber of Horrors. She said it was so interesting to see how ordinary criminals looked. There's a little woman there who was a nurse, such a smiling rosy little body, but she killed goodness knows how many babies and threw them into the river.'

'Mrs Dyer,' murmured Crook knowledgeably.

'If she'd applied to you for a job,' Imogen continued, 'you wouldn't have had any hesitation . . .'

'Presumably they didn't, the kids' mothers, I mean. Mostly born the wrong side of the blanket,' he added.

'I didn't like it,' Imogen confessed. 'But I enjoyed the comic mirrors. They could make even Miss Plum look fat. I don't think she liked that much.'

'She didn't mind going round the Horrors on her owney-oh?'

'Oh no. Anyway, it's always crowded. I said to her once how could she bear to contemplate so many examples of man's inhumanity to man, and she just looked at me in that birdlike way she had and said, "I believe in facing facts." '

'Wouldn't surprise me to know she believed in making other people face 'em, too,' Crook agreed. 'Been to the PO this time, had she?'

Imogen looked reproachful. 'She didn't have time, Mr Crook. I mean, she fell out of the window the first night. But she was going the next day, she said so. Remind me I must call at Baker Street tomorrow, she said. Not that she was likely to forget. She never forgot things like that.'

'I'll say,' Crook murmured. 'Ever have any visitors in London?'

'She used to go off sometimes on her own. I'm meeting a friend, she'd say. I didn't mind. I liked being on my own, too. There's such a lot to see in London, it must be the biggest free show in the world. If it was wet I'd go to a cinema—and it's all very well to say Londoners are stand-offish, but, Mr Crook, it simply isn't true. They're more friendly than country-folk. Charles wouldn't agree, of course, but then Charles is the local Member, naturally everyone wants to talk to him, but if you hadn't lived about a hundred years in the same village, you're regarded as an outsider. I don't suppose you agree,' she added half-apologetically to Dora, 'but then you're different. You're like London, sort of the hub of the universe.'

'And if ever they make you a Dame you won't get a better compliment,' observed Crook enthusiastically to Dora. 'And I couldn't agree with you more, Sugar, on all heads. Well, it'll be interesting to know what the rozzers make of all this.'

'You mean, you're going to tell the police where she is?' Dora sounded outraged.

'Citizen's duty, the same Nelson says England expects every man to do. Besides, why should she go on hiding? You ain't broken no laws, none of the ones on the Statute Book, anyway,' he corrected himself.

'What will happen?'

'I daresay they'll come to see you.'

'See me?' repeated Dora. 'Why on earth . . .? I mean, they can see me at any time. Surely it's Imogen they'll come for.'

'You'll find it comes to the same thing,' Crook assured her consolingly. 'Beside,' he added to his new client, 'once they know where you are you'll be a free agent, be able to go where you like.'

'I like to stay here,' said Imogen simply.

'If I'm acting for you—and it was your suggestion, remember,' he added severely to Dora, 'I call the tune.'

'I expect Mr Crook's more up to their tricks—the police, I mean—than we could be,' Dora assured her guest.

So it was that Crook used the telephone and contacted the local station. The officer in charge of the case was off duty but Crook said that was OK, his client was also off duty, so to speak, and tomorrow would do very nicely. Yes, naturally Miss Garland would be available, what on earth had she got to hide, and like jesting Pilate, he didn't wait for an answer.

'What about Charles and Flora?' Imogen asked. 'I don't suppose they want me to go back there . . .'

'Let them have a quiet night,' Crook suggested. 'I want to follow up a hunch or two on my own account and then I'll go round and have a word. And remember, when the fuzz does arrive, if they get difficult, there's the famous trilogy of a notable KC. I wasn't there. I don't remember. Everything went blank.'

And merry as a sandboy he got back into the Superb and drove away.

After he had gone Imogen said solemnly, 'I was thinking —about all the people who deserve medals and never get them. There's Mr Crook going to face Charles *and* Flora single-handed, and taking it as part of the day's work. I'd sooner be Daniel in the lions' den myself. Lions can only ROAR.'

'They can devour you,' Dora pointed out.

'Even lions can't bite through armour-plating.'

'If he's got your brother and his wife, you've got the police.'

'Why should I be afraid of them?' Imogen enquired. 'I've only got to answer their questions. I've done that already. They can hardly blame me if they didn't ask the right ones.'

'They may have suspicions.' Dora's hiss wouldn't have disgraced a king cobra.

'Suspicions are like viruses. They all exist in the mind, and seeing they're in the official mind, and not mine, why should I worry? Now, Dora, let's have a lovely cup of tea—I'd have suggested it to Mr Crook but he doesn't look a T-set sort of man—and then we can go to bed.'

'But the police . . .'

'You heard what he said. They're not coming round tonight.'

'You can't ever be sure with them.'

'Then we'll block the bell. It's quite easy, just a bit of paper under the clapper. You don't have a knocker, and I don't think even the police—what did Mr Crook call them? the fuzz? The young man in the Park called them that, too —I don't think even they are allowed to break in unless you're a wanted criminal.'

'They might even think you were that.' Dora's voice was dark, but Imogen's was confident.

'Not with Mr Crook behind me they won't.'

'If it hadn't been for Mr Crook they'd never have known you were here,' Dora grumbled.

'I expect they'd have found out, they're not fools. Anyway, I couldn't have stayed hidden for ever.' She spoke more truly than even she knew. Even without the obliging Mr Crook's assistance, the fuzz would have been on the trail by morning.

At about the time that Crook reached the Ditcham cottage, Dr Ambrose Martin left his flat in Albany and strolled round to what he referred to as his club. This wasn't the Mausoleum, of which he was a member, and to which he ungratefully referred as the Living Graveyard, but a snug little pub called the Angel Sisters, where Crook would have found himself at home, but where the clientèle contrived to be reasonably exclusive. By no means a den of vice, a number of its unofficial members discussed vice from a variety of (personal) angles.

The first man the doctor saw as he moved towards the bar—it was all very democratic, no velvet-footed waiters with bunions bringing you a thimbleful of dregs on a silver salver (Crook's definition of drinking with the nobs, though it wasn't a thing he often did himself), chaps fetched their own drinks and there was no putting them on the slate. The room was small and darkish to match the secrets that were frequently believed to be ventilated there, and anyone who didn't want to be chatted up could sit in a quiet corner and probably go unrecognized for as long as he pleased. The first man, then, whom Dr Martin recognized was a square-set individual in a coat any New York tycoon might have envied, who was drinking beer, it being a place where the beer's as dependable as the whisky.

'Having a spot of bother, I understand, Henry?' suggested Martin, ordering whisky and soda. He'd had a busy day but, like Mr Crook, he had the sort of mind that, like Clapham Junction, can go all ways at once.

'What cloud did you drop out of?' demanded Superintendent Henry Jorrocks. 'Saw a picture of you flying to Nuremberg or something.'

'Amsterdam,' corrected Martin. 'Breeding session there, breeding a lot of new drugs.' He frowned.

'No likee?' asked the superintendent.

'Tell me, why do we have such a large police force? And don't remind me that it's not large enough. I'll put it another way. Why do we need such a large police force?'

'Because there are so many villains about.'

'Ah, but if you knew the way they were going to work you could be ready for them. The trouble is crime isn't a nice, straightforward affair, you can't count on it toeing the line. Murder—burglary, arson—grievous bodily harm—blackmail. If you could isolate all those your job would be comparatively simple. OK, Henry, I only said comparatively. Well, it's the same with drugs. You discover an antibiotic called A, which will alleviate or even cure a certain condition—call that B—but in so doing you may well set up side-effects that produce a different disability if not actually a disease in your patient . . .'

'Which is just as likely to kill him in the end?'

'The trouble is you can only prove your case by trial and error. And you can try it out on rats and mice and still find you're wrong when it comes to the human animal. A woman in my hospital said to me the other day, "If God had meant me to be a guinea-pig he'd have given me four feet." '

'One sees her point,' agreed Jorrocks politely. 'And I suppose I see yours. Every sick body's different, like every criminal. But there are certain basic similarities . . .'

'You're not lecturing to your young rookies now,' said Martin. 'My fault, I get carried away. Trouble with the National Health is it tends to depersonalize the patients, and goes half-way towards depersonalizing the doctors. About this case of yours—your vanishing lady.'

'Miss Garland?' The superintendent looked frankly

astounded. 'Not a friend of yours, I take it. This interest in crime is surely new. I've heard it said of you that you're probably the one man in the country who wouldn't recognize Sherlock Holmes if he walked in.'

'I saw her, I'm convinced of it,' Martin told him. 'Saw the pair of them come to that. Miss Garland was making all and sundry a present of her name, she called the other one Miss Plum . . .'

'Hold everything,' interjected Jorrocks. 'Where was this?'

'A little station called Penton on the Southern Region, and if you haven't heard of it no one could blame you. How Beeching overlooked it when he was shutting up stations all over the country—I can only assume it was so insignificant he didn't know it was there.'

'What were you doing at a station like that?'

'I was seeing a patient who couldn't come up to Harley Street, and didn't trust anyone but me to see him off to Kingdom Come. Always a ditherer,' he added, in a tone of faint scorn. 'Kept his mother waiting twenty-four hours before he came into the world, never got married because it's better to be safe than sorry and now can't make up his mind whether to live or die. Anyway, his shuvver, who called for me—oh yes, he likes to do the thing in style—fell down in the local and broke his leg, anyway, that's his story—so I volunteered to come up by train.'

'Try anything once,' agreed the superintendent.

'And once is enough. Anyway, here I was this wet afternoon, and there, too, were Miss Garland and her friend.'

'When was this?'

'Oh, two, three months ago. I could check it in my diary. Anyway, one of them was the woman who reappears as the defenestration victim . . .'

'You're not in Harley Street now,' Jorrocks reminded him in some disgust. 'Plain English is good enough for me. The one who fell out of a window. Who else was around?'

'There was a scruffy young chap who took himself off

quite early in the proceedings, and there was a fellow who looked like a professional bruiser. If he isn't a chucker-out at some rumbustious pub he's missed his vocation.'

'So?'

'Miss Garland was talking to this other woman . . .'

'Miss Styles?'

'No, not her. There was a third woman, no, I don't know her name . . .'

'Do your patients pay you by the minute in Harley Street?' enquired Jorrocks offensively. 'Didn't this lady have the decency to mention her name?'

'No, but she was telling all and sundry she'd just bought a cottage in the neighbourhood, and Miss Garland said did she know it was haunted, so X said, "You must come down and see it some time—Miss Styles had gone to the comfort station . . ." ' (Jorrocks winced.) 'Before she went she asked Miss X to keep an eye on her friend.'

'Why? Did she think the lady was moronic?'

'In view of what happened later she may have had her reasons. When the train did come in Miss Garland and her companion went up to the front, and the next minute there was a terrific tamasha. So far as I could gather Miss Garland had either slipped or tried to throw herself under the train.'

'And you dashed forward . . .'

'Not likely. The bruiser and Miss X were on their heels, for a minute it was anyone's guess which of them went under the wheels, the ticket chap came out and read the Riot Act—the scruffy lad had jumped into a carriage, I doubt if he saw anything—didn't seem to be anything useful I could do, and to tell you the truth I didn't think much about it till I saw the news in the paper when I got back this afternoon.'

The superintendent looked less grateful than might have been expected. 'Where precisely do you think that gets us?'

'You're looking for this woman, aren't you? She's not at home, she can't be in an hotel, without luggage, you've got your alerts out, and in this weather she's hardly likely to be camping under a hedge. Why shouldn't she have gone to pay her promised visit to the Haunted Cottage?'

'Doesn't occur to you the owner might notify us?'

'If this Miss Garland threw herself on her mercy? Not likely.'

'So perhaps you can supply her name?'

'There's helplessness for you. Surprises me to know you can go to the bathroom by yourself, Henry. Well, think, man. How many cottages, complete with ghost, are likely to have changed hands in that neighbourhood—and Penton must be the nearest station or Miss X wouldn't have been waiting for her London train there—during the past two-three months? Get the local chaps on to it, they'll have the smell of the neighbourhood. One or two of them may even have shaken hands with the ghost themselves.'

'There have been enough ghosts in this case,' grumbled Jorrocks. 'What I want is a flesh-and-blood person able to give me specific evidence.'

'I never promised you that,' Martin observed. 'I wouldn't put it past those two to have joined a witch's coven, they still have 'em in that part of the world. But cheer up, there's still the ticket chap, in a remote place like Penton someone trying to put herself under a train or stop someone else putting her there, don't ask me which, must give quite a tang to the day. And, of course, there's the chucker-out, if you can find him. Any number of strings to your bow. And now, if there's nothing more I can do to assist you, I'm dining with a man . . .' And he was gone.

Loss to the criminal classes, reflected Jorrocks, ordering the second half of his beer. Any chap who can move at that speed could make his fortune the other side of the fence.

A minute or two later it occurred to him that Dr Martin was probably making it on the right side, so swallowing the contents of his glass, he proceeded to get in touch with the authorities in whose manor Penton lay.

And learned that a man called Arthur Crook had just telephoned, announcing that he represented the missing woman, supplying her address, and suggesting a meeting the next day.

'What's wrong with tonight?' snapped Jorrocks.

'Mr Crook won't allow his client to be interviewed without her solicitor present,' was the glib reply. 'And he'll be going to Ditcham tomorrow. We've got a man keeping the cottage under surveillance,' he added. 'There's no chance of the lady giving us the slip.'

'I'm not concerned with the lady,' Jorrocks assured them. 'It's Crook. That man could make an eel look like a feather-boa. If you're going to keep anyone under surveillance he's the chap to keep your eye on.'

It was typical of Crook, he reflected as he hung up, to oil through a hedge or crawl out of a hole in the ground and get in first. He wondered what airy-fairy edifice the fellow was building to make mugs of Authority.

CHAPTER SIX

'GOOD GRIEF!' exclaimed Charles Garland, slamming the door of his car at noon the following day, and striding up the path with all the arrogance of a Regency buck, 'it's news to me they've started putting the police into fancy dress.'

The rotund figure in striking brown habiliments, who was standing on the front doorstep, turned enthusiastically.

'Don't let them hear you say that,' he warned in his buoyant way. 'You might find 'em camped around like the hosts of Midian any minute now. I'm the advance-guard, so to speak.' He hauled a fantastically large card from his pocket and handed it to the fascinated Charles, who was searching for an apparently truant latch-key.

Charles glanced at the card, grinned and shook his head. Then, finding the key, he started to fit it into the lock.

'You're about a dozen years too late,' he said. 'Our boy's at the 'Varsity where, by all accounts, they do their own conjuring tricks.'

'Keep it for the fuzz,' suggested Crook, 'the bit about the conjuring tricks, I mean. I ain't in the public entertainment racket, well, not officially. Fact is, I'm representing your sister, legally, that is.'

'It's news to me my sister needs representation,' said Charles mildly. 'No one's so far accused her of any crime.'

'Not for want of trying,' Crook assured him heartily. 'Well, naturally they want to pull someone in for Miss Plum's death, and it's nothing to them who they get so long as they can make the charge stick. Besides, anyone the police are interested in needs representation. It was Miss Chester pulled me in,' he added.

Charles seemed suddenly to open his eyes. 'Are you telling

me you know where my sister is? Here, you'd better come in. If we go on yammering on the steps chaps 'ull get the notion you're the MP, and I'm doing a bit of canvassing.' He opened the door and pulled Crook into the hall. 'Who's this Miss Chester?'

'Bought a cottage in Ditcham. Haunted. By pigs or something.' Crook looked about him with frank delight. The place had everything, a lordly staircase, oil paintings, old oak chest, all the doings you heard of in ghost stories and saw in mystery films.

'I know the place,' said Charles. 'I'll call my wife. Female angle, you know.' His look said he wasn't sure that Crook really did, but Crook put him in his place by telling him, 'You're talking to the man who's forgotten more about it than most chaps ever know.' He indicated the staircase. 'One of England's Stately Homes?'

'I'm still waiting for some chap to pay me half-a-crown to go over it. Ah, here's my wife. Flo, this is Mr —?'

'Crook.'

'He's brought us news of Dotty. She's staying with that foreigner who bought old Tom Marsh's cottage at Ditcham.'

'Couldn't be in better hands,' Crook assured them. 'Sugar, I mean, no, the cottage. And if you're wondering where I come in,' he added, 'put it down to Providence.' He explained about the meeting on Penton Station. 'I'd back Miss Chester against a whole posse of police. Tell you the truth, I began to feel quite sorry for the chaps, facing those two. Y'see, Miss Garland don't answer the question she thinks the police have in mind, like most of them do, she answers the actual question. You ask your criminal—suppose you're investigatin' the death of a cow, say—Did you notice the cow when you crossed the field this morning? and he'll hand you a lot of spiel about noticing it because it was behaving in a very rum manner, convulsions or something, and he did wonder should he say anything to the farmer, but your sister she'll just say Yes, she saw the cow, and if the chap tries to press her into an opinion as to how it was behaving, she'll just tell him that, not being a cow, she don't know the right way a cow should behave. That floors 'em. They ain't used to the truth, it has the same effect on them as whisky on a total abstainer. No, you don't have to worry about her.'

'I can scarcely take it in,' murmured Flora. 'Hidden away like—like an exile within a stone's throw of her own home.'

'Wasn't sure how long it 'ud continue to be her home if she brought the rozzers back with her like Bo-Peep's sheep,' Crook explained. 'And you don't have to worry, she'll be as right as rain with Miss Chester. Trouble with spinsters,' he continued thoughtfully, 'is they learn to think for themselves, having no one to do their thinking for them, and since their processes move on lines no sane fellow could apprehend—well, it makes it tricky for us as well as for the police.'

'What did Dotty tell you that she didn't tell the police?' enquired Charles curiously.

'Don't get her wrong, or me either, come to that,' said Crook. 'She told the fuzz everything they asked. 'Tain't her fault if they didn't ask the right questions. Chief point of interest was what she had to say about Miss Plum's brother.'

'Her brother?' The two Garlands regarded him with amazement. 'That's a new one to me,' said Charles.

Crook lifted his eyebrows in Flora's direction. 'I never recall her mentioning one,' Lady Garland said.

'It's what Sugar told me, nobody knew about him except her—and Miss Plum, of course. She'd know because she invented him.'

'I suppose some of this makes sense,' murmured Charles in resigned tones.

'Sugar had the same idea, about you not knowing, I mean.'

'Sugar?' That was Flora, reminiscent of the icing variety.

'Oh well, if you want to make it formal . . .'

'Let the chap tell it in his own way,' suggested Charles, in the resigned tone of one who has suffered from many constituents.

'She says Miss Plum—Miss Styles to you,' he added scrupulously, 'told her about Brother as a deathly secret. She got the idea he might be a bad hat, battening on hard-working Sis . . .'

'In that case she kept remarkably quiet about it,' said Flora unsympathetically.

'Could have had her reasons,' suggested Charles.

'I'll say she had her reasons,' Crook agreed. 'My ADC, name of Bill Parsons, has been doing a bit of head-hunting for me, and just before I came along I called him up from the local where I'm staying. Miss Styles was the only child of a respectable couple, Daddy was a schoolmaster, living in Kent. One parent died in 'thirty-five, the other in 'thirty-eight.'

'Bang goes Big Brother,' murmured Charles.

'And bang goes Sugar's theory that Miss Plum was writing to him under the rose via the Oakhill PO. So—who was she writing to?'

'If she was writing to anyone,' was Flora's dry comment.

'Sugar says so, and Sugar's my client. Anyway, the police have established that she did go to Oakhill to call for letters addressed to V.S. No idea who she might be writing to, I suppose?'

Flora looked startled. 'How on earth should I know?'

'Well, you knew her before any of the rest of us.'

'I met her during the war. We were working in the same unit.'

'MI 5?' suggested Mr Crook, looking intelligent.

'Something of that nature.'

'And she seems to have carried that into her private life. Well, you must admit she's a bit of a mystery. Or are you holding out on us?'

'I've no reason to hold out, as you put it. As for her being a woman of mystery, I gather she was as much of a mystery to herself as to anyone else.'

'This is like living in a treacle-well,' cried Crook.

'My wife means that Miss Styles suffered from amnesia for some years after the war as the result of being blown up by a torpedo.'

'You mean,' hinted Crook, 'she disappeared from mortal ken?'

'It was after our Headquarters were destroyed by enemy action,' Flora amplified. 'We suffered a good many casualties including our CO. The survivors were all sent on different missions. The only news I heard about Vicky was that she had been on a ship that was torpedoed, and her name wasn't among the survivors. This was in 1944. It was an odd thing about the war, it doesn't and didn't seem like a part of one's personal life. A curtain fell in 1939 and was lifted six years later, but the history within the confines of those curtains was a separate existence. Nothing that happened to me during that time, particularly after the unit went to France, seems to have any connection with myself, the woman who is Sir Charles Garland's wife and Timothy Garland's mother—step-mother, actually, but he doesn't remember his own—It's like a thick cut out of the middle of a loaf . . .'

'And Miss Plum only existed in the thick slice, so to speak?'

'Yes. Until she suddenly reappeared about six years ago. I really did wonder if I was seeing a ghost, though I've never believed in them.'

'You don't want to say that sort of thing outside these four walls,' her husband warned her. 'Very ghost-ridden part of the county, this. That cottage where Dotty's staying—wouldn't surprise me to know they set an extra cup for their ghost at every meal.'

'Didn't surface while I was there,' said Crook respectfully. 'But maybe he's not the pushing kind.'

'I came back to the car park that morning after shopping at the WI Market, and there she was standing beside the car,' continued Flora steadily.

'How come she knew which was yours?' intervened Crook.

'She said she'd discovered where I lived and rung the house and someone had told her I'd gone to the WI. That was true,' she added defensively. 'Mrs Price, who was our housekeeper then, remembers the call. And when she got to the car park she asked the attendant—Mrs Price had said a big cream car—I knew what it meant when it said you were knocked down by a feather. I said, "But it can't be Vicky Styles, you were reported missing when your transport was sunk." You know how you blurt things out under the influence of shock.'

'Never had any doubt of her identity?' suggested Crook.

'Oh no, she hadn't so much grown older as just grown up on the same lines. There was always something birdlike about her . . .'

'That's what your sister said,' agreed Crook, nodding in Charles's direction.

'You can't tell me anything about birds,' retorted Charles grimly. 'Look as if worms wouldn't melt in their mouths, and pick out Mummy's eyes before breakfast if her worm looks a bit more succulent than theirs. Fact,' he added, seeing Crook's expression of surprise. 'All this Robin Redbreast malarky about him getting his nice red waistcoat from Our Saviour's blood, it's all on a par with the Flopsy Bunnies in coloured hats and white pinnies. Rabbits are vermin and birds put us chaps to shame when it comes to defending their own interests. And my wife's right when she says Miss Styles made her think of a bird.'

'Ever say why she'd waited so long to look you up?' Crook wondered.

'She explained that. She'd been suffering from amnesia—when the transport was bombed she was picked up by a

French fishing vessel—the French were our allies again by that time—and landed on the French coast. She told me the first thing she remembered was finding herself on some remote Normandy farm . . .'

'No name? No address?' That was sceptical Charles.

'I didn't ask for one. I was trying to get used to the situation. Vicky, whom I'd thought dead all these years . . .'

'It's not a new story,' murmured Crook, sounding almost apologetic. 'I've known chaps aplenty who've had clouded memory and simply don't recall they were doing bird for the past ten years. Of course, there are records . . .' he added. 'You were saying, Lady Garland?'

'Vicky said something about the Day of Resurrection and then told me about the farm. She couldn't remember exactly how long she'd been there, because she said there was a kind of timelessness about it, you could only tell the time of day and the month of the year by the light and the seasons. Naturally, all her papers had gone down with the ship, everything was scattered, the end of the war everybody at home had been anticipating would be a matter of weeks only, seemed to recede . . .'

'What did she do on the farm?'

'She worked. Even you, Charles, who've never really been fair to her, must admit she was a good worker.'

'Ever explain how she managed to stay all that time without a work permit? They're fussy about these things on the Continong.'

'I don't suppose the farmer ever reported her. It was a very remote farm, the French were madly short of labour, so many men being in German labour camps or—or conscripted—he could probably do with a willing pair of hands and no questions asked.'

'Just as well,' agreed Charles, 'seeing she didn't know any of the answers.'

'Anyway at that time of the war—it was soon after D-Day—there must have been any number of refugees wandering around, no one had the time, even if they had the inclination, to round them up.'

'I must say this is the first time I've heard this yarn in detail,' acknowledged Charles frankly. 'How long did she live in her Peasants' Paradise?'

'I told you, there was no way of measuring time. Then the men started to come back, and she realized the war must be over. She did say that it was like being in a wood or a desert, some place without land-marks, and after a while she got the feeling this wasn't *her* place, but she didn't know where her place was. And then—it was dramatic really, though it sounds so simple—one day a big car drew up at the farm and a woman asked a question in English. Vicky hadn't heard English spoken for years, no one at the farm talked anything but French, and of course she had three languages—in our job you had to . . .'

'If they were Normandy peasants could she understand them?'

'Seeing our work took us among every sort of person you had to know dialects, and Vicky had been one of the best in our unit. But when she heard English again—well, American really, but you know what I mean—she said it was like waiting for a day to break.'

'Another minute and you'll be telling me she wrote poetry in her spare time,' Charles said.

'You were telling us about the light breaking,' suggested Crook.

'Some woman had taken the wrong road and wanted to get back on to the main one. So she stopped at the farm to ask the way. The peasants didn't understand a word, but Vicky could help her. This woman was a GI widow, travelling in a big American car . . .'

'On her owney-oh?'

'She was making for Italy, where she had a villa.'

'What was she doing in Normandy?'

'I asked Vicky that, she said she'd come to see her husband's grave. Well, to cut a long story short, she—the widow—wanted someone who could drive and speak the language, and the authorities were beginning to wake up a bit, and anyway the French were coming back—I dare say the parting didn't break anyone's heart.'

'She told it very nice,' said Crook respectfully. 'Did she explain how she got a passport into Italy—and out of France, of course?'

'She said the American pulled strings—they generally can, can't they?—and anyway, money talks everywhere.'

'Could be,' agreed Charles grudgingly. 'And then, she was dealing with frogs.'

'What a lucky girl!' enthused Crook. 'Nice safe farm in Normandy when the war hotted up, and then sunny Italy. Why didn't she stay there? Or did she have another black-out?'

'The widow married again, an Italian, and they had a little girl. Vicky stayed on for a time, during which the matter of her identity seems to have got cleared up. She was rather vague about that part of it.'

'Shouldn't wonder,' Mr Crook agreed.

'Then the American's father died and she came into the property, so she decided to go back to America—for keeps, Vicky thinks—and the husband and little girl went with her, and the villa was put up for sale.'

'No place for Miss Plum in New York?'

'I don't know if it was ever suggested, but anyway she had begun to feel homesick. The wife gave her a parting present and said if ever she found herself in New York to be sure to look them up, and off they went. Vicky said they didn't even bother to pack all the child's toys, and there were little piles of lire left in all the ash-trays.'

'I don't suppose they'd be much use in the States,' said Charles drily.

'When Vicky came back she tried to trace some of the old gang, she'd completely lost touch, you see, but I suppose some were dead and others married and changed their names, and she kept drawing blanks.'

'You'd changed your name,' her husband pointed out, 'but she ran you to earth.'

'Maybe the lady knew her onions,' suggested Crook respectfully.

'Knew . . .?'

'Well, she didn't come all that way just to enquire after your health,' Crook explained. 'And if you'd been living on the pension, say, or workin' in a shop—what I mean,' he added, thinking how dumb can you be?—'is—it's like that wartime question—Is Your Journey Really Necessary? Is your journey really worth while?'

'You mean she came to make a touch,' cried Charles. He looked enquiringly at his wife.

'She found post-war England as strange to her as a jungle,' Flora insisted again. 'She had to work—anyway, you can't imagine Vicky sitting with folded hands . . .' Crook repressed the thought that folded hands don't get you far when you're out for a fortune, as he presumed Miss Styles was. 'Anyway, she had a chance of going into partnership with this friend—or acquaintance—who was running an hotel on the West Coast, somewhere near Torminster, she said.'

'And she wanted the golden handshake?' Crook supposed.

'Oh, she said the American woman had been generous, she had some capital, though of course money melts fast when you haven't got a job and no one to—to back you till you get started. She thought it might prove a goldmine—she would do the cooking—you must admit, Charles, her cooking was absolute cordon bleu—'

'All this dressing-up of food,' grumbled her husband. 'If it was all right in the first place why do you have to disguise it with a lot of foreign fal-lals?'

'I used to wonder where she'd learnt,' continued Flora, undaunted. 'Perhaps the farm . . .'

'If there ever was a farm it's news to me that peasants have cordon bleu cooking. Still, she wasn't bad . . .'

'You know she was first-rate. She could have done much better for herself than staying here as housekeeper-cum-nursemaid,' cried Flora rashly.

But it wasn't easy to silence Charles. Crook began to realize why he had (1) got into the House of Commons and (2) gave every sign of staying there.

'In that case, one wonders why she hasn't moved on,' he observed. 'She could do better for herself, surely.'

'Depends what you mean by better,' said Crook. 'Maybe you could offer her something she couldn't get for all the gold in Araby. Well, let's have it,' he added in encouraging tones. 'You put up the dibs. Any question of repayment?'

'None,' said Flora shortly. 'It's not much of a boon to start a new business with a load of debt round your neck, like that famous albatross.'

'You've kept this very dark,' said Charles in injured tones.

'Oh, it was about the time you were standing for the division, you had enough on your plate, I didn't want you worried.' She couldn't have said more clearly that it was her money, so actually no concern of his. 'And then—in a way my life in France during the war was like something that was separate from my civilian existence, and the people I met there belonged to that private world. I can't conceive of any of them fitting in here.'

'Till Miss Plum turned up.'

'And she was a square peg in a round hole,' Charles insisted. 'Yes, Flo, of course she was.'

'She was very useful to us,' flashed his wife. 'Our housekeeper had just decided to marry again, and it's almost impossible to get reliable service these days, particularly in a politician's house, where all the times are haywire.'

'But what went wrong?' insisted Crook. 'I mean, there she was, all set up in her igloo or whatever—don't tell me she found it too much for her. She made me think of that old saying about the Gates of Hell not prevailing against her.'

'It was the partner, proved dishonest, falsified the books —Miss Styles did the cooking and so forth, the paper-work was done by the partner—who just upped and left, leaving bills everywhere and the whole set-up in a state of confusion.'

'Any idea where the wicked partner went?' Crook wondered.

'Vicky thought abroad.'

'So why didn't she follow?' demanded Charles, voicing Crook's thought. 'She had a passport, or had something mysterious happened to that?'

'She had to stay and close the hotel. Well, clearly she couldn't carry on by herself, and there were debts left, right and centre. She told me she'd managed to settle them all . . .'

'No other old wartime friend prepared with the ready?' asked Charles nastily.

'I don't think she wanted to carry on, I think it had been a shock. And if she did get an extradition order, how would it have helped? You could be sure she wouldn't see the money again. Besides . . .' she hesitated.

'Give,' Crook encouraged her.

'I always thought there was something she didn't want to reveal, I thought—which is odd considering the kind of woman she was—she was afraid of something . . .'

'Or someone.'

'But why?'

'Because all the gold in the world don't get a man a meal if he's alone on a desert island, without even a butterfly-net to catch gulls. And a million a week can't keep a chap alive if he's got a mortal disease. It's like I was suggesting a bit earlier—she might have got an easier job or a more gilded one, I wouldn't know—but what she wanted was a background. Well, stands to reason. A maiden lady living on her own in Camden Town, say, is a lot easier target than the same lady sharing the house of the local nobs. Mind you, it ain't worked out quite the way she expected, but if you was to see the statistics of not-so-young dames living on their own and being found banged up—why, they're a gift to all the young thugs who're out for an easy play.'

'But why?' asked Flora, with wrinkled brows. 'She wouldn't have anything worth stealing—or running such a risk for. And she was such an enterprising woman, not the kind you imagine being taken in by a hard luck story.'

'Enterprising she may have been,' put in Charles, 'but all the same she got herself pitched out of a window. And whoever did it didn't even snatch her handbag. No, what Mr Crook's getting at is that she had enemies—or one enemy anyway—and knew it, and thought she'd be safer with us than probably anywhere else.'

'Even your sister fitted into the picture,' agreed Crook. 'Of course dames in pairs do sometimes get run down by the same car, but it don't happen nearly so often. Never strike you as rum that, with a perfectly good address and a buzzer in the hall, to say nothing of one on the Green, she had to go two miles to Oakhill to collect her mail or chat up a mate?'

'Don't forget Imogen was always around, and she may have preferred privacy,' Flora said. 'Even quite innocent conversations . . .'

'What Mr Crook's hinting is they likely weren't quite innocent conversations. And those letters . . .' He looked across at Crook. 'Anything significant about her going to the waxworks whenever she came to town?'

'That was to please Imogen surely,' Flora said.

'That ain't the way she tells it. She preferred to stop outside and squint in the funny mirrors.'

'While Miss Styles kept her appointments—all a bit melodramatic, wouldn't you say?'

'I'd say being pushed out of a window was a bit melodramatic, too. And then there's the money question. When Miss Plum sends money it ain't in the form of a cheque, but a postal order, though she has a checking account. It's Operation Cover-Up all the way for her. You can't be anonymous about a cheque, but a PO's a different matter.'

'But you haven't explained yet why she should want to remain anonymous.'

'I'd say that dame always had her reasons. Case of big fleas and little fleas, I wouldn't wonder.'

Charles, who liked to think he could follow the most devious conversation, thanks to his political experience, elaborated. 'You think she was putting the black on X, and Y was returning the compliment? So she used Oakhill—she could have been using another name . . .'

'We know she had the Oakhill letters addressed to V.S.—the police uncovered that one—wouldn't surprise me if she had another account somewhere else—they never uncovered a PO bank book that I recall—the Baker Street branch might be able to help. No law to say you can't open half-a-dozen Post Office accounts in different names.'

'Like the man who followed a tiger and never realized that another tiger was following him,' said Charles soberly.

'Well, not till it jumped.'

'But you're talking about Vicky Styles,' protested Flora. 'Not Mata Hari.'

'Oh, I wouldn't be too sure,' said Crook. 'My guess is that, like the Apostle Paul, she stood in jeopardy every hour, *and knew it*. All this sympathy for having to go around with Sugar—why, your sister was as good as a bodyguard any day, and the protection worked till she went out of her way to dispense with said bodyguard. Ever stopped to wonder why she suggested a bath before dinner, contrary to normal usage, when they were going to dine downstairs? You don't travel in cattle trucks any longer, you don't arrive at the Great Metrop speckled with smuts. No, no, you take my word—Miss Plum planned it like a general. Room in the most private part of the hotel, companion in bath—she heard voices, remember.'

'Even above the bath-water and the radio,' acknowledged Charles. 'Mind you, Miss Styles was a sergeant-major lost to posterity. You really think she might have invited her murderer for a tête-à-tête?'

'Wouldn't the receptionist remember someone asking?' Flora wondered.

'Not if X knew the number of the room, and if it was a date she'd tell him. She wouldn't want to attract attention any more than he would. And nothing simpler than for him to slip up the stairs, knock on the door—if anything goes wrong and Sugar ain't retired he'll say, "Beg pardon, wrong room—" '

'It all sounds very involved,' Flora confessed. 'I suppose there's no possibility it was an accident?'

'Miss Plum leaning over the sill falls to her doom? It don't sound a very likely story to me. From all accounts it 'ud take a pretty hefty shove to have got her off terra firma. And if you're expecting Sugar, then why? She's a grown woman, if she don't want to submit to being followed around by a baby-sitter she's only got to say so.'

'I'm sure Imogen wouldn't deliberately hurt anyone,' defended Flora warmly. 'But it really is better for her to go about with someone else, she has such an odd sense of humour. Do you know, when the new curate was expected —he was a middle-aged man who'd taken orders rather late in life—we got word that he was in bed with pneumonia and Imogen went round in a black cassock and a shovel-hat she'd found in the attics . . .'

'Relicts of my Uncle Ben,' put in Charles hurriedly taking over from his wife.

'Made half the parish look fools,' she continued. 'Well, the ones who'd been taken in weren't going to pass the word round they'd been had for mugs—Dotty was in her element.'

'She even collected some subscriptions for the Mission Field,' Flora added.

'I told her she could have been had up for obtaining money by false pretences, but she said that was all right, she left it on the hall table on the way out. The fact is she's like that stuff you get in a thermometer, never know where you are with it.'

'Takes all sorts,' said Crook philosophically, who had enjoyed the recital. 'Still, I better drop her a hint about trying to guy the fuzz. They're models of most of the virtues, I dare say, but a sense of humour ain't one of them. Now let's get back to Miss Plum. She's the heart of our mystery. Don't it seem to you rum that in a world where most people have the usual number of eyes and ears, so little's known about her? Or put it another way. So few people who knew her are prepared to come into the limelight? She's like the bird that flew into a lighted tent out of the darkness, and then back into the night, without uttering so much as a squawk.' (This classical allusion left both Garlands dumb.) Crook continued fluently, 'Take the case of the brother. You didn't know she had one, but she confided in Miss Garland. Yes, I know what she confided was untrue, but that's not the point. She did confide. Now about this guest-house of hers. If you were a shareholder . . .' He looked Flora full in the eye.

'I wasn't a shareholder. I'd far too many interests to be concerned in a seaside hotel.'

'Anyone actually set eyes on the hotel?' asked Crook curiously.

'She sent me a photograph. It was near Torminster, on the coast. It looked just like a dozen others.'

'I might send you a photograph of Buck House but that wouldn't mean I'm Prince Philip. What happened to it? Did she sell the goodwill, or what?'

'I don't think she ever went into details. I gather there were a good many debts outstanding.'

'I thought she was such a good business woman,' cut in Charles.

'I thought so, too.'

'You mean, you just handed over a sizeable slab without even seeing the property?' Crook looked scandalized—and incredulous. 'She might have been leading you up the garden.'

'There was no point in her inventing the hotel.'

'What does that mean?' demanded Charles suspiciously, but Crook was way ahead of him.

'Meaning you'd have shelled out whatever reason she gave?'

Flora drew a deep breath that seemed to echo on the attentive air. 'I suppose I shall have to dig up the whole story,' she said. 'The fact is, she saved my life when we were in France. You don't forget a thing like that.'

'Miss Plum clearly didn't.'

Charles sounded less satisfied. 'I suppose you mean she hauled you out from under the rubble when the HQ collapsed. But, hang it all, I thought that was part of the occupational hazard of fighting a war. And even a war hero don't come back and ask for the VC fifteen years after the event.'

'I fancy it was a bit more complicated than rescuing a comrade,' said Crook, and now his voice was as sober as a proverbial judge. 'And my guess 'ud be she didn't ask for a loan, she demanded a down payment and you were in no position to refuse her.'

'Mind your tongue,' growled Charles.

'If it hadn't been for her I might have died in a most unpleasant way,' said Flora steadily. 'And even if I hadn't, I wouldn't be your wife, Charles.'

'You can't leave it at that,' Charles assured her, and

Crook broke in, speaking in a voice so quiet both hearers were warned, 'What had she got on you, Lady Garland? Something that 'ud stick after fifteen years.'

Flora hesitated for another moment. Then she said, 'I'm sorry, Charles, I didn't mean you to know this, but you may as well hear the truth from me, at least it won't be garbled. But I'm afraid you must prepare yourself for a shock. But for Vicky Styles, I might have been charged with murder.'

'You don't believe in half measures, do you?' murmured Crook. 'Who might you have murdered?'

'My husband, Ernest Sinclair,' Flora said.

There was a moment's complete silence. Whatever Crook had expected it hadn't been that. But it was Charles who broke through the silence.

'Do think what you're saying, Flo. You always told me he was killed when the Germans bombed your Headquarters.'

'I said he was killed the day the Germans bombed us. It's true they killed half our personnel, including the CO, but Ernest was dead before they arrived.'

'And Miss Plum could have made people think you were responsible?'

'In a way, I suppose I was. Whether I actually killed him or not . . .'

'Oh, come, Flo!' Charles's voice was rough with anxiety. 'You must know whether you killed the feller or not.'

'Oh, in a sense you could say I killed him, but how far it was deliberate—how can you tell when things happen so quickly; it's like being in a vat of whirling crystals—no time for thought, and so much at stake.'

'How much was that?' asked Crook, wooden as a chopping-block.

'His good name, my future, the whole unit—I'll try and clarify the issue a bit.'

'It would help,' agreed Charles in the same tone. 'At the

moment I feel as though I were conducting a conversation in Choctaw.'

'Well, at least we've got our interpreter.' Crook indicated Flora, who had turned as pale as the famous ash.

'It was just after D-Day. We were in one of the Secret Service units, not exactly MI 5, not Commandos, but akin to both. I'd met my husband in France and married him there, more or less unofficially. Married women weren't well looked upon in the unit. Our position was rather that of celibate priests—unmarried, you could be sent anywhere, no personal considerations to take into account. A married woman might start a baby, have a miscarriage, anything. I've wondered so often since if, but for the war, I'd ever have married Ernest. But everything went by so fast in those days, it was like one of the old Keystone Cops films, you lived for the day and were glad if you were there to wake in the morning. Our personnel changed a bit, of course, there were inevitable casualties and replacements, but just about that time, June 1944, suspicions began to flash like warning signals. It was a dangerous job, most jobs are dangerous in war, but it did begin to seem as though there were rather too many coincidences. I mean, the enemy may be lucky in one guess, but when he continues to be lucky and pluck the heart out of every mystery, then it becomes impossible to continue to turn a blind eye. Besides, we couldn't afford the casualties—some of our best men and women.'

'What you mean,' said Crook, who didn't believe in using words of two syllables where one would do, 'is that someone was selling you down the river.'

'In an outfit like that it's terribly difficult to pick out a traitor, you all work so closely together, everyone knows practically everything, but it doesn't do any good for A to suspect B, and C to look askance at A.'

'Don't tell me,' pleaded Crook. 'You discovered the truth—and the traitor was your husband.'

'I wondered afterwards if I should have suspected, but it didn't seem possible. He was the man I'd married, we'd taken mutual vows . . .'

'It's news to me,' said Crook unpardonably, 'that the marriage service says anything about not selling your country.'

'Well, of course, it doesn't. But it's just one of the things that doesn't occur to you. I had had thoughts about one or two other members of the unit and then, by sheer accident on my part and perhaps a little carelessness on his, I—so to speak—caught him red-handed—hidden transmitter, the lot. It was all like a rather bad film, I'd got back a bit early from duty and he was in his hut, where he was supposed to be sending messages to a second unit. I didn't want to interrupt him and I stayed where I was for a minute, till I realized—I suppose the shock slowed up my thought processes. Then I moved, and in an instant he was on his feet. When he saw who I was he began to laugh. "Mission completed?" he said. "If you've got a minute to spare there's still some coffee . . ."

'I said, "I heard you. So it's been you all along." I thought he'd deny it, fly into a tearing rage, but he just stood perfectly still for a moment, then he said, "That's a bit of bad luck. You should keep to your timetable, darling." I was thunder-struck. I said, "But you've been betraying us—our unit, I mean—to the enemy. People have died, Liza and Rupert and—oh, there were others—it's a kind of murder," I said. "All war's a kind of murder," he said. Then he explained. England couldn't win the war, any steps he took would help to shorten it. It was bad luck about Liza and Rupert and the rest, but far more lives would be saved.'

'Not win the war—in 1944?' Charles stared. 'Fellow must have been round the bend.'

'I knew we had an exercise planned for that night—we'd had another about ten days previously, and the members of that party had run into an ambush and only two had come back out of eight. I was sure he'd been passing on the details. I turned to go, there didn't seem anything more for me to say. "Where are you going?" my husband asked me. "To tell the Colonel, of course," I said. "You don't think I'm going to let our lot walk into a second ambush blindfold?" He said, "Oh, I wouldn't do that." And then—this is where it began to resemble a very bad film—he dropped his hand into a drawer and there he was—the Bad Man with the gun.' She made a sound, something between a choke and a sob.

'Take it easy,' said Charles. 'I suppose you tried to get it away and he got the business end of it.'

Takes it pretty cool, reflected Crook, seeing it's his own wife. But I suppose being in the House of Commons toughens you up.

Aloud he said, 'I thought it was all karate at that stage of the war.'

'Karate's all right in given circumstances, but there are times when nothing's so lethal as a gun. People on special missions were issued with them . . . I didn't really think he was going to shoot, not me, anyway. Then he said, "Just think how it would look. I come in and discover the identity of the traitor and I do the only possible thing. Well, I couldn't see my wife put up against a wall and shot, could I? And in a war guns can go off by accident, and there's been enough publicity about security breaches in the press, without the boss wanting to add to it." He really meant it, Mr Crook—Charles—' Her eyes went from one man to the other. 'He would have shot me and made it seem as though he'd taken the only possible way out—but he'd have finished putting his message through before he "discovered" what had happened. He was very thorough in his own way.'

'Is Sir Charles right?' asked Crook, resolved not to increase the emotional pressure by even a gesture. 'Did you jump for the gun?'

'I suppose I must have done,' Flora agreed. 'I remember a struggle and a report, and Ernest was down. It wasn't till then I realized the sirens were sounding to warn us of a raid. We had to go down into the shelter, and take any incriminating documents or records with us. I snatched up the transmitter—I couldn't let him be found with traces of his treachery, he was my husband, that's something you can't forget, I dashed out. There was no one in sight, I thought they'd all gone to the shelter, so I went too. In the shelter they took the roll-call, everyone was there except Ernest. The CO wouldn't let anyone go up and look for him, he said he couldn't afford any more loss of life, and anyway it didn't matter because the HQ got a practically direct hit. We were lucky the shelter escaped. When we came up after the raid the place was a shambles. Someone got to Ernest's hut before I did, I heard a voice call, "He's here, keep Flora back." Someone caught my arm, it was Vicky Styles. "You can't do anything now," she said. I was remembering the gun, if that was found questions might be asked. I tried to push forward. Then Vicky said, "It's all right, he died a hero's death." I wanted to laugh—and laugh. I ought to have said—He was transmitting to the enemy—it didn't occur to me they'd come back. But they did. They just gave us sufficient time to feel secure and then they returned. We lost half our personnel, including the CO. Our wireless system was destroyed, but of course we had instructions what to do in just such an emergency. We were destroying the papers the Germans hadn't destroyed when Vicky came up and stood beside me and said in a perfectly normal voice, "It's all right, you don't have to worry about Ernest, I've got the gun." I was so staggered that for a minute I didn't speak, and then I said, "I don't know what you're talking about." She said, "There's going to be a mass funeral, Ernest will have died as a hero, and probably lie cheek by jowl with what's left of the Colonel. Someone has a very odd sense of humour." I said, "Give me the gun," and she said, "Oh, I don't think that would be a good idea. You might be tempted to use it again." And then she told me. She'd been coming to warn him about the siren—she didn't know I'd got back, I was on my way to report to the CO when I found out about Ernest—and she'd heard it all. I asked, "What good will it do you to blacken a dead man's name?" and she said hadn't the others a right to know?'

'And that's what she's been holding over you? From more than twenty years ago?' Crook sounded puzzled.

'You still don't understand,' said Flora. 'A few days later we got our new assignments, she hadn't said a word to anyone, but she watched me like a hawk, and I was almost afraid to let her out of my sight. Then I heard that the transport she'd been on had been sunk and her name wasn't among the survivors. I wouldn't have been human if I hadn't been thankful. Then the war was over and I came home, and went back to civilian life. Ernest had only one living relative so far as I knew, his aunt, Miss Marian Sinclair. I wrote to her when we got married and sent her a snapshot of myself, and when I went on leave I went to see her. She was a very down-to-earth person, fairly old and looked fragile, but in herself she was as tough as British oak. When she saw me she said, "I'm glad to see my nephew's tastes have changed for the better." I asked Ernest when I got back what she meant, and he laughed and said, "I've done myself a bit of good, marrying you, my girl." I thought then it was a sort of joke, not one I much appreciated, I must admit. Afterwards I began to wonder . . .'

'After what?'

'Miss Sinclair told me that after that first meeting she'd changed her will and reinstated Ernest as her heir, with reversion to his widow if he predeceased her. "Though if I know anything of my nephew," she said, "he'll come riding back at the head of all the King's horses and all the King's men. He likes to do everything on the big scale." When Ernest was—killed—' she stumbled momentarily over the word—'she was told he'd died in the course of duty or whatever the official phrase is. I used to think how he'd have enjoyed that. He was a consummate actor, he used to say if he came out of the war alive he might Have a Go. Of course, we had to make our own entertainments, everything in the unit was too hush hush for us even to have ENSA for our spare hours, but Ernest topped us all, head and shoulders. Perhaps if he hadn't been such a good actor he wouldn't have got away with—what he did.'

'Was that the aunt whose money you inherited?' Charles said.

'She lived in Bournemouth with a nurse companion. I have an idea this woman hoped to inherit everything; in the event she got five hundred pounds. Miss Sinclair died a year or two later, slipped on the stairs in her own house and broke her neck. They say, don't they, there are more fatal accidents in houses than even on the roads.'

'When you start believing all you hear you might as well turn on the gas,' said Mr Crook in his outspoken way. 'You know the old saying—liars, damn' liars, and statistics. What was Nursie doing?'

'It was a Thursday afternoon. She always went out on Thursdays. Sometimes I used to go over, because she liked visitors, sometimes a neighbour dropped in. It wasn't often she was alone. That Thursday I was going to a French film, I telephoned and asked if I should come later, but she said No, she'd get a Mrs—Mrs—I can't recall the name—to come in if she wanted anyone. It so happened this Mrs X was out that afternoon, and when Nurse came in she found the poor old lady, she'd fallen on the stairs.'

'Been living in the same house for long?' enquired the sceptical Mr Crook.

'Years, I think. She used to live there with a sister, but the sister had died some years before.'

'Did she fall downstairs, too?'

'She died in hospital.'

'And Nursie rang the doctor?'

'She rang me, too, but I wasn't in at the time. As soon as I heard I went over, but there wasn't much I could do.'

'No mention of a string stretched across the top of the staircase, I suppose?' murmured the unscrupulous Mr Crook. 'What time did Nursie get back?'

'About seven, I think. She explained she felt worried . . .'

'Always feel worried on a Thursday?'

'It might have been a premonition.' But Flora sounded doubtful.

'So it might,' said Crook in his hearty way. 'What sort of a woman was Nursie?'

'Nothing particular. She seemed quite attached to Miss Sinclair.'

'What sort of age?'

'Mid-forties, possibly a year or two more. I didn't take special notice.'

'Ever hear what happened to her?'

'The lawyers told me she got married quite soon afterwards, a man younger than herself.'

'Didn't hear anything after that?'

'No. Why should I?'

'Lady of what's called uncertain age—not that I ever understood why, normally it's all too certain—hankering not to have Miss writ on her tombstone—five hundred pounds in—what year was this?'

'About 1948, no, the beginning of '49. I re-married myself soon afterwards, to tell you the truth I never thought of her again. It never occurred to me it could be anything but an accident.'

'And maybe it was,' Crook acknowledged. 'Second nature to me to snuffle round like a hog looking for truffles.' He didn't seem to recognize the uncomplimentary nature of the simile. 'Now, coming back to your predicament . . .'

'My wife doesn't have to submit to your cross-examination,' Charles pointed out sharply.

'Not cross,' murmured Crook, 'seeing no one else has done any examining to date. Anyway, I was only thinking I might be able to give her a wrinkle or two if questions should be asked.'

'My wife is perfectly capable of telling the facts to anyone in a position to demand them.'

Charles's voice made a poker sound as pliant as a willow-bough.

'It ain't so much the facts as the construction the authorities put on 'em,' Crook explained. 'I knew a KC once, had to defend a woman on a shooting charge, victim was a chap who'd treated her bad (not that she was an innocent little plant herself), and he knew that everything 'ud depend on a certain question the Prosecution would put to her, and not on the question alone, but on the phrasing. There were twelve alternate ways it could be phrased, and each way wanted a slightly different answer. If she gave the right answer she was in the clear, if not she was for it. He didn't worry about anything else. Time came, she was in the box, Prosecution puts its question, she gave the right answer and out she sailed, a free woman. Mind you,' he added in parenthesis, 'I've always had doubts myself, but if she did shoot the chap she was highly provoked.'

'Just as well this isn't a court of morals,' remarked Charles drily.

'If it was that, you'd probably be looking for a Bishop, not a fellow like me. Still, I dare say there were no questions asked . . .'

'I remember thinking how—inconsequential—life is. If I hadn't gone to that film, and it wasn't such a good film, after all, I'd have been with her . . .'

'And she could still have slipped,' said Crook. 'You can't undo history. About Miss Plum. Never dropped a hint, the way a lady drops her purse and finds out too late? No visitors? No phone calls?'

'You said it yourself,' Flora reminded him. 'She was like the bird that flies out of the dark, circles round in the light for a minute or so, and goes back to the darkness. She had no one.'

'And yet she fell out of a window. And not by accident, but because someone meant her to. Wonder if Sugar could help.'

'She'd hardly have told my sister,' Charles put in, still as grim as a winter dawn. 'Dotty doesn't know the meaning of the proverb that says silence is golden. And I'll tell you something else. If she'd pushed Miss Styles out of that window she wouldn't hold her tongue about it, she'd have a perfectly good reason, so good to her that it wouldn't occur to her she couldn't convince the rest of the world.'

'Well, but we've agreed she didn't do it,' argued Crook. 'She's my client, so she can't have done. Trouble is that whoever knows the bit we're after ain't likely to talk. It wouldn't surprise me if there was something at the Baker Street PO, only I don't think any of her clientèle, if that's the word, would be crazy enough to sign their names.'

'If there had been someone at the Montblanc surely he or she would have noticed,' Flora urged.

'You should ask your sister-in-law about that. She says that Miss Plum liked going to the Chamber of Horrors because the men and women there, convicted murderers, mark you, looked so like everybody else. That's the murderer's strength, that he don't wear the brand of Cain on his forehead any more. And he wouldn't do anything to make himself look particular, like wear a Bishop's robes or a sable mini-skirt, he'd look just like you and me. Why, there's even been cases where the chap's disguised himself as a rozzer, but not this time, I fancy. Someone would remember seeing him.'

'I suppose the police have already sorted out all the people who were in the hotel that evening,' Flora reflected.

'Well, but how can they? They can isolate the residents, but there's a bar there that's open to anyone. Chaps come in, have a gargle, go out. Who's going to remember them? Not the barman, any more than the casualty officer in a hospital will remember a chap coming in with a hand he's cut on a broken milk-bottle. Of course, if it was a notable, that's different, but he wouldn't be crazy enough to take the chance.'

'So—where do we go from here? How do you find out the guilty person?'

Crook looked surprised. 'You're mixing me up with the police. I don't have to do their work for them.'

'Suppose they decide that Imogen is guilty?'

'That 'ud be too easy,' objected Crook. 'Still, if they did, then I'd have to get cracking, and seeing I couldn't prove she didn't do it—pity she wasn't still in the bath when that Harlequin character banged on the door—then I'd have to try to find a substititue.'

Flora said steadfastly, 'And I can guess your first choice.'

'Hold hard, old girl,' exclaimed Charles.

'I'm sure the thought has passed through Mr Crook's mind. Vicky was round my neck like that dead albatross . . .'

'How could you have been anywhere near the Montblanc that night?' Charles protested. 'You were lecturing to that bloody girls' school.'

'Only till five o'clock. What time did Vicky fall from the window?'

'Round about six o'clock, as I remember.'

'Then I could have done it. In point of fact, I went to a coffee-bar—but I could have taken a bus or the subway to Sloane Square . . .'

'You always travel by taxi when you're in town.'

'Ah, but Mr Crook will point out that I wouldn't do anything that would call attention to my arrival. I even knew the number of the room, because she showed me the management's letter, I could have gone up in the lift—is there a liftman or is it automatic?'

'Automatic, according to Sugar. Anyway, no one's heard a mention of a liftman . . .'

'And if I could do it, so could anyone else. Oh, there must be some sort of record of her correspondents. Cheques, for instance . . .'

'Only if they're ripe for the nuthouse,' Crook assured her. 'Never sign your name to anything. No, I'd say payments were strictly cash. She wasn't one of the big criminals, you know, I dare say it was fifty pounds here, twenty pounds there, well, if she was in the big money she wouldn't have stayed on here, she could have hired a private bodyguard. Anyway, it's seldom if ever the Big Man who gets knifed or doped or pushed under a car—different in the States during the days of Gang Warfare, of course, but I don't think there was much of Legs Diamond or Al Capone about Miss Plum.'

'Do the police know about the Baker Street hide-out?' Charles demanded.

Crook glanced at his watch. 'If they haven't found out for themselves. Sugar will have told them by now. And it wouldn't surprise me if they came around to you to dot the i's and cross the t's. Very formal, the police, left, right, left, right, keep in line. And Sugar won't see any reason for not telling them. Come to that,' he added casually, 'I wouldn't mind knowing myself.'

'You're not going surely?' suggested Flora, politely.

'Somehow I don't think the fuzz will want to find me here. A case of absence making the heart grow fonder.'

'Why should they come here?' Charles sounded belligerent.

'Where else is there for them to go at this stage? It's like the old song—Nowhere to go but up. Up the pole, I shouldn't wonder.'

And he bowed himself out, like a brown tweed croquet-hoop.

'What was the object of that exercise?' Charles demanded, wrathfully, when he and his wife were alone. 'I shouldn't have thought that sort of chap needed any ideas putting into his head. You could watch 'em spawning like frogs without you taking a hand.'

'I didn't put the idea into his head, it was there from the start, and before he could drop some casual hint about having an alibi for the time Vicky fell from the window, which I haven't got, I thought I'd play my own hand.'

'You can never tell with a chap like that, he'd see us all strung up to get his client off.' Charles sounded pessimistic. 'I must say, Flo, you've given me a pretty average shock! You paying blackmail!'

'What would you have had me do? Let her tell her story? Can't you see how she'd have told it? Oh, I'd have shot Ernest, but not because he was a traitor but because he'd discovered I was one. I suppose she heard the shot and came to see what had happened. The others had all gone down to the shelter. She had no proof, the story could have gone either way, but how could I risk it being made public? It wasn't only you, there was Tim. No one is crueller than one child to another, compassion is strictly reserved for animals at that age, and not always then. I'd been luckier than I could have dreamed, finding you after that appalling first marriage and when I was no longer a young woman—the risks were too great. What was a little money?'

'But you must have known it was a cumulative process. It was like paying the Danegeld of old. If you don't pay it we shall attack. And if it's paid the same demand comes . . .'

'I know, I know,' cried Flora, all but wringing her hands. 'But what alternative was there? I used to think: People pick up germs, get run over by buses, are in train or plane accidents, why shouldn't it be her? Only it never was.'

'And you didn't have to make a present of the situation to that Crook fellow,' Charles reiterated.

'Men like that don't wait to have things handed to them, they go out and grab. Charles, you don't think Dotty could conceivably . . .?'

'My dear girl, we've already agreed that if Dotty had done the job, and I, for one, would sympathize most heartily with her, she'd have had half a dozen good reasons, and expected everyone else, including the police, to appreciate them. What does bug me,' he added, scowling, 'is how you could let a woman with such a history go round with Dotty, who in a way is the most defencelesss creature living.'

'Vicky would never have hurt her,' cried Flora impatiently. 'She counted on us, our background, rather. Mr Crook was right, she didn't come here for love, but because she was being threatened.'

'Never dropped you a hint?' wondered Charles dubiously.

'I suppose she thought I'd have the wits to work that one out. But there must be some record somewhere.'

'So well hidden the police haven't tripped over it yet. I could do with a drink,' he added rather roughly. 'It's been an afternoon of shocks and I'm not the chap I once was. I don't care what time of day it is,' he amplified, 'in any case, all the times are out of joint. Good God, Flo, I can't get accustomed to the idea that all these years you've been in her power, and you never breathed a word to your own husband.'

CHAPTER SEVEN

At about the same time as Crook stamped off to the Superb, two police officers were leaving the Haunted Cottage.

'I don't trust that woman an inch,' remarked the elder, 'and the friend's not much better. No one, not under restraint, could be as moronic as Miss Garland, no wonder her brother hired someone to keep her under surveillance. Not that she's a fool by any manner of means, but what was to hinder her pushing this poor lady out of the window and then going back and turning on the tap? And no sense blaming the deceased, you don't expect your own dog to round on you and take a piece out of your leg.'

'So where do we go from here?'

'To Oakhill, in case the sub-postmaster there can help us. Miss Garland's not a type to be easily forgotten. And by this time there may be more information the other end. I never trust a case with Arthur Crook in it. It's well known if he can't find the needful evidence he'll manufacture it, and add it on to the real story so neatly you can't detect the join.'

'How about a word with the Member? He is the brother.'

'That won't count for much, the last person to know about a relative is another relative. And if this one can't handle the situation better than the rest of the chaps in Parliament, talking to him's just a waste of time.'

The poor man had an attack of acidosis coming on, and to find Crook and a first-class moron united against him was a challenge you'd have thought even Heaven would be ashamed to think up.

'Now they've gone we might take a little walk and I'll introduce you to the village,' offered Dora brightly, as the police car drew away.

Imogen looked surprised. 'Aren't you afraid of our being Mobbed?' she asked.

'You must know everyone's on tiptoe to Hear More,' reproached Dora. 'And surely it's better to meet people Out In The Open than have them crawling through the undergrowth or skulking under the gate.' Her lively imagination conjured up visions of faces, chalk-white and inhuman, pressed against dark window-glass, the telephone ringing and mysterious voices hissing threats, or even bricks coming through the window with messages tied round them. Nothing of that sort had happened yet, but she wasn't particularly anxious that it should.

In the churchyard they found Mr Bunyan vigorously attacking the weeds that almost obscured a tombstone.

'Where darnel grows and thorn!' quoted Dora.

The rector straightened up to give them the time of day. 'The poor fellow!' he said compassionately, referring to the dust beneath the stone and not to the author of Dora's quotation. 'A man of straw in life and a stumbling-block in death.' He slashed away with an ancient scythe. 'There's a verse on the stone,' he continued affably, 'though you'd be hard put to decipher it nowadays.

All ye who pass this way along
Think on how sudden I was gone.
God does not always warning give,
Therefore be careful how you live.

I've always thought Jane Eyre had the edge on all of us there,' he continued, irrepressibly. 'I can say that to you ladies knowing you won't ask me who Jane Eyre was, though there's plenty, it seems, never heard of Charlotte Brontë these days. You mind she was asked what she should do to escape damnation, and she said, I must keep in good health and not die. You'd not get a better answer than that in a month of Sundays. So you've brought a friend to stay among us,' he ran on, never pausing in his labours. 'It's always a pleasure to see a new face, Miss Chester. I'd offer to shake hands but mine are cumbered with churchyard mould.'

'Dust to dust,' quoted Imogen aptly, putting out her hand. 'We've been admiring your gravestones.'

'They're a grand show,' the rector agreed simply. 'And no entrance fee. Plus good advice and all for nothing.'

'My brother doesn't hold with gravestones,' Dora confided. 'He says the Almighty remembers without any reminder from us, but I tell him it's not the Almighty we're thinking about. We want the world to remember us now and again. But he calls that human vanity.'

'You should tell him to read Thackeray,' said Mr Bunyan. 'Let us thank God for imparting to us poor weak mortals the inestimable blessing of vanity. You didn't mention your friend's name.'

'She thought you'd know it,' Imogen explained, identifying herself. 'She's putting me up for a few days, till Charles and Flora get used to the idea of me being a suspect, or till the police make up their minds I really did push Miss Plum out of that window.'

'The police are a very underrated body of men,' the rector concurred. 'The ideas they get into their noddles 'ud surprise the Archangel Gabriel.'

'Of course, I wouldn't have done such a thing to Miss Plum,' continued Imogen earnestly. 'It was a terrible thing to happen . . .'

'Perhaps her time was up,' offered the rector. Dora had the idea that if he heard the bell ringing for Judgment Day, he'd drop his scythe, call out to someone in the sky, 'Come ing, sir, just have to wash my hands,' with no more emotion than if he had to answer the phone.

'Even so,' she murmured reprovingly, 'there are less shocking ways.'

'Hospital bed and the odour of sanctity? Ah, but the ways of the Lord are not our ways, and windows have a peculiar sanctity of their own. Windows of the soul . . .'

'Windows into Heaven,' contributed Imogen eagerly.

'Storied windows richly dight, Casting a dim religious light,' offered Dora.

They continued to vie with each other for another minute or so, before the rector recalled his scythe and the task in hand.

'I'm introducing Imogen to the village,' Dora explained.

Mr Bunyan nodded. 'When shall we three meet again? May it be soon. Oh, and Miss Chester, you remember that cockerel of mine?'

'The one that went AWOL?'

'That's the one. Well, he's back again and as noisy as ever. There's some locally who raise objections, but who's to say the crowing of the cock isn't as acceptable to the Lord as the psalmist in his glory? There was St Benno and the frogs . . .' He explained about St Benno.

'And to think,' marvelled Imogen, as they moved on to buy Dora's groceries from Mr Masters, 'I've lived for years with Charles, and never known we had a centre of culture on our doorstep.'

When he had cleared away sufficient grass and weeds to reveal the memorial's existence, thereby preventing any casual visitor from falling over the mossy stone rim, Mr Bunyan decided he had earned a drink, so he went into the local inn, the Stud and Links. It hadn't been long opened for the evening and almost the only customer was a man resembling a large brown bear, who stood at the counter. Mr Bunyan's errant fancy started to consider what the world would be like if all animals stood on their hind-legs wearing human accoutrements and all men went on all fours, in their pelts. The publican introduced the two men with the grace the occasion demanded.

'Mr Crook down from London, come to stand by Miss Garland, we hear, seeing she's no man of her own.' His voice implied that, though she had a brother, Charles was Flora's man, and she wasn't the kind to share.

'I've just been talking to the lady,' Mr Bunyan said in agreeable tones. 'Not about the tragedy, of course, or only *en passant*, but I was in Willy Masters's shop the night the paper carried the story, and I saw Miss Chester, the lady she's staying with—well, I saw it meant more to her than just a melodramatic item of news.'

'Pure gold,' agreed Mr Crook. 'And they don't come better than that.'

'I have a sister, lives near Surbiton,' Mr Bunyan went on implacable as the gently-smiling stream that bears all our sins away. 'Half of the best bitter, please, Jim . . . She insists on sending me her local newspaper. I have endeavoured in vain to make her realize that human nature is not materially affected by environment . . .'

'You've got the Harley Street johnnies against you there,' Mr Crook warned him.

'You mistake my meaning,' murmured Mr Bunyan courteously. 'I mean that saints and criminals abound on all sides. Who was it who said that hearts as brave and fair could beat in Berkeley Square as in—was it Seven Dials? My point precisely. To suppose that because I live in a rural neighbourhood the atmosphere is one of innocence and peace while in Surbiton life is a continuous whirl of activity, much of it misdirected . . .'

'I get you,' said Crook, feeling this had gone on long enough. 'But where does Surbiton come in?'

'This Mrs Huth—the lady, you will recall, who actually saw the body descend from the hotel window . . .'

'She lives in Surbiton?'

'Precisely. And the local paper has, as they say, gone to town on her. My sister knows Mrs Huth, that is, they shop in the same supermarket and occasionally play bridge together—naturally she takes an especial interest in the affair. And since Mrs Huth has, so to speak, opened her grief to the local editor, I have had an opportunity to—well, I believe the expression is to mull over the mystery.'

'And in a minute you're going to tell me what conclusions you've come to,' Mr Crook encouraged.

'I wonder,' said Mr Bunyan, 'if you ever watch TV.'

'Well, not often,' confessed Mr Crook. 'I always have an uncomfortable feeling that when I turn that knob the set's watching me.' He added hurriedly, 'Electronic age and all that, you know.'

'It was my sister who drew attention to the point,' explained the rector conscientiously. 'She's a great devotee of the box, and she has noticed in the plays and serials that whenever a character needs to telephone, whether a policeman or a villain, there's always an empty box handy. Whereas in real life every box within a radius of a quarter of a mile is occupied by immigrants from the four corners of the globe trying to obtain accommodation or persons wishing to lay bets. If a box is by chance free it's because it's out of order.'

'She should write to the BBC, they could do with a bit of advice,' suggested Mr Crook unsympathetically. He ordered a second pint, signed to the barman to refill his companion's tankard and draw himself whatever he fancied.

'Oh, she wasn't complaining,' Mr Bunyan said. 'But she did make the point that here was a true case, where a witness—to wit, Mrs Huth—looked for a telephone box, and it was occupied.'

Mr Crook set down his newly-filled tankard with a bang that almost jolted the contents over the rim.

'Your sister's got her head screwed on all right,' he told Mr Bunyan handsomely. 'Why didn't I think of that? Of course. Now.' He made a wide enveloping gesture reminiscent of a conservative general outlining a campaign. 'What exactly did Mrs Huth say? That she was coming up the street with her thoughts elsewhere when she was startled to see what proved to be a body descending rapidly towards the pavement.'

'I don't think you can blame the lady for being startled,' demurred the rector.

'I'd be more inclined to blame her if she wasn't. I've heard of it raining cats and dogs and hailstones like lumps of rock, but bodies—of course she was shocked. Take her the best part of a minute, I'd say, to realize what was happenin'. Reactions not likely to be too quick, seeing she was worried about hubby and probably the fact that she'd spent too much money at the sales—oh yes, she had, they always do, a lot of fal-lals. Then—she's flabbergasted, hesitates, goes forward to make sure, not able to believe the evidence of her eyes. Shock does that, slows things down, doesn't sharpen 'em up the way you might expect. Then and only then she starts looking about for someone, anyone, only there ain't anyone. Her thought crystallizes, what she wants is a rozzer.'

'Not a doctor?' suggested Mr Bunyan.

'Dames who've had a shock of that dimension don't argue logically. First thing the lady 'ud do would be to want to share the responsibility with someone else, and with dames that's a rozzer. Well, it's what they're paid for, to take responsibility, to know how to deal with the unusual situation, and that surely covers bodies falling out of windows. And there was no one, in or out of uniform. Ain't that what she said?'

'So far as I recall, yes.'

'So—we come to the phone box.'

'She looked across the road and there was a box, but it was occupied.'

'She don't say by whom, so far as my memory serves me.'

'She was probably still feeling—confused,' the rector reminded him.

'I wonder how close to the hotel the box was,' brooded Mr Crook.

'I think she said practically opposite.'

'Easy to check anyway. Now say X—the occupant of the box—had been there when the body came down ker-splosh on the pavement, surely he or she 'ud realize something out of the usual had happened. I know about the sounds of traffic, but a body falling on to the pavement from the third or fourth floor don't sound like a car going by or even like an electric drill. But—X don't move, just carries on steadily with what he's saying.'

'He could be hard of hearing,' suggested the resourceful Mr Bunyan.

'In that case why choose a phone so near the high road? Even if the Post Office was shut the pubs 'ud be open . . .'

'If it was a lady . . .' began the rector.

'I didn't know we had any more of those,' said Crook. 'Well, either we've got a robot, or we've got someone who don't want to know—or Mrs Huth has pulled a boner. And I don't think it's the last, because if the box was empty she'd have poured herself into it, like that Sherlock Holmes snake—or do I mean Conan Doyle?'

'You are thinking that X plays an integral part in the crime,' suggested Mr Bunyan.

It was on the tip of Mr Crook's tongue to assure his companion he was wasted in this dump, but he prudently shut his great mouth. Human nature's the same everywhere, the rector had observed, and he might well have a point there.

So instead he continued, 'He don't do any of the things you might expect. Just goes on chatting up his girl or whatever. And—mark this—when the crowd pops up, does he emerge and say . . .' He paused. 'Come to that, what could he say? I wonder if anyone else tried to get into the box? I mean, a body falling out of a hotel in what's practically London's West End is good for a couple of pars.'

'There is a story by G. K. Chesterton,' Mr Bunyan reminded him. 'A lady falls down a lift to her death and the only person who shows no sign of disturbance and no apparent knowledge of what has occurred is a self-styled prophet communing with the Absolute . . .'

'With both ears a-cock?' supplemented Mr Crook. 'Meaning he knew what was coming, so he don't have no sense of shock. Now, if that's the case, he'd see Mrs Huth beetle into the hotel and before the alarm's properly given he's out of the box and mingling with the crowd. Or even nipping into the nearest local for a b. and s. Now, no one has spoken of a chap coming out of the box, so the odds are no one noticed him. It's a fact that most people see what they expect to see —we'd agreed that already, hadn't we?'

'So what's the next step?' enquired Mr Bunyan. 'Or shouldn't I ask?'

'I can't do any more down here at the moment, Sugar will be safe under Miss Chester's wing, her own family know where she is, it 'ud be a brave rozzer who'd set himself against that trio, so I think I'll go townwards and check up on one or two ideas you've given me, and when I come back,' he added, handsomely, 'we'll do a bit of arithmetic and see what kind of a total we've got.'

'A most interesting character, Jim,' Mr Bunyan observed to the barman after Crook had flashed away. 'I wonder if there are many of that ilk in London.'

'Not even London could hold two of them,' opined Jim. 'How about a small whisky, sir? I'm sure Mr Crook would have offered it, if it had gone through his mind.'

'Treat not with the spirits,' the rector adjured him, 'at all events not before Evensong. And that reminds me, if I don't hurry I shall be late, and punctuality is the politeness of princes. Miss Chester sometimes attends,' he added gravely. 'A matter of civility, I fancy, but not unappreciated.'

Lumme, reflected Jim, watching the rector trot busily away, he's picking it up from Mr Crook. At this rate, we'll all be round the bend by Sunday.

Up in London Mr Crook went straight to the Montblanc Hotel. Mr Harlequin regarded him with the utmost suspicion. Since the Tragedy (with a capital T) they'd had some very queer visitors, but none to equal this one. He looked at Mr Crook's grotesque card with the suspicion of the routine mind for the eccentric.

'Just checking up on Miss Garland's behalf,' Crook explained. 'You're sure no one came asking for Miss Styles that evening?'

'I've answered all the police's questions to the best of my ability,' retorted the harassed manager.

'Maybe mine won't be the same questions, or if they are I won't draw the same conclusions from your replies. What ain't arguable is that somebody went to Room 39 that night and shortly afterwards Miss Styles came hurtling out of her window.'

'We've no proof of that,' snapped Mr Harlequin.

'Meaning you favour the Miss Garland version? Well, I can't accept that, I'm representing her and my clients are always innocent. Now, supposing an intending visitor knew the number of Miss Styles's room. I take it he could walk up without attracting any attention?'

'There was no message left at the desk,' insisted a wooden-faced Mr Harlequin.

'Which only goes to show that Miss Styles didn't want the world and his wife worming in on her secret. It all fits, man. She comes to a hotel where neither of them is known, she persuades Miss Garland to take a bath at an unusual hour, what's to hinder her visitor arriving unnoticed—lady knew the number of her room—before she came?'

'She asked particularly for a room at the side, saying Miss Garland was a poor sleeper.'

'First time anyone's mentioned that,' said Mr Crook. 'Anyway, you told her the number?'

'There seemed no harm,' snapped Mr Harlequin.

'No harm in the world,' agreed Mr Crook smoothly. 'Now, say A comes up unnoticed. You've got a printed invitation to non-residents to use the bar and the dining-room, no one's likely to notice one particular stranger. Miss Styles is waiting—Miss Garland says she thinks she remembers voices, though I dare say a good counsel could make that sound like a load of cods-wallop if it ever got as far as the witness-box, there are words, Miss Styles goes out of the window and X whirls down the stairs and into the phone box opposite. It was his luck there wasn't anyone about except this Mrs Huth, but if there'd been a crowd it wouldn't have mattered. Mrs Huth, so far as we know, didn't see anyone go into the box, but she's like the rest of us, she can only see one thing at a time, and what she saw was Miss Styles. Then by the time she looked around the box was occupied.'

'That wouldn't help him,' said Mr Harlequin heavily. 'That phone's been out of order for more than a week.'

If Mr Crook had had the right sort of ears they'd have pricked as sharp as a thistle.

'Sure of that?'

'I ought to be. Number of chaps who've come in, asked if they could use one of the hotel phones—we have a couple of pay phones here for visitors who haven't got an instrument in their rooms—very urgent, they say. There's a Post Office a hundred yards along the main road, I tell them, we're not a public convenience.'

'And if you nip into a phone box and find it ain't working you don't stay there to shelter from the cold,' ruminated Mr Crook. 'You get out—what time was this?'

'Six o'clock or thereabouts.' Poor Mr Harlequin seemed quite bemused.

'PO might be shut,' Crook reflected. 'But there are pubs or, as you say, there's your good self. Only whoever it was didn't come in. And when he came out he can't have overlooked the crowd, the flurry, ambulance, the bundle. And it's agin human nature to slink off and pretend you've seen nothing, unless you've something to hide.'

'And you think that whoever Mrs Huth saw in the box could have told us something about Miss Styles's death. But, Mr Crook, even suppose the lady really did see someone there, and there's only her word for it . . .'

'She saw someone all right,' confirmed Crook, 'or she'd have beetled into the box herself.'

'Could it be done in the time?' pursued Mr Harlequin.

'We thought of that one. Lady sees a body falling from a height. Can't have been just under it or she'd have gone down like a stone. Can't even have been very close or she'd have got splashed, there'd be quite a lot of blood about. Say half a minute for shock, then half a minute to come up and realize what's happened; even when she's recovered she don't make a bolt for the hotel, looks around for someone to share the buck, no one in sight, sees or remembers there's a phone booth, takes a step or two I shouldn't wonder, only that's no go because there's someone there. It 'ud be taking a chance, I admit, but say someone came out of your hotel and under cover of the lady's natural confusion crossed the street—I see the box is just above the part of the hotel where the body 'ud fall—didn't mention if it appeared to be male or female, I suppose—no matter, we can check on that—anyway in these days of interchangeable gear it ain't always easy to tell—one way is to look at the feet, big feet are a chap, smaller shoes a dame, though you can't always be dead sure even then—still, she'd hardly be able to see the feet in the circs—then when Mrs H has come belting into the hotel, and before she's made herself clear X beetles out of the box into the main road, jumps a bus, hails a taxi, or just crosses the street. Dead certain about the phone being out of order that night, I suppose?'

'So far as I know it's out of order still,' retorted the manager rather bitterly. 'But try for yourself. Though where the fun is dismantling a phone when a life might depend on it, search me.'

'Might as well check,' Mr Crook agreed. 'You ain't got my experience of the police, Mr Harlequin. They wouldn't take the Archangel Gabriel's word for anything, not without he offered proof, and when I've got their corroboration, I'll do a bit of ferreting round, see if Mrs Huth remembers in tranquillity, like the poet says, anything fresh about the body in the box.'

'It will be a relief to me to get the matter cleared up,' Mr Harlequin said sourly. 'I can tell you, Mr Crook, it's not doing my hotel any good.'

'It wasn't exactly a picnic for Miss Styles or Miss Garland,' Crook acknowledged, 'nor her family ain't exactly enjoying the publicity.'

'Is there any proof . . .?'

'Of what? Come to think of it, I don't believe there is.'

In fact, the entire case seemed to rest on the word of a woman whose family called her Dotty.

Mrs Huth didn't like the look of her unexpected visitor, and hadn't the nous to conceal the fact.

'I've had the police,' she said, desperately—if only, she thought, he'd called at a time when her daily was on the premises and could have said she wasn't at home.

'I'm the Harlequinade,' Mr Crook told her sunnily. He saw she hadn't a notion what he was talking about. 'Acting on behalf of Miss Garland,' he amplified.

'Oh yes.' But even now she hardly believed him. 'She's the one who pushed Miss Styles out of the window.'

Crook looked shocked. 'You see her?'

'Well, of course not.'

'Then how come you're so sure she did it?'

'I mean, the one the police think did it.'

'Praise the pigs, I ain't responsible for what the police think. And they ain't brought a case against her yet, and if I win my bet, they never will. Even if they were sure . . . they must know their case wouldn't stand up five minutes in a court.'

'But who else could it have been?' demanded a bewildered Mrs Huth.

'If I knew the answer to that one there wouldn't be any mystery, would there? No, that's for me to find out.'

'So why come to me?'

'Because you're the one who knows the phone booth was occupied that evening.'

'I only saw someone there,' Mrs Huth defended herself breathlessly.

'That's what I said.'

'I don't know who or what he was doing . . .'

'Sure it was he?'

'Well, no. I just supposed . . .'

'As to what he was doing, he was making like an honest man, ringing his wife or his girl-friend, only we happen to know he wasn't doing anything of the sort because the phone was out of order and still is. I've been on to the engineers, they're sending today, work all behindhand because of the 'flu, and if it hadn't been the 'flu,' he added unkindly, 'the manager would have had elephantiasis or something. Now, think hard. You didn't happen to notice anyone goin' into the box?'

Mrs Huth stared. 'I didn't notice anything except this poor woman falling. And she might have come from the roof, only why should she be on the roof? I was worried about my husband—I told the police—I'd have crossed the road only my car was parked that side. I do remember thinking, Thank goodness she didn't fall on that. Only I didn't tell them that, of course. They'd only have thought How callous. They don't understand about Percy and the car.'

'They ain't paid to understand,' Crook pointed out gently. 'Now, you're sure whoever it was didn't open the door or call out or cross the street . . .'

'If he had I'd have made him get the manager or the police or whatever. Nobody moved, Mr Crook. I remember thinking, Why should it be me? Still, no one would try and say it was my fault.'

'Not even Percy?'

'How did you guess? Oh, he doesn't blame me for the woman falling out of the window, even he isn't that unreasonable, but he did make the point that if I'd started home at what he calls a reasonable hour, I'd have missed the whole drama. Only some of the shops stay open till six of a Friday, and I'd gone rather further than I meant, and King's Road is so crowded at that hour . . .'

'Ah well,' Mr Crook comforted her philosophically, 'that's husbands for you. No cross, no crown. I suppose you wouldn't remember someone shoving into the hotel vestibule immediately after you?'

'People seemed to be shoving everywhere. Someone pushed past me, a porter I think it was, and there was a doctor, he made me sit down and someone rang Percy. I suppose you might say I was in a state of shock, over what had happened and being worried about him, he doesn't like me being late . . .'

'Well,' said Crook brutally, 'you weren't as late as the late Miss Styles. Don't remember if it was a man or a woman in the box, I suppose?'

'I was in a state of shock,' Mrs Huth reminded him. 'Anyway, why should the person in the telephone box be responsible? Why shouldn't it be Miss Garland?'

'Because it don't make sense,' said Crook. 'Why should

she suddenly go berserk and push the lady out of the window? She must know she'd be the first suspect, person on the spot . . .'

'Perhaps she had a brainstorm. She did run away.'

'She left the hotel. Nothing that says you can't do that.'

'Oh well,' said Mrs Huth pettishly, 'if you're going to argue like that.'

'She's my client, ain't she?' asked Crook. 'I mean, I'm representing her.'

'If she wasn't guilty she wouldn't need a representative. Anyway, if you don't know who the person in the box was, how on earth do you hope to make the police believe he was even there?'

'That's where you come in,' said Mr Crook.

'I can't help you, I don't know who it was. And Percy . . .'

'To hell with Percy,' said Crook pleasantly. 'As to how we find this chap, ever hear the recipe for climbing a mountain? One foot in front of the other, one foot in front of the other, and so on till you reach the summit. They tell me,' he added casually, 'you get a very nice view from a mountain-top.'

After Crook had gone she thought resentfully, If I'd just got into the car and driven away no one would ever have known I was there. And I wouldn't have got involved. This is what comes of trying to behave like a Christian.

On his way back to his office Crook called at the Baker Street Post Office.

'Letter for V.S.?' said a suspicious clerk. 'You're a bit late. It was collected a while back—by the police.'

'Thanks, chum, said Mr Crook, beaming. 'That's all I needed to know.'

The newly-rescued envelope had contained a Post Office Savings Book in the name of Vera Summer, and an address that proved to be that of a small shop where letters could be sent. The woman in charge said she couldn't remember names, it wasn't her job, but when she realized she was talking to the police, she demanded fiercely, 'How was I to know? I'm sure she looked respectable enough. I thought at first she might have a boy-friend, you never can tell, it takes all types, only then the handwritings were different. No, she never said what was in them, and I never asked. She paid the usual charge for services rendered.' No, she said in reply to a final question, there were no letters waiting now. The fuzz could come and look for themselves if they didn't believe her.

'But, of course,' said Jorrocks when he heard the report, 'that's not to say she didn't dispose of any after the story broke. Whoever sent 'em would lie low, and once her name was in the press there'd be no more letters, and general rejoicing.'

CHAPTER EIGHT

Unlike Mr Crook, Dr Martin had no faith in a Providence that sets a man in a particular situation for its own inscrutable purposes. He had been on Penton Station, had seen the two women, caught a glimpse of Crook, and had dismissed the whole matter from his mind. Had he been told that he was to become intimately involved in the sequel he would have regarded it as so much poppycock.

'Trouble with the Brains is they don't give Providence credit for a sense of humour,' Crook used to say.

On an evening two or three days after the Montblanc affair and while the police were still groping in the dark, Martin was dining at his club, popularly known as the Mausoleum. He was entertaining a bigwig who considered he was doing his host a favour by encouraging him to contribute to a symposium of learned medical opinion. Martin, no fool, had too good an opinion of himself and his abilities to feel any particular compliment was being offered him.

Something else the old boy hopes to get for nothing, he reflected.

The room that more modern clubs would have described as a lounge was very large, inexpressibly gloomy, while its furnishings might have been lifted straight out of one of the lesser great houses of the Victorian era. Although there were seven or eight members dotted about in various chairs as far as possible from one another, the place gave the impression of being empty. When the doctor had been there for about five minutes—his own guest was the type of man who is always too busy to keep appointments to time—a new member came in. He looked a glossy sort of specimen, probably some sort of PRO, or one of those professionals whose chief gift is an ability to work the confidence trick. The fellow looked round expectantly but if he had anticipated seeing an acquaintance he was disappointed. No one took the least notice of him. Martin held his evening paper in front of his face and unobtrusively pushed his chair a little further back into the shadow of the heavy velvet curtains that wouldn't have disgraced a funeral parlour. The newcomer rang a bell and when one of the club servants appeared ordered a drink, adding, 'I'm expecting a guest. Wheel him in as soon as he arrives, will you?'

The servant gave him the look of one who remembers a less democratic and far more gracious age and retreated. The drink arrived, Martin's visitor delayed, a rather famous but by now slightly moth-eaten Law Lord snored gently by the fireplace, the other figures remained supine as though waiting for the mortician's van to come and collect them. A good enough place for them, too, Martin reflected. When they were planted, as Crook would have put it, they'd find scarcely any difference between this place and the grave.

A few minutes later the manservant returned, followed by a cocky little fellow who, heedless of the man's 'Your guest, sir,' marched up to the new member, saying, 'You're Ponting, aren't you? No, don't tell me. As if I didn't know. Mind if I take a pew?'

It was obvious to Martin that whoever Mr Ponting had been expecting it hadn't been this little chap. He sat upright, his eyes goggled, then he blurted out, 'I think there has been some mistake.'

'That's for you to say, of course,' agreed the little man, taking the chair he hadn't been offered. 'But don't try and kid me your name's not Ponting. I've seen you too often to make that error.'

'So far as I'm aware I've never set eyes on you in my life,' Mr Ponting said.

'More people know Tom Fool than Tom Fool knows,' quipped the little fellow merrily. 'Like me to refresh your memory? For instance, where were you ten o'clock Saturday morning?'

'Saturday morning?' Ponting sounded like a flabbergasted parrot.

'You can't have forgotten already. Still, always ready to oblige.' His voice changed suddenly, like the voices of amateur entertainers who imagine they're being some famous music-hall star to the life. 'Seen any good murderers lately?'

'I don't know why you're here,' Ponting began, but by now even the aloof doctor had started to smell a rat.

'Quite absorbed you were,' the little voice went on. 'Dr Crippen this time, wasn't it? Now, there's a man who never got justice. In any humane state he could have cut his wife's throat and got away with culpable homicide, but that's not British justice, oh no. Mind you, I always thought he only gave her hyoscine just to keep her quiet for the evening, it was a new drug, then, and he had the bad luck to give her an overdose . . .'

'I take it,' interrupted Mr Ponting, and his voice had a brittle sound, 'you didn't come here tonight, uninvited—incidentally, I am expecting a guest at any moment—in order to discuss Dr Crippen.'

'Just explaining how I know where you were last Saturday. My name's Gray, by the way. Not that it wouldn't be all one to you if it was Black or White or Green. I don't take cheques, any more than the lady did.'

Mr Ponting looked wildly about him as if searching for a bell. 'Going to order me a gargle?' wondered Mr Gray easily. 'Not to worry. I've had a couple and I've got another chap to see. Now, no need to go into details, is there? I know where you were on Saturday morning, and I know why you were there—to meet a certain little lady. Quite a neat rendezvous, if you come to think of it. Always a Saturday—well, I suppose most of her lot were working during the week—and the place is always packed with kiddos, so who's going to notice a lady and gent having a few words alongside old Mrs Dyer or the chap who drowned six wives in a bath.'

'I deny it absolutely,' declared Mr Ponting, more firmly. 'I don't know who you are, I don't know who you saw on Saturday at Madame Tussaud's, and I suggest you get out before I ring for one of the servants to throw you out.'

'You wouldn't do that,' affirmed Mr Gray confidently, 'not in a classy club like this. Think of the scandal.'

'In any case, I deny your story in its entirety. I don't say you weren't in Madame Tussaud's and that you didn't see someone with Miss Styles . . .'

'Hey! Hey!' said the little man. 'Who said her name was Styles?'

'It's been obvious from the start whom you're talking about,' Ponting insisted. 'And come to that, it might interest the authorities to know what you were doing there.'

'Well, not what you're thinking,' said Mr Gray. 'I never paid the lady a penny in my life, which isn't to say I couldn't give you a list of quite a lot of the chaps who did. Now, why don't we come to some amicable agreement over this? It's not going to cost you, not more than it's done to date, I mean . . .'

'You must be mad coming here,' Ponting exclaimed in a low, infuriated voice.

'Where, then? Better than your office, I thought. I never trust these lady secretaries, always know more for your good than they do for their own. Of course, there's your home address, but I don't know how far your lady wife's in your confidence. Oh not to worry,' he added soothingly. 'No one's going to pay any attention to us. For one thing, it wouldn't be the act of a gentleman, would it now, trying to listen in to some other member's conversation, and for another they're all so moribund it 'ud take the Angel of Death to wake them. Look at that one there.' He indicated Martin, who had let himself fall into a sprawling attitude, his paper half-covering his face, his breathing heavy and threatening at any moment to break into a snore. 'This mean anything to you?'

He opened his wallet and produced a photostat of a postcard. "M.T. 10 o'clock Saturday,' it read.

Ponting turned it over. 'It's not addressed to anyone.'

'Ah, but the envelope containing it was. But I daresay you destroyed that right away. Don't bother to go on saying No like all the good girls—and take it from me, there's not one doesn't say Yes in the end. I could tell you which days you came up and what you brought.'

'I suppose you realize this is blackmail,' muttered Ponting thickly.

'What's in a name?' Mr Gray shrugged. 'It's just a matter of business. I've got something to sell—my silence—you've got the cash to buy. I'm not putting up any of the prices, just think of it as continuing with a covenant payment, only the original payee's gone and you're paying to the partner.'

'So that's what you call yourself? And, of course—' light broke so violently you could almost hear the clash—'you had something on her. I wonder,' he added more softly, 'if you'd care to explain to the police what you were doing on Saturday?'

'Any rule against a chap going to see the Horror on the Hooks or whatever it's called? Funny how the kids always make for that, that and the chap in a cage you wouldn't dare keep a canary-bird in in this country. Mind you, I had one of the worst shocks of my life when I heard about that poor girl, like being told the bottom's dropped out of the stock market, when all you have to live on is your dividends.'

'I wonder how you heard,' murmured Mr Ponting.

'When she wasn't there on time I began to wonder. Whatever you like to say about her, she was always punctual to the dot. I saw you, of course . . .'

'If,' intervened Mr Ponting, 'you're considering tying me up with her mysterious death, let me put to you that I'd hardly have kept the appointment if I'd known she couldn't be there.'

'Might be the smart thing to do,' murmured Gray. 'What *did* you think?'

'I supposed something had happened to prevent her coming. Perhaps that crazy woman she used to take around had had some accident . . .'

'Didn't call her hotel or anything?'

'I didn't even know which hotel she stayed in. And if you were thinking of telling the police you saw me there . . .'

'Always a mistake to drag them in,' Mr Gray warned him. 'Mind you, if you think you've got a charge to press, go right ahead and don't let me stop you. I dare say a chap with your brains can explain away how you came to be involved in smuggling hashish, do they call it, or am I old-fashioned? Whatever it was, it meant a packet for you. And I don't think your business buddies would be quite so keen on your company if they knew as much about you as some of the rest of us.'

'How many more of you are there?' demanded Mr Ponting bitterly.

'The smaller the company the bigger the share. I don't say it wasn't cruel bad luck that letter falling into the lady's hands, but you know as well as me that it 'ud stand up in a court of law as well today as it would have done three years ago.'

'And if I don't care for your proposition?'

'The authorities might start wondering how it happened that our Miss S fell out of a window—oh, I know they've got their eye on this crazy dame, but that's a waste of time, now she's dragged Crook in.'

'Who's Crook?' asked Mr Ponting.

Mr Gray made a sympathetic clucking noise. 'It's a shame to take the money,' he said. 'He's only Sherlock Holmes and the CID and Lady Molly of Scotland Yard rolled into one.

Seeing you're so blame innocent, you might think up a yarn about what you were doing Friday night.'

'In point of fact, I was starting a heavy cold and stayed at home.'

'And Wifie 'ull back up the story? Too bad the police are such a suspicious lot. A wife's evidence doesn't really count, and that goes for the girl-friend, too,' he added shrewdly.

'I've told you already, I had no idea where she was staying. Our meetings weren't of a social nature. Were you always in attendance?' he asked sarcastically.

'You had to get up in the morning very early to keep abreast of Vicky Styles,' Mr Gray told him.

'And, of course, you had to be sure of getting your cut.'

'Never look at your firm's audited accounts, I suppose?' suggested Mr Gray.

'You could have had a motive,' suggested Mr Ponting shrewdly.

'Such as? No, old man, that one won't wash. Why slay the goose that lays the golden eggs? Besides, we understood one another, Vicky and me.'

'If you were blackmailing her . . .'

'Did I say that? We just ran a two-man enterprise. By the way, did I ever see you at that hotel she ran at Postman's Bay?'

'I've never even heard of the place.'

'Nice secluded little hide-out on the cliffs. Pity she had to give it up really, but you could say she had no choice. Still, it was a regular goldmine while it lasted.'

'Why are you telling me all this?'

'So that if the police should start asking questions you can't say you never heard of it. Look, don't let's waste any more time. I've got a chap to see and I dare say you're waiting for someone—well, you wouldn't be in the Black Hole of Calcutta without you had some good reason. I don't suppose you brought the wad with you, but you'll hardly have had time to spend it since Saturday, so—let's say the Governor's Arms—know it? Next to Harboro' Hill Station, all to-ing and fro-ing, chaps dashing in for a quick one before they catch the train back to the suburbs, if you walked in in your birthday suit you'd hardly be noticed. And if you should be asked about Friday evening, have something under your hat. Didn't your lady wife ring the doctor, seeing you had such a heavy cold?'

'My wife happened to be staying with her mother at Basingstoke.'

Mr Gray looked at him almost with admiration in his eyes. 'It's true what they say then, there's one born every minute. And—steer clear of that chap, Crook. He's the real nigger in the woodpile. If it wasn't for him the police 'ud be quite happy to tinker around with the companion or whatever she was called, and for all I know they could be right.'

'Even your famous Mr Crook can't disprove evidence,' Ponting pointed out.

'You have to be joking,' said Gray. 'If there were six witnesses who'd seen Miss Whatsit push her friend through the window and they all came round with affidavits a yard long, Crook 'ud tear the whole caboodle into little bits and use what was left to decorate his Sunday-go-to-meeting hat. It wouldn't surprise me if he was to winkle you out and do some of the police's job for them. I'm just giving you the word, brother. Now, if someone could push Crook out of a window . . . Still, if it could happen to Vicky it could happen to anyone—might bear it in mind. Hallo! Must be feeding-time. All the ostriches are beginning to take their heads out of the sand. If this is the one you're waiting for,' he added as the aged retainer returned, followed by a man who could have gone to a fancy-dress party as a Viking just the way he was, 'I'll beetle off. Don't forget—the Governor's Arms, say, Tuesday, six? And if you can't make it, not to worry, I'll come round to your place later that same evening.'

He marched out as jauntily as he had come in. The Viking, who proved to be Martin's guest, and whose arrival had apparently roused the doctor, since a minute earlier he'd been slumped back in his chair with half a newspaper over his face, remarked genially that they were getting a rum type of member here these days, to which Martin replied agreeably that you could say just the same of the Lords, as the Viking, whose name was Tranter, presumably knew.

It was fortunate that Tranter was the kind of guest who likes to do all the talking, and doesn't notice whether his companion replies or not, for throughout the meal Martin scarcely opened his mouth except to put food into it. He was surprised to realize, when at last his huge visitor rose to leave the club, that he had tamely agreed to contribute the article —a minor thesis, Tranter called it in his booming voice. Something far more important was occupying the doctor's mind. While he wouldn't be prepared to swear to every charge or rebuttal in the conversation he had overheard between Ponting and the odious Mr Gray, he realized it cast a completely new light on the situation. He could tell himself it was no concern of his, and it was simply his word against that of both the other men, for he realized that the two would gang up on him without hesitation, but he found he couldn't so easily abrogate his feeling of responsibility. Nevertheless, he had an unsympathetic vision of Jorrocks's face when he heard the story. Nary a ha'porth of proof, a few bits and pieces overheard in what was called a gentlemen's club, upon which, no doubt, more than one construction could easily be put. Even an optimist like Crook would hardly expect a police officer to go into the box with that sort of yarn. He wondered about the mysterious hotel at Postman's Bay, but even if there'd been hotel registers there was no guessing how many of the names recorded there were the real McCoy, or even if, at this date, they still existed.

All the same, thought Martin, uneasily, I can't sit by like the notorious Tar Baby and do nuffin.

It was then that he had his second and startling idea, and promptly proceeded to put it into action.

Mr Crook had been back from his favourite port of call for about half an hour and was considering calling it a day when his telephone rang, and a voice he didn't recognize enquired, 'Mr Crook? If you've, say, twenty minutes to spare—yes, of course I mean tonight—I might have some information that would interest you.'

They were all the same, thought Crook, though this chap's voice was smooth enough to arouse suspicion, all trying to give the impression that you were on the receiving end and they were doing you a favour.

'How much?' he asked cautiously, and the voice sharpened a bit and said, 'It's not for sale, it's not that sort of information.'

'I mean—how much would you expect it to interest me?'

'Depends how much Miss Garland's security means to you.'

'I didn't know it was being threatened, not more than usual,' Crook told him.

'I said security—not safety.'

The penny dropped. 'Meaning my safety? I should koko. If I've heard that record once I've heard it a couple of hundred times.'

'Records do get broken,' said the voice gently.

It was the gentleness that persuaded him. Maniacs don't use that tone.

'I'll buy it,' he said. 'Does Mahomet come to the mountain or . . .'

'Be with you in fifteen minutes,' promised the voice crisply, and the telephone went dead.

Crook wondered. In his experience the later the hour the

more dubious the job on hand. Still, without being more conceited than most, he knew there was a covey of fellows in the London area alone who'd take a lot of trouble to see he didn't go prematurely underground, and not just because he was their favourite man.

It was fifteen minutes to the dot when he heard steps, purposeful without being menacing, coming easily up the stairs. They didn't mean a thing to Crook, though he'd been known to say that a man's walk often gave him away more completely than his face. You can change the colour of your hair and add or subtract a lot of facial decoration, but walks are like ears, they're as good as identity cards. When the bell rang he reminded himself that man can survive anything but death, and that, as is well-known, cometh to all soon or late, and went to answer the summons. When he saw who his visitor was he whistled softly.

'Well, blow me down!' he said. 'No lilac domino, no firearms? Just as well. The landlord don't allow them on the premises.'

'He'd have to supply me with one before I could tout it along,' returned Martin pleasantly.

'So—come into my parlour,' invited Crook.

And the fly, every inch an aristocrat, strode into the web.

Crook poured beer for the pair of them. 'Now, give!' he offered, 'and remember I'm one of the square types that like a story to start at Chapter One. And if you can stick to words of not more than two syllables, so much the better.'

When he had heard the doctor's story he remarked candidly, 'Not surprised you didn't care to take this to Jorrocks, they do like a spot of proof, and they have a word for eavesdropping that ain't mentioned in polite society.'

'If I'd had proof,' commented Martin coolly, 'I'd have lodged it with the Director of Public Prosecutions, but I'm assured a little thing like that doesn't worry you. Mind you,

I don't know anything about these two chaps, except that one of them's called Ponting, and he's a new member, and the other . . .'

'Interesting,' said Mr Crook, replenishing their glasses. 'Funny no one's thought of this before. It's like the old saying about the man who's following a tiger and never thinks that another tiger may be following him.'

'Meaning,' suggested Martin brilliantly, 'he had something on her.'

'Interesting to know what that was. Or, of course, they could just be partners, with about as much trust between them as you could hide under a pre-war threepenny bit. And you know the one about when thieves fall out. Wouldn't surprise me to know she was trying to double-cross him, he went to sort things out and she got the worst of it. If they were partners, then he'd know the names of her clientèle and he could get to work on them on his own account.'

'You make it sound so simple,' sighed Dr Martin.

'Murder's generally simple. It's the consequences that get so tangled up. Didn't get any more info about this hotel?—come to think of it, there aren't many better settings for running a blackmail racket, not if you specialize in your clients.'

'He spoke of Postman's Bay, somewhere along the coast, I gathered.'

'Quite a lot of coast around Britain,' acknowledged Crook agreeably. 'Still . . .' he picked up the telephone receiver.

'That you, Bill?' he enquired an instant later. 'Ever heard of a place called Postman's Bay? No? Well, you do that and ring me back. If you can get any gen on who ran an hotel there . . . Well, I shouldn't think there'd be many. It sounds like the other end of Nowhere.

'What Bill don't know and can't find out ain't worth worrying over,' Crook confided to his visitor, returning the receiver to its rest. 'Incidentally, feel like declaring an interest? I mean, we're always hearing how overworked the profession is and more than half of them on the bread-line, so why this interest in a pair of females you wouldn't know from Eve.'

'You're forgetting, aren't you,' suggested the doctor, rather stiffly, 'I saw both ladies on Penton Station.'

'Well, you thought that one up nice,' Crook congratulated him.

'And I happen to know Jorrocks.'

'So—he ain't going to be delighted when he hears you've seceded to the enemy—oh yes, that's the way they regard me. Wonder what did go on at that hotel? Can't just be a rendezvous for unlicensed *amants*—when Big Brother comes to stay and, praise the pigs, I'll be in my sarcophagus by that time, anything more than fraternal feeling may be an infringement of the law, but no one as yet, except maybe a wife, can haul a chap up for meeting his true love at a place with such an unlikely name as Postman's Bay. One thing, whatever the racket was, that little chap knows a lot about it. Come to think of it, Lady Flora said something about a dishonest partner busting things up and going off with the takings. I wondered at the time why the lady didn't try for an extradition order—maybe it was a bit more complicated. Or, of course,' he added in his casual way, 'Miss Plum may have found she was being double-crossed and taken the law into her own hands and this fellow—what did you say his name was—Gray?—is the invisible witness and don't see why he shouldn't cash in.'

'Your imagination does you credit,' said the doctor drily.

'As you've just pointed out, where there ain't no proof you have to make use of the next best thing.'

The telephone rang and it was Bill on the line. 'About five miles out from a place called Torminster,' he said. 'Torminster's fifteen miles from Bournemouth. Name of hotel the Pendragon, closed now, compulsory purchase, I understand. Postman's Bay consists of about fourteen houses, a pub and a couple of shops. Population, at a rough guess, about a hundred.'

'One of these days civilization, God save the word, will take Bill over as a computer,' said Mr Crook piously, hanging up the receiver. 'Don't ask me how he does it. You never did tell me what your special interest was, and don't tell me love of justice because I shan't believe you.'

'When I was a boy,' said the doctor primly, 'my father always made us finish a job we'd begun, whether it was carpentry or reading a book or writing a letter.'

'My mum was the same,' agreed Crook enthusiastically. 'Only with her it was our dinner. If you had a belly-ache. OK, don't pull out your chair, I'll give you something to settle that. But she didn't let you muck up a plateful of stew or a liver dumpling—no need to look so prissy, my mum's liver dumplings were famous for miles round—if you start you leave a clean plate. And I don't mind telling you,' wound up Mr Crook generously. 'I've got a stomach a food disposal unit might envy. Even the muck doctors hand out couldn't disturb it.'

'I'll remember that one of these days,' Martin promised. 'I can't help wondering what induced that nice-looking girl to get herself involved. I mean, what's Imogen Garland to her?'

'Just another human being,' offered Crook. 'I only hope she don't find herself drowning in the consommé before she's through. She's like most women—more zeal than discretion. I wouldn't put it past her to go down on her own account and try to solve the mystery of the Hotel Pendragon.'

'You couldn't let her do that,' cried Dr Martin.

'What makes you believe you or any man could stop any dame doing what she'd set her mind to? Matter of fact, it might be quite an idea. When did this Pendragon place close down? Two years? That fits. It's about two years since Miss Plum came to live with the Garlands; everybody wondered why, but if it was security she needed . . . Putting on the black may be a very paying job but it's about as safe as playing with a black mamba.'

'And Miss Garland?'

'She'd take her along, of course. Good as a police dog any day, better maybe. Looks a moron, but ain't, and there's no tougher armour than that.'

'But they'd be recognized—or hadn't you thought of that?' demanded the doctor. 'There's been one violent death to date . . .'

'That's what you think,' Crook told him. 'But the story goes 'way back—oh, say twenty-five years. Chap whose name you probably never heard. Case of big fleas and little fleas,' he added unoriginally. 'But that's what blackmail's about. You bite A's ear, B gets to know about it, and before you can say Hey presto—' he paused—'it's a funny thing, but I've never heard a chap say Hey presto—you find you're having a sizeable chunk taken out of your own. Illogical body of men, the police. I don't say they approve of murder, but they can and even do find excuses, though it don't do X much good, but when it comes to putting on the black—well, the Wars of the Roses ain't in it.'

'Every word you say convinces me it's sheer madness to think of letting these two women get involved. That Miss Chester . . .'

'Well, there ain't been much about her in the press,' Crook soothed him, 'and the other can buy a wig and change her name—Ivy Garden or Beryl Bookay or something—and anyhow women don't get involved, they start that way. And if you knew half as much about the sex as I do, you'd realize that's how they like it. If they didn't they wouldn't get themselves into the messes they do. Life to a dame is like a ball of wool to a kitten. Unless it's a picturesque tangle, they ain't interested. Now, if you or me was to turn up at Postman's Bay asking questions, the whole community 'ud shut its big silly trap and hardly give us the time of day. But two females, especially when one of them's my client that could make even a giraffe give tongue—ever teach you in Med. School the giraffe's the only animal that can't utter?—they wouldn't actually stay in Postman's Bay, of course—hotels full of garrulous females, widows, spinsters and the sort that drive a man to emigrate at dead of night —all burning to find a fresh audience . . .'

'I repeat, you can't let that girl take the risk.'

'Like I said, what makes you suppose that you or me or a whole regiment of the Guards could make her or any other dame, not do what she'd set her mind on? She'd take Dotty with her naturally—if the rumour goes round you're not quite *compos mentis*, it's surprising how many chaps will open their grief to you, as the prayer-book hath it.'

'And if and when they both come back in one piece?' Martin still sounded truculent.

'We'll hope that, like Bo-Peep they'll bring their flock alongside, wagging their tails behind them. Me, I want to know where this man of mystery fits in. He had some hold over Miss Plum, no question about that.'

'If you're right and he was doing the blackmailing, why should he have been at Madame Tussaud's on the Saturday?'

'Keeping tabs on the lady,' returned Crook, briefly. 'Never was a falser truism than the one about honour among thieves. He'd want to make sure of his commission, wouldn't he?'

'But why on earth should he want Miss Styles out of the way?'

'She might have been doing a bit of extra homework. What we need is a bit of info about the gentleman, and our precious pair are just the ones to get it for us. Bound to be someone in the neighbourhood who'll remember this hotel —can't be so many in a place that boasts one pub and half-a-dozen shops—you take my word for it, those two girls together 'ull gather enough straw to build a wigwam.' He clapped his companion on the shoulder. 'Cheer up, mate,' he advised. 'Only a zany commits murder in the presence of a witness, so if the two girls stick together . . .'

'If that bounder's keeping an eye on things, he might follow them,' objected Martin.

'If he does that they'll pick him out quicker than you or me would find a needle in a haystack. In fact, the chap I wouldn't want to be in that set-up is Gray himself. Like St Paul, if he's loony enough to follow in their footsteps, he'll find he stands in jeopardy every hour, and lucky if he can keep his feet for as long as that.'

As he rose to go the doctor added, 'By the way, there's one more thing. Just as he was leaving the Mausoleum the little runt said, "The chap you want to get after is Arthur Crook," or words to that effect. "With him out of the picture things 'ull start to cool down." I'm paraphrasing a bit, of course. Just thought I'd mention it.'

'Don't let the thought keep you awake,' said Crook in his gracious way. 'Don't they always tell you the meaty bit of any letter is in the postscript? But thanks for the warning just the same.'

'What are you going to do about it?' enquired the doctor curiously.

Crook stared. 'What had you in mind?'

'I suppose you might ask for police protection.'

'The day I do that I add myself to the bread-line. Why, that's what most of my clients hire me for, they don't like the way the police are looking at them. If I was to ask for protection it 'ud be as bad as going over to the enemy. Not that I think there's all that danger,' he added in his candid way. 'If anything was to happen to me crime-wise you'd need double the police force to protect the chap responsible. Fact. There's a lot to be said for having some right villains on your list. Chaps like that have their own sense of justice, and it wouldn't suit their book for me to start pushing up the daisies before my time. Regular bodyguard they'd be.

I tell you this, Doctor, I've had anonymous messages before now, mostly on the blower, where a chap don't have to sign his name, just repeatin' a rumour and hanging up before I could ask any questions.'

'Practical joke?' hazarded Martin.

'Only if you think six feet of earth and the conquering worm's a joke. Some of them don't have much in the bank, but there's other ways of settling accounts besides hard cash. Thanks for the tip, though.'

'Been a pleasure to meet you—officially, I mean,' the doctor assured him.

And meant it.

CHAPTER NINE

Mrs Anstruther, a handsome woman with well-curled white hair and a searching brown eye liked to refer to herself as the doyen of the Homestead Hotel, Torminster. 'Mrs Anstruther says' . . . 'In Mrs Anstruther's opinion' . . . 'Might be a good idea to ask Phoebe Anstruther'—she took it all as her due. She had come to the Homestead after her husband's death for four weeks' change and convalescence, and five years later had become the self-styled doyen, occupying the favourite window-table, with a slightly larger vase of flowers than the rest. And she took it for granted that when the tea-trolley was rolled in she should 'dispense', as she called it. A companion, said to be a poor relation, saw to it that she had first choice of the toasted tea-cakes and gateaux, and she sometimes irritated her fellow-guests by sorting the post and calling out, 'One for you, Mrs Hines, Mrs Metcalfe two, and you're not forgotten either, Mr Joseph.' Mr Joseph was one of the few male residents, a retired solicitor with a hearing aid that conveniently didn't work when he didn't want to listen.

The Homestead wasn't one of those ports of call where people came for a fortnight and then vanished into limbo. Many made it a permanent home, though the less affluent found it convenient to stay with relatives during the summer season when prices went up by 50 per cent and even single rooms became doubles. Mrs Anstruther never moved, nor were her prices increased. 'In return for favours received,' said Mrs Hines, though no one was quite sure what she meant.

The arrival of two new visitors, one of them young (by Homestead standards) and the other barely middle-aged, was bound to excite interest in so circumscribed a gathering. Dora, given a free hand, had worked wonders with Imogen.

'You don't want all that hair flying round your face like a Skye terrier,' she had urged, and took her to a good shop in Brigham where she had it cut and shaped and washed with a brightening rinse.

'It's too bad they've stopped women going on the game,' was Flora's pithy comment. 'Imogen looks positively dishy.'

'The expressions women use!' Charles said. 'Point is, she doesn't look like Dotty. Your Miss Plum never did anything like that for her.'

'She wasn't going to be dangled as a bait in those days,' Flora pointed out. 'Well, of course that's the idea. Why do you suppose she and the Chester woman are going down to Torminster if it's not to try and pick up a bit of dirt about Vicky Styles?'

'If she opens her mouth about Miss Plum she'll be identified pronto,' phophesied Charles.

'She's registering as Miss Garth. Luckily you don't have to show a passport in British hotels. Miss Chester hasn't really been in the limelight, so she can stick to her own name.'

'You're all taking it for granted this blasted hotel did exist,' said Charles.

'Oh, I don't think there's much doubt of that. She said she was a partner in an hotel on the coast.'

'Then let's hope her ghost doesn't haunt it. Those two women are perfectly capable of raising the dead. I hope Crook knows what he's doing.'

'Miss Chester seems balanced enough, and Dotty appears to have taken to her.'

'Dotty would take to an earthworm if it tried to show her any affection. She's the least discerning creature in the world.'

'I wonder,' remarked Mrs Anstruther reflectively to Maud

Pardon, her companion, who was, in fact, the daughter of a distant cousin, 'why those two women chose to come here.'

'It's good value for money,' Maud reminded her. 'I've heard you say so a dozen times.'

'Have you managed to find out anything about them, Maud?'

'Oh, Cousin Phoebe, they've only been here two days. Besides, you're the one who Draws People Out.'

'Naturally,' announced Mrs Anstruther, 'one doesn't wish to appear inquisitive. It's my experience that, given half a chance, People Reveal Themselves.'

So at tea-time that day the new-comers were given their half-chance.

It began when Dotty, seeing the patient Maud carrying round the plates, jumped up to lend a hand. She snatched at the dish of hot tea-cakes before Mrs Anstruther had an opportunity of picking the butteriest for herself. Then, when the doyen had said, 'Thank you, but Miss Pardon likes to take charge of those,' Imogen offered, 'I'll carry round the cups, shall I? Are they all the same or are some sugared?'

'We generally permit guests to sugar their own tea,' Mrs Anstruther told her loftily.

'Oh dear!' Imogen sank back on the sofa, laughing. 'I've put my foot in it, haven't I? Both feet, in fact. What a good thing I'm not a centipede.'

An extraordinary sound, like a crow starting to caw, surprised everyone. It was Mr Joseph, accompanying Dotty's mirth.

'I'm afraid,' began Mrs Anstruther, giving her version of Queen Victoria not being amused, but she got no further, for the intolerable man said, 'Don't you get it? Fancy having a hundred feet to put into things.'

'Or there are millipedes, of course,' reflected Imogen. 'They must have a thousand feet, though I don't know whoever counted them. They must be very *long* creatures.'

'I really don't think this conversation about creepy-crawlies is very suitable for tea-time,' objected a tart Mrs Anstruther.

'But He Who made the lamb made them,' insisted Imogen. 'William Blake. Of course, he was talking about a tiger, but it comes to the same thing.'

Mrs A quite clearly hadn't a notion what she was talking about. 'Maud,' she said reproachfully, 'I think Mrs Hines would like a refill.'

Maud Parsons said in a voice that staggered the doyen, 'Oh, I didn't hear her ask.'

Which only went to show what happens when bad influences get into hotels.

Mrs Anstruther, having rebuked her companion, turned graciously to Dora. You didn't have to possess second sight to see what she was making of the situation. A nurse out of uniform in charge of someone who was no more than ninepence in the shilling, as they said.

'Do you know this part of the world, Miss Chester?'

'I've never actually stayed here,' answered Dora truthfully, 'but there's a place just along the coast, called Postman's Bay—an extraordinary name.'

The human rook cawed afresh. 'You could call it a play on the words,' he offered. 'It was a smuggling resort at one time.'

'With postmen?' asked Imogen innocently.

'It's a cruel piece of coast,' confided Mr Joseph. 'Very rocky. That's the reason it's never caught on as a tourists' resort. No bathing, no sailing, I've always wondered what made that Sumner couple open their hotel there—what was its name? Ah yes, the Pendragon. It must have been obvious to a blind man there was something fishy going on.'

'Isn't that rather a dangerous statement from a lawyer?' enquired Mrs Anstruther, who wasn't accustomed to being done out of even a ray of limelight.

'It's a question of common sense,' retorted Mr Joseph

equably. 'What was the attraction of that bit of coast, smugglers apart, of course?'

Imogen leaned forward, beaming. 'Perhaps that's what they were—smugglers.'

Mr Joseph shook his head. 'Too chancy—oh, right enough at the time when all you had to do was hang a torch round your moke's neck and stand on the edge of the most dangerous cliff available—and if you can believe that you'll believe anything—and watch the vessels founder on the rocks. Then your gang went down and collected the loot. Nowadays planes are quicker and offer much less risk. No, no, I never believed smuggling was the answer.'

Dora leaned forward in her turn. 'Did this Mrs Sumner—you did say Sumner?'

'That's right.'

'Were they the first people to have the hotel?'

It was originally a nursing home,' interposed Mrs Anstruther crisply.

'With its own private cemetery?' enquired Mr Joseph, who was a man after Crook's own heart. 'Who on earth would want to convalesce in that desolate spot?'

'I dare say they weren't consulted,' observed Dora shrewdly. 'It sounds an awfully convenient sort of place to send your relations if they were being difficult or you wanted them out of the way.'

'In these enlightened days, my dear young lady, you can't just put up a plate and announce you're at home to mentally deficient patients.'

Imogen nodded. 'There was that nurse in Epsom—you remember, Dora? And it turned out she was only a sort of glorified ward-maid. I wonder if she's in the Chamber of Horrors, too.'

'All the same, Mr Joseph is right,' mused Mrs Anstruther in the deep tones of one who sees somewhat further than the rest of humanity. 'There was something very queer about the Sumners, if that really was their name.'

'Why shouldn't it be?' asked Imogen.

'Sometimes people have good reasons for wanting to change their names,' the doyen announced triumphantly.

'No law to prevent you doing that, provided it's not with criminal intent,' Mr Joseph assured them. 'Impersonation, for instance.'

'There was all that talk when he disappeared,' put in Mrs Metcalfe, who was a suffragan bishop's widow and seemed to think that gave her special qualifications.

'You mean, he left her?' asked Dora.

'I mean, he disappeared and was never seen again.'

'Well, not in this locality,' agreed Mrs Anstruther graciously. 'Mind you, I've often wondered if the police weren't behind it.'

'In that case, why didn't they move in?' demanded Mr Joseph obtusely.

'There was some rumour about his having fallen from a cliff,' breathed Mrs Metcalfe.

'Why should he do that?' enquired innocent Dotty. 'Or do you mean he was pushed?' Her eyes blazed with excitement.

'A most dangerous suggestion,' pontificated Mrs Anstruther. 'No body was ever found.'

'With the sort of tides you get round that bit of coast you'd hardly expect it,' Mr Joseph reminded them. 'Odds are a corpse 'ud be swept out to sea, and by the time he was swept in again, if ever, his own mother wouldn't know him.'

'But surely his wife would report his disappearance?' insisted another guest.

'Perhaps she was the one who pushed him,' offered Dora.

'Ridiculous!' snorted Mrs Anstruther.

'I don't know so much about that.' Mr Joseph sounded tolerant. 'I dare say that kind of thing happens a lot more than anyone knows, but if every wife who was annoyed with her husband pushed him off a cliff or down a flight of stairs or whatever was most convenient, you'd need an additional Ministry to deal with widows' pensions.'

Dora heaved a luxurious sigh. It was almost as good as listening to Mr Crook.

'It doesn't sound very reasonable,' she offered. 'I mean, if she couldn't prove death she couldn't draw the widow's pension, and if it was just that they didn't get on they simply had to separate, nobody can force you to go on living with someone you don't like, so pushing him off a cliff does seem like pushing things a bit far—I'm sorry, I didn't mean to make a pun.'

'Oh, but it didn't have to be like that,' urged Dotty, her face brighter than ever. 'He might have known something about her, something not quite convenient, I mean.'

'I'm afraid,' boomed Mrs Anstruther, 'some people have been watching too much TV.'

'Oh yes?' murmured Dotty politely. 'Dora and I don't care for it much. Mr Crook—that's a friend of ours—says nothing happens on stage or screen that hasn't happened already in real life and we find real life quite fascinating, don't we, Dora?'

'She'd need a motive certainly,' mused Maud Pardon, to whom all this was like champagne. It wasn't often anyone had the temerity to stand up to Mrs A.

'Mr Crook says that, according to the police, just being the married partner is motive enough,' said Dotty, 'and I'm sure I've heard husbands can be very provoking.'

'But even if he did know something about her,' urged Mrs Metcalfe, 'I'm sure I've heard that married couples can't be made to give evidence against one another.' She thought. 'Of course, if a third party was involved . . .'

'Why drag in a third party?' Mr Joseph asked. 'My own opinion is that the little lady knew exactly what was going on. And when she'd closed down the hotel—and don't believe any yarn you may hear about bankruptcy, I understand she paid up every penny—she joined him, wherever he might be. And no doubt with good reason. I believe there was enough fish fried on the premises to turn it into a fish-and-chips shop.'

'We still don't know why they chose that particular locality,' brooded Dora, drinking all this in like an addict on meth.

'Do you suppose—' Dotty came in like the non-serving partner on a tennis court—'that perhaps the hotel was for people who wanted to—well, lie low for a time, who couldn't afford the limelight? Didn't I hear the charges were abnormally high, but even so the limelight might have cost still more. I mean, if the fuzz—that's a word they use in London meaning the police—were on their trail they wouldn't dare risk trying to leave the country because the ports and airfields would all be watched and then passports are such a problem, getting new ones, I mean—a place like Postman's Bay would be ideal. You couldn't go to your relations, even if they'd have you, because that would be the first place the police would look. I dare say it was a little goldmine,' she wound up enthusiastically.

Mrs Anstruther looked appalled. 'Really, Miss—er—Garth, you must appreciate this is nothing but speculation.'

'Ah, but who are the millionaires in this world?' demanded Dotty triumphantly. 'Speculators to a man.'

'You seem remarkably interested in the Sumners,' continued Mrs Anstruther.

But Dotty was equal even to that one. 'You know how it is if you live in the country,' she explained apologetically. 'We don't actually have linkmen to light our lanes after dark, though sometimes I wish we did, but everything's very quiet and—and humdrum (guiltily she avoided Dora's eye), so to find a mystery on your doorstep, so to speak . . . Did anyone ever discover why they really left?'

'Because we don't live in the Land of the Free any longer, whatever politicians would like you to believe,' Mr Joseph assured her. 'The War Department wanted the site for a missile base or something, and since the hotel stood just outside the village it meant that the dozen or so old codgers who'd lived there all their lives could stop on with their general-store and their ale-house . . .'

'I dare say she was no loser on the transaction,' contributed Mrs Anstruther smoothly.

'Which shows how little you know of the workings of the authoritarian mind,' Mr Joseph assured her in grim tones. 'They offer you a price, and seeing it's never up to your own valuation of the site you sit back and prepare to bargain. And what do you find? That's our figure, take it or leave it, please yourself, it's a free country, but either way you go out by the front door as we come in by the back. Probably ruined the place by now,' he added gloomily. 'What a Government Department can achieve in just under two years when it puts its mind to it . . .'

'There was never very much to ruin,' Mrs Anstruther said. 'I remember remarking to my friend—you recall it, Maud?' Her frozen smile, straight from the refrigerator, warned poor Maudie it would cost her her job to forget. 'I can understand siting a nursing home there, particularly if it's for the less—er—social diseases—but for a holiday resort—I mean, what's wrong with Torminster? Shops, concerts, an excellent little theatre, good restaurants, if you want to entertain away from the hotel—and the sea, of course. No, I'm convinced in my own mind that couple were there for no good purpose. It really might be quite interesting to learn what did happen to them.'

'Didn't you ever try to find out?' Dotty asked.

'Really, Miss Garth, their affairs were their own concern.'

'That's what everybody thinks, but it doesn't always work out that way. I wonder if the War Department thought of digging up the garden when they took over the property.'

'Seeing their ultimate idea is to blow the whole lot of us sky-high, why give themselves the trouble?' demanded a balding ferret-faced retired bank manager, who sometimes wondered why he'd bothered to retire, the inhabitants of the Homestead being absolute replicas of the half-crazy clients he used to interview at the bank—and at least there he'd been paid for his trouble.

'There was that Bulgarian Miss Plum used to talk about—she was someone I met when I was in another part of the country, not with Miss Chester,' she added in explanatory tones.

'In an hotel?' demanded Mrs Anstruther acutely.

'Well—more like a house really.'

Just what I suspected, Mrs Anstruther thought. A bit wanting, poor thing, probably a very suitable applicant for Pendragon in the old days when it had been a nursing home for the slightly peculiar.

'What happened to the Bulgarian?' enquired Maud Pardon. 'You do seem to have known some interesting people, Miss Garth.'

'Oh, if I'd known him I wouldn't be here now. He used to advertise for servant-girls, and when they answered his advertisement he strangled them and buried them in the garden.'

'What an extraordinary idea of entertainment,' said Mrs Anstruther, more convinced than ever that they'd got a real nutcase in their midst.

'I don't think entertainment was the idea, not their entertainment anyway. His name was Kiss, isn't that a funny name for a murderer?'

'It's a funny name for anyone,' suggested Mr Trevor, the bank official.

'How did they catch him in the end?' enquired Mrs Metcalfe avidly. 'I don't wish to sound morbid but my husband did at one time contemplate work in the Mission field.'

'Mr Kiss doesn't sound the sort of person who'd ever have gone near a Mission.'

'Wasn't there a Mrs Kiss—or was she underground, too?'

'Oh no. She was his partner—well, the law made her that

by marriage—and the dictionary says partner means a helpmeet, and anyway, she told the police she never really approved, but she didn't want to be found in one of the jars—oh yes, when the garden was full he started putting them in jars in the cellar. I suppose the smell gave them away in the end,' she added seriously.

'Wouldn't have expected the Bulgarians to have noticed that,' said Mr Trevor. 'Went there once as a young man—smells abounding . . .'

'So if the War Department had dug up the garden,' continued Dotty, resolute as a terrier digging out a fox, 'they might have found poor Mr Sumner.'

'Only thing is it seems a great waste of energy to dig a grave—this is chalk and not so easy to work, not for a woman on her own—when the place is—was—balanced on a cliff-edge. How long have the War Department been there?' Mr Trevor added.

'About two years—that's when the hotel closed down.' Mr Joseph pulled out his watch. 'Time for a little refresher,' he announced, as he always did at 5.30. Never ordered a drink on the premises, though the hotel was licensed, but went into the town to a common pub where doubtless he met common men and drank with them. 'Care for something a little stronger than tea?' continued the lawyer cheerfully, addressing Dotty and Dora.

Both women thought it a splendid idea. 'See you at dinner,' Dotty beamed at the open-mouthed company. Because it was the first time in living memory Mr Joseph had ever invited a female to accompany him for a drink.

'I wouldn't be too sure of that,' prophesied Mrs Anstruther unsympathetically, as the door closed behind them. 'I know that type. One glass and they're over the windmill. I only hope that crazy one won't start singing in the middle of the night and get the place a bad name.'

Mr Joseph and his two lady guests didn't return to the

Homestead until the dinner gong was being sounded, and immediately the meal was over and when the Old Gang were united in a resolve to pluck out the heart of the mystery Dora and Dotty foiled them by saying they were rather tired and would turn in early.

'Mr Crook should give us each a putty medal,' Dora remarked, having turned the key in the door and left it in place, on the chance that curiosity might overcome if not actually kill one of the hotel cats. 'Think what we've found out. That Miss Plum down here wasn't Miss Plum at all, and that her defaulting partner wasn't a woman as Flora supposed . . .'

'I thought your sister-in-law was the sort of person who knew everything,' Dora murmured.

'Oh, she does,' Dotty agreed, 'but she's only human, so sometimes she knows it wrong. I was wondering—that little man, he knew about the hotel and Miss Plum's connection with it—do you suppose he could be the missing Mr Sumner?'

'But in that case, why should he have pushed Miss Plum out of the window? I mean, there is that thing about motive.'

'She might have been threatening him, and believe me, she was a woman of her word. No, I've got a better idea. Suppose Miss Plum did push her partner over the cliff—*and the Little Man knew it*?'

'And had been blackmailing her? That's a good point, Dotty. She wouldn't dare go to the police, and she wouldn't have any illusions . . .' Her brow furrowed. They might have been two Foreign Secretaries, wondering how to avert a Third World War. That, Crook used to say, was the sex's main charm for him. Unlike the Laodiceans of Pauline fame, they never blew lukewarm—piping hot or ice-cold, and either could be a challenge. 'I suppose she couldn't have been secretly married to Sumner?'

'Oh no,' said Dotty decisively, 'if she had been, Mr

Crook would have found out. He's the kind of man who finds out everything. Well, look how he discovered that the envelope the police collected from Baker Street held a Post Office Savings Book in the name of Vera Sumner. You don't suppose the police rang him up and told him, do you?'

'You've made your point,' Dora agreed.

'What I thought,' Imogen continued, 'was that we might do a bit of enquiring on our own account. We're supposed to be here for a few days' sea change and fresh air, so it's natural we should make a few excursions. You heard what Mr Joseph said, there's still the core of the old village left at Postman's Bay, someone must be left who'll remember the couple and there can't be much to talk about . . . I mean, people don't disappear suddenly over cliffs every day of the week even in a place like London and in an enclosed community like Postman's Bay . . . It might even be quite fun playing detective.'

'We're not really down here for fun,' pointed out the conscientious Dora. 'Still, I suppose there's no reason why we shouldn't take any that comes our way.'

'I'm beginning to feel sorry for Miss Plum,' admitted Imogen. 'Of course, blackmail's indefensible, but if someone was demanding money she had to get it from somewhere. To hear some people talk you'd think it grew on trees.'

'I'd like to have heard Miss Plum trying to explain that to the police,' remarked Dora frankly.

'Oh, I shouldn't think even Miss Plum would have tried that. The police aren't like you and me, Dora. They take it for granted people want to keep the law. And she couldn't have paid much blackmail out of what Flora gave her. I always did wonder why she stayed on.'

'For security's sake, perhaps,' Dora said.

'That's a very good suggestion. I mean, it would be a very bold murderer who would even attempt to slay her on Charles's doorstep. He may look mild, but he's a tiger when he's roused. Besides, a scandal would cause an upset locally, and even his political opponents don't want to see Charles murdered, only sent into the wilderness for good—with the pelicans and basilisks,' she wound up vaguely.

Postman's Bay had undergone a startling change since the so-called Sumners ran their suspect hotel. The coming of the War Department had turned the place into two opposing camps—on one side, the Army, which had its own NAAFI, and could afford to import girls from Torminster or even Bournemouth for army dances, and the old hamlet that stood well back from the cliff and seemed as unreal as a legend. At first it wasn't easy to get anyone to speak, but old Mrs Wenham, who ran the wool shop, welcomed strangers who might prove to be customers. Oh yes, she remembered the Pendragon all right, always something funny about it. Half-empty sometimes, but an outsider couldn't just walk in and book a room. She'd known them as had tried.

'And that's no way to run an hotel,' the old woman nodded. 'No vacancies, they'd be told. Town people thinking anyone who doesn't live in a city must be daft. I mean, you can't go against the milkman, can you? And if he finds a note saying six pints when he's used to delivering twelve, you have to think, don't you? And fussy! No children and no dogs. That's no way to run a seaside hotel. Mind you, you never saw one of these little match-box cars there, great huge things you'd have slept a family in, but all the catering done in Torminster when they didn't go into Bournemouth.'

'That can't have made them very popular,' suggested Dora sedately.

'Well, of course it didn't. If you live in a holiday resort you do count on getting something out of the visitors. But these Sumners, they hardly so much as acknowledged your existence. I don't believe half the folk would have recognized them if they'd met them face to face. Believe me, my dear, I hardly so much as sold an extra ball of wool during the season. That shows you the kind of people they must have been. For what is there to do of an evening if you don't knit? It's not as though we can get the television here, though I hear it's good enough at Torminster. Something to do with the hills, they say.'

'I wanted some wool,' said Imogen, rather wildly. 'To make a dressing-jacket—for a Dean's relict—that's what they call a widow in theological circles—white with that silver thread in it, and long sleeves because for years they worked in the Coloured Countries though you aren't allowed to call them that any more. Oh, and would you have a pattern? Rather loose sleeves—aren't they called raglan?—because she suffers from swollen joints.'

Seeing that neither of them knew how to put a row of stitches on a needle, Dora thought she was putting up rather a good show.

'And queer!' old Mrs Wenham went on, ruffling through a tatty old box of paper patterns. 'The talk there was when he went off. Oh, I know there were some said it was a case of cherchez the femme, but I think it's a lot more likely it's the takings he went off with.'

'Didn't the police ever find out?' asked Dotty innocently. 'Are those the right size needles for a bed-jacket? I've never made one before. My sister-in-law always gives me one for Christmas, she gets it from the Conservative Association Christmas Bazaar. All I can ever contribute is netted purses. I don't know what happens to them.'

'They go in the bran tub, dear,' said knowledgeable Mrs Wenham.

The door of the shop opened a few inches and a man's head appeared. 'I beg pardon,' he said quickly. 'I was looking for the Post Office.'

'That's in Mr Cater, the general store,' said Mrs Wenham.

'For a minute,' said Dora, 'I thought he was a ghost—the ghost of the missing Mr Sumner, perhaps.'

'It's not likely he'd come back here.' Mrs Wenham wrote

some figures on a bit of paper and carefully began to add them up.

'He must have been quite someone,' reflected Dora. 'I mean, it's two years ago, and they're still talking about him at the Homestead. That's where we're staying—we were recommended.'

'I dare say they've nothing better to talk about,' Mrs Wenham conceded.

Dotty paid for the wool and the couple left the shop.

CHAPTER TEN

There was no sign of the little man when they emerged into the narrow street, but Imogen, turning to her companion, said, 'Dora, did you notice him? The one who pretended he was looking for the Post Office?'

'How can you be so sure he was pretending?'

'Because there's a notice over Cater's shop, a blind man couldn't miss it. He looked in to make certain we hadn't left by a back door or something.'

'Really, Dotty!'

'He was on the bus this morning,' Imogen continued.

'If he wanted to come to Postman's Bay that was his only choice, unless he was going to walk or had a car.'

'I'm sure I've seen him on the promenade, too, always on his own.'

'Who was the poet saw Heaven in a wild flower—or was it a grain of sand? You can see a criminal at every turn.'

'It's why we're down here, after all, but what does a solitary little creature like that want with a place like Torminster?'

'You think he's the spy who came in from the cold?'

'There was that little man in Dr Martin's club. Oh Dora, you don't think he could be the real Mr Sumner?'

'If he was, this is surely the last place he'd come to.'

'I'll tell you what,' offered Dotty. 'We'll stop at the Copper Kettle—I wonder why they always call them that, when they're all-electric nowadays and hardly ever copper—we've got twenty-five minutes before the bus goes back, and what would you like to bet that he fancies a cup of tea, too?'

'Most people do this hour of the day,' returned Dora, unmoved, 'and there isn't anywhere else to go.'

Sure enough, they'd no sooner given their order than the door was rather nervously opened and in came the man who had peered through Mrs Wenham's door. There was nothing particularly jaunty about him, in fact his raincoat had definitely seen better days. He took a table in the corner and asked for 'the full tea'.

'I've been thinking,' said Dotty reflectively. 'Oh Dora, one of the things I like about you is that you don't look as though I'd made a joke when I say a thing like that. Flora always begins to laugh and says, "We'd better get out our life-belts." '

'If you're going to start bothering about what relations say,' retorted Dora scornfully. 'My brother would have me in Bedlam like winking if it weren't that it wouldn't sound well for a Dean to have a demented sister. Tell me what you were thinking?'

'That this little man—if he isn't the missing Mr Sumner—could know more about what happened to him—Mr S, I mean—than suited Miss Plum's convenience.'

'But in that case, why should she be the one who fell out of the window? She was a source of income to him.'

'You didn't know her as I did, in fact you didn't really know her at all, did you? She wasn't the type to go on taking orders for ever. She'd wait her chance, and then she'd be perfectly ruthless.'

'Which makes it all the odder that she should be the one to come to a sticky end.'

'Even Miss Plum's plans must occasionally have gone astray. At all events, we know she was expecting someone that night at the Montblanc, which is why she suggested a bath—she knows I take simply hours in a bath—and the wrong one fell, if you know what I mean.'

They finished their tea and walked towards the bus stop. 'I'm not sure it wouldn't be a good idea if we separated tomorrow,' Imogen suggested. 'Now don't look so horrified, I shall be perfectly safe. He can't attack me with a knife on the promenade, but if he's really interested in either of us, and it's not just coincidence, then the one he must be after is me, because you never knew Miss Plum, whereas I was living more or less on top of her for two years, and he can't be sure what I winkled out.'

'Or what she told you.'

'I shouldn't think she talked in her sleep, I never heard her, and that's the only way you'd ever have learned anything she didn't want you to know. And then you remember what Mr Crook said once, it's not just what you know, it's what someone else may believe you know, even if you don't know you know it yourself. It sounds a bit involved, but I dare say you get me. And then we don't really look the sort of people who'd come to Torminster for a spring holiday. I mean, what's wrong with Venice?'

'I still don't see the point of your being alone,' insisted Dora.

'Anyone can see they'd get no more out of you than a Trappist sphinx, but if he is the one the doctor saw, the one who used to go to Madame Tussaud's, then he might easily have noticed me and thought I was one of the half-wits, who really find the distorting mirrors amusing. And I do,' she wound up candidly.

'I still don't like it, Dotty. We're both assuming he belongs to the criminal classes . . .'

'All the more reason why he wouldn't run unnecessary risks, he'd know he'd have you on his tail, and behind you there's Mr Crook, and most people would sooner face the Judge Advocate than the pair of you. But I'm different. You know the way grown-ups talk in front of children, thinking they're too young or too silly to be on the ball, well, don't you think he might give himself away? And, let's face it, we haven't made much progress so far. We don't even know whether the little man is the one Dr Martin saw in the club—and you can't absolutely discount the possibility that he's the missing Mr Sumner. You heard what the old lady said—he'd hardly be recognized in Torminster—and if he wore a wig . . . Of course, if Mr Crook could see him for himself it would be different.'

'But Mr Crook never saw him in London,' objected Dora.

'That wouldn't make any difference to him. Or, of course, the doctor might know him again.'

'You don't expect much, do you?' murmured Dora. 'Doctors are seeing people all the time, I sometimes wonder how they differentiate between one patient and the next. And a little man seen for five minutes in a dingy club . . .'

'I didn't mean so much remember his face, but his voice, the way he walked—Mr Crook says, though people can change their appearance it's very hard for them to change their walk, unless they get a wooden leg or something. The same with ears, unless you acquire a cauliflower ear, and that isn't always as easy as it sounds. No, Dora, there's only one thing for it, somehow he must be persuaded to Give Himself Away.'

'Sometimes I wonder if you really are dotty,' Dora told her frankly. 'How on earth do you propose we're going to make him do that?'

'I didn't say we. I meant me. You see, if he catches me on my own—well, if he is in any plot he'll know I'm the one who knew Miss Plum, so he'll be watching me like a hawk. If it's you he's after, well, he'll just follow you, won't he? But I don't think he will. And if we're wrong about him altogether he won't follow either of us. And if I could lure him into conversation, though I dare say he won't need much luring—have you ever noticed that if you don't appear too bright people are apt to tell you things, often without realizing they have told you?'

'So what's your plan?' enquired patient Dora.

'I thought tomorrow we might set out together as we always do—if we go separately someone's bound to suggest coming just for the company, that Maud Pardon's had her eye on me from the start. So we'll go off in the direction of the cliffs—it's all right, Dora, I'm a big girl now, I can look after myself—and you can go to Ell Woods and sketch that fern they were talking about—it's indigenous to the district and goodness knows when we'll be in this part of the world again. I'll take a book and settle on a bench somewhere, not too near the hotel—no one from the Homestead is likely to walk up the cliff road, it's a bit steep for one thing, and then there aren't any shops or cafés—and he—if he—comes strolling along to say what a lovely morning it is—let's hope it will be or our plan will fall apart—we shall know there's something in the wind.'

'I don't know what you intend to tell him . . .'

'It's what he tells me that's going to be important.'

Dora groaned. 'You mean, you're going to play it by ear? Well, just remember, Dotty, that if anything should happen to you we might as well make it a double funeral, Mr Crook would never forgive me and I'd as soon face the Day of Wrath as his displeasure.'

The next day the weather co-operated like a doubles player. Dora and her companion set off together, as planned, disregarding a bright remark that perhaps they'd all meet up at the Blue Cockatoo later. When the winding uphill road turned inland Dora departed, with her paint-box and folding stool. Imogen climbed higher and established herself on an uncomfortable wooden seat set a little way back from the cliff-edge. To her right the cliffs stretched as far as eye could see; below, just out of sight, the waters dashed enthusiastically in the direction of the land. The tide was coming in fast and furious. Imogen, who had an imagination a witch might envy, pictured the indomitable Miss Plum and her husband-partner standing here, admiring the view, not a soul in sight, she perhaps calling his attention to something that would cause him to turn his head away for an instant . . . Or, of course, reflected the ingenious Imogen, she could drop her purse, and when he stooped to pick it up . . . He was a small man and Imogen recalled those powerful, pitiless hands. There was no protective fencing at the cliff-edge here, and she remembered hearing talk of the steady erosion of the sea at this point. One thing, a guest had observed, they'll never try and build a bungalow town there.

Imogen opened her book, handed her at random by Miss Pardon, who sensed some mystery in this rather odd visitor, and was dying to pluck out the heart of it.

'A warning to us single girls,' she'd giggled, handing it over. It turned out to be the story of Frederick Seddon, that gentlemanly-looking insurance agent who was hanged in 1912 for the murder of his unappetizing but by no means penurious lodger, Eliza Barrow. Miss Plum should be reading this, not me, Imogen reflected, and then a new thought came. Miss Barrow appeared to have been simple almost to the point of lunacy—so it seemed to Imogen—but for all her wits and foresight, Miss Plum had come to just as sticky an end. Within ten minutes Imogen was absorbed in the book. Poor toad-like Miss Barrow, she thought, how she must have congratulated herself on her own good sense in taking her landlord's advice, and making over her small fortune to him—shares and the lease of a public-house—in exchange for a roof over her head, food and reasonable care for the rest of her life.

And I dare say he seemed as respectable as—oh, as Flora, Imogen decided. She could visualize the house, the polished hall, the dark pitch-pine doors, coloured glass panels in the entry (though the book didn't mention any of these).

They probably even protected the stair-carpet with druggetting, Imogen decided.

And yet—it was a rather dreadful story really, even for a murder record. Because the only passion in it had been Seddon's passion for possession. There hadn't been a scrap of human feeling behind all that deferential manner and outward concern. So deep was she in the story, which had all the fascination of a tale that had all the thrill of fiction and the horror of truth, that it came as a shock to her when a voice enquired, 'Mind if I take a pew?' and looking up, she saw the Little Man beaming down at her.

'Not much joy being on your owney-oh on a day like this,' continued the voice gaily. 'I always say, when you find a lady reading, it's because she's got to pass the time somehow.'

'I'm filling in time till my friend joins me,' agreed Imogen meekly.

'Nice love tale?' chuckled the Little Man, and she turned the spine of the book so that he could read the title.

'Well, not exactly what I'd choose for holiday reading,' he confessed. 'Not with all this sun and—just look at that sea, a lovely colour.'

'But so restless,' objected Imogen. 'It always seems to be rebuking one for being idle, though what good it does, just going up and down . . .'

'Must be contagious,' offered the little man humorously. 'I mean, it's what most of us do. What's so interesting about this one?'

'I suppose really the fact that he looked exactly like everybody else. I mean, you could have sat next to him in a train or bus and you'd never guess—and somehow an insurance agent sounds so—so reassuring.'

'I wouldn't go for that in a big way,' her companion told her. 'I mean, ravening wolves can look like sheep compared with some of these chaps who try to sell you insurance. I'd have expected even an old girl like that Miss Barrow to have recognized a spider when she saw one.'

'It's very difficult to understand how a man can look like a ravening wolf and a spider at the same time,' murmured Imogen. 'I think his real charm for her was that he made her think he was interested in her just for herself. I always think that's the mark of the great doctor, it's not so much that he knows which instruments to use and how to use them, of course, but the one who makes you feel like a person and, while you're with him, the only person in the world who counts.'

'I can see you're a regular philosopher,' observed her companion. 'Been down here long, Miss—Er . . .'

'Garth. I'm staying with a friend at the Homestead, it was recommended to her by a cousin. Not that she'd stayed there herself, she'd stopped at an hotel at Postman's Bay. Well, of course!' She paused, beaming. 'I knew I'd seen you somewhere before. You were in the tea-shop yesterday.'

'Quite right,' said the little man admiringly. 'I will say this for you, Miss Garth, you're no slouch. You must forgive me if I didn't twig right away, but anyone can see you've got all your wits about you.'

'You mustn't blame yourself,' said Imogen modestly. 'It's different for me. I'm what some people would call a private investigator. I'm working for a firm of solicitors, who are interested in the whereabouts of a man called Sumner who used to live in these parts.'

'And you think you'll winkle him out?'

'I can only do that if he's still here, but it seemed quite a notion to put up at the Homestead, where the residents are what might be described as a long-living lot, and having no real affairs of their own, naturally they're interested in other people's.'

'Well, you could have foxed me,' said the little man frankly. 'Do you mean to say you think you've solved the mystery?'

'I've got certain facts I was sent to find, if possible,' acknowledged Imogen modestly. 'What my employers will do with them is no concern of mine, of course. It's like buying in a supermarket. You can see what the customer is paying for, but you've no idea what she's going to make with the ingredients. You or I might think a pound of candles were for lighting purposes, but she may be going to make a waxen image and stick pins in it.'

'I've sometimes had that notion myself,' the little chap agreed. 'But my Grannie taught me temptation is there to be avoided.'

'It seems such a negative thing to be created for,' Imogen demurred. 'If a tree's only on a landscape just in order that you shan't run into it, how much simpler if it wasn't there at all. I suppose you haven't heard any talk about this Mr Sumner,' she added wistfully. 'I mean, a friend of mine says you can pick up more useful gossip from men in a public-house than you could from a whole Bench of Bishops.'

'Sorry I can't help. Who is this chap Sumner, anyway?'

'That's just the point—is or was. They kept an hotel, he and Mrs Sumner, at Postman's Bay where the War Department have their base now, and it's said he just walked out one night. I suppose Mrs Sumner didn't do anything about it at the time because she thought he'd just walk back, but he never did, and now she doesn't know if she's entitled to a widow's pension and there's something about a legacy—they don't tell me everything, of course—that depends on her being a widow, so naturally she wants to know.'

'I thought these lawyer wallahs advertised for missing people—learn something to your advantage—you know.'

'I suppose they have—without any results. Naturally, if he's dead he can't come forward, but he might be living in South America, say, with a millionaire's daughter or something.'

'And how long ago did you say this happened?'

'I don't think I did, but it was about two years.'

'The police—' began the man, but Imogen interrupted. 'We don't really know it's a case for the police, do we? Anyway, Mrs Sumner doesn't seem to have contacted the police, so she can't have thought there was anything—sinister—about his disappearance.'

'And you've got some actual proof?' His voice sounded casual enough, but now there was a wary note in it.

'I wasn't sent to get actual proof,' Imogen repeated, 'only to get certain facts. What the lawyers do with them isn't my affair at all. Oh look, isn't that beautiful!'

Her enthusiastic gaze was turned seaward. A yacht, beautiful as a sailing bird, had just appeared round the curve of the cliff. The little man's face underwent an instant change.

'That's the life,' he whispered. 'No rates, no wallahs always coming round for instalments, no neighbours, no radio, no coming home five nights a week on the five-forty, just going on and on for ever and ever.'

'*Lucky Lady*,' read Imogen thoughtfully. 'I wonder whose luck, though.'

'Anyone's luck who owned her,' said the little man. 'Just think of it, a whole world of your own.'

'Rather a poky world,' suggested Imogen. 'I mean, every street's different but the sea's the same wherever it is. And though fish may be very clever, you can't pretend they'd be very interesting companions. Besides, have you ever noticed, ships are like swans, lovely on the water, but somehow clumsy-looking on land. Which, I suppose, is a hint that we should all remain in our true element.'

He looked at her as though he thought she really was round the bend.

'But she's beautiful!' he urged in incredulous tones. 'You can't see her properly from there. Come a bit nearer the edge—it's all right, I won't let you fall over.' He chuckled suddenly. 'Never do to have two mysteries in two years on the same bit of coast, would it?'

'I can see quite well from here,' affirmed Imogen sturdily. 'Anyway, I haven't a great head for heights. Good heavens! Is it really nearly lunch-time? My friend will be worried if I don't turn up, she thinks I'm so woolly-minded I might walk into the sea without noticing, till it was too late, I mean. She was quite nervous about my coming up here today, but really the Parade gets so noisy, and then people will come up and talk, residents from the hotel, I mean, and then it's all parish pump.'

'Down from London perhaps for a bit of ozone?' suggested the little man affably.

'Oh no. We live in the country, my friend and I, a place called Ditcham. Oh please, you mustn't worry yourself to walk back with me. I'm particularly all there today.'

He put out his hand and took the book from under her arm. 'Allow me!' he said with an exaggerated courtesy.

Imogen felt a sudden shiver, which was absurd, seeing the sun was as bright as ever, no threatening clouds overcast the alabaster sky—it was as though fear had touched her with a finger.

'In any case,' the little man went on, 'I can show you a short cut.'

'I never really believe in short cuts,' Imogen confessed. 'They nearly always turn out longer in the end.'

'This one won't,' he promised confidently. 'I came on it quite by chance a day or two ago. Up here—this way you miss all the noise of the traffic. It's a bit brambly and rough underfoot, but I'll see you don't come to any harm. You'll get an amazing view from up here,' he added encouragingly. 'Never see anything like it down below.'

Willy-nilly, she found herself following in his wake. If I were Dora, thought Imogen rather miserably, I should so contrive it that if it came to a struggle he'd be the one to fall over the edge, but though he was smaller than she and probably weighed less she knew she wouldn't stand a chance. Overhead two gulls screamed—a warning? a derisory cheer?—I'm sure I don't know why we think we're superior to the birds, Imogen reflected. We can't even levitate.

The path led dangerously near the cliff-edge. Once, as they turned a corner, Imogen caught a glimpse of a wall of solid white, not with chalk but with gulls on their nests. At any other time the view would have enthralled her.

Now she only thought that, however loud she screamed as she fell, a passer-by would only think it was another of those maddening birds. There didn't seem to be any other sign of human life. She toyed with the idea of stooping to adjust a shoe and somehow managing to retreat towards the lower road, but realized this might give him the very opportunity he anticipated. She lingered, her wits as bewildered as a ball of wool after a kitten's done its worst.

'Late for din-dins!' called that odious voice. And then, like a miracle, came a fresh interruption. From the brambly heath behind them resounded the noise of a heavy step, and a springer spaniel surged into view, followed by a young woman who might have been the original of the Amazons. Wildly Imogen waved her hand.

'Jane!' she called. 'Jane!'

The young woman not surprisingly stopped dead, stared at Imogen as though she were some sort of figment of the imagination and prepared to continue on her striding way.

'Oh Jane,' panted Imogen, 'if you're going back to the Homestead, would you let my friend, Miss Chester, know I'm on my way back, but I may be a few minutes late. I got beguiled into conversation with another visitor—' she waved towards the outraged little man—'Mr Smyth with a Y,' she improvised—'very interested in murderers and the Chamber of Horrors. If you could just let her know—or leave a message at the desk.'

Her eyes, that Flora had sometimes remarked made the poor girl look positively goofy, shone like the Delphic oracle. The girl addressed as Jane said in a hearty voice that seemed to suit the springer even more than herself, 'Will do. Miss Chester. Yes, I know. Are you bringing Mr Smyth with a Y back to lunch?'

'I'm afraid he can't accept,' said Imogen. 'He's really coming out of his way to escort me back to the Homestead.'

'He's taking you a long way round, you'd do better to stick to the lower road.'

'It is rather rough,' acknowledged Imogen gratefully. 'But you mustn't let me deprive you of your wonderful view, Mr Smyth. I know my way perfectly from here.'

Mr Smyth (presumably travelling incog.) sketched the most casual of salutes. 'See you again, perhaps. Mind you watch out for your Mr Seddon. He could be lurking round any corner, you know.'

'I suppose he told you he was an ex-Serviceman,' remarked the girl (whose name wasn't Jane but Valerie) rather scornfully. 'As if everyone of his generation couldn't say that. But—it's an odd thing—I bet you eight times out of ten he makes a touch.'

'He didn't say anything about the war to me,' confessed Imogen honestly. 'And he was joking about Mr Seddon.'

But it was obvious that the young woman knew no more about Frederick Seddon than, say, the history of the Ottoman Turks.

'I'll say this for you, you've got your wits about you,' she remarked generously. 'Though if he wasn't trying to make a touch, what did you think he was going to do? He didn't look like a rapist to me.'

'He was talking about wolves looking like sheep or spiders,' proffered Imogen hazily.

'I suppose it makes sense,' said Jane-Valerie soothingly. 'Anyway, I got the message, loud and clear, and I'll tell your friend. I must get on now, or Bouncer will be half-way to Bournemouth and for some reason he doesn't like policemen.'

And off she strode, wearing the morning like her dress, thought romantic Imogen. Lovely to be so supple and strong and looking as though you swung the earth a trinket at your wrist.

Dora was waiting in the lobby of the hotel when Imogen arrived. 'Well, you've set the cat among the pigeons,' she announced. 'Someone looking like Diana of the Ephesians came striding in and announced to all and sundry that you you were on your way, but had been held up by a Mr Smith.'

'Spelt with a Y,' amended Imogen.

'I think she forgot that bit. Miss Pardon's green with envy. She thinks you're a dark horse. I really don't believe she'd be surprised if you turned out to be the missing Mrs Sumner. You know, Dotty, I think I'll ring Mr Crook presently and see what he thinks. My impression is we've been here long enough.'

'Did you have any luck?' enquired Imogen as they drank their after-lunch coffee.

'After I'd done my sketching, I went to Claudine to have my hair done, there's a girl there—they're all girls up to sixty—who remembered the Pendragon but she said all the site was fit for was an open prison, seeing there was nowhere to walk except off the edge of the cliff. I asked innocently if anyone ever had, and she said some people thought Mr Sumner might have mistaken the road one dark night, but in her job if you started believing what people told you you'd believe in Noah's Ark.'

'I've always loved the idea of Noah's Ark,' confessed Imogen, 'but I could never understand how the mastodons, say, managed to avoid squashing the spiders. Do you notice how often history books avoid giving you just those details you'd most like to know?'

'How are your turtle-doves getting on at Torminster?' Martin asked Crook, whom he met a few hours later, in consequence of Dora's telephone call.

'If they go on at their present rate they'll turn into a pair of eagles soaring into the blue. Trouble is, they don't always remember that in their kind of game you want eyes before and behind. Fact, they've soared so far they're almost out of view, and my sight ain't of the weakest.'

Martin looked instantly concerned. 'You really believe they could be in danger?'

'Dames are in danger from the day they're born,' Crook told him in resigned tones. 'Most of them seem to have no sense of self-preservation at all. Show them a lioness with about fourteen cubs, and they'll say, What a pretty cat! and go up to stroke it. And then they're surprised when the lioness yanks an arm off.'

'Very temperate of her to be satisfied with one arm if she's got fourteen cubs to feed,' said the doctor smoothly.

'And these two,' continued Crook, as though he hadn't spoken, 'are more of a liability than most, because they don't even try to cover up. And they're persistent. Sooner or later it's going to occur to someone they'd be safer in the morgue and that's the minute I'm waiting for.'

'So that you can identify them,' asked Martin, with deceptive gentleness.

'So that I can reach the morgue first,' corrected Crook. 'If they do discover anything I wouldn't put it past X to throw a hand grenade through the window of their carriage and to hell with the rest of the passengers.'

'When do they plan to come back?'

'My dear chap, women don't plan, not women like Sugar and the Garland. They're like those chaps who saw a star in the East and set out willy-nilly on a two-year journey.'

'Tell 'em to come back on Saturday,' Dr Martin said, surprising himself as much as his companion. 'Even my unreasonable patients allow me an occasional Saturday off. I'll go down and fetch 'em.'

'That'll give the Homestead something to talk about,' agreed Mr Crook in jubilant tones. 'Mind you, they'll probably think you run a private bin and are collecting two of your patients.'

'Sometimes,' said Martin in a rather gloomy voice, 'I think that's virtually what I do.'

'Feel like declaring an interest?' asked buoyant Mr Crook.

'In a way you could say I'm responsible for their being at Torminster at all. If I hadn't unearthed that little monster at the Mausoleum . . .'

'We don't even know it's the same little monster.'

'We haven't actually found anyone who saw Miss Styles being pushed through a window, but that hasn't stopped us from drawing the obvious conclusions.'

'You'd not only talk the hind-leg off a goat, you'd give the beast a transplant at the same time,' said Crook generously.

'Will you phone them?' the doctor asked. 'They're more likely to listen to you. I often wonder why women consult doctors, if consult is the word, unless it's for the pleasure of disagreeing with everything they say.'

'We shall be leaving before lunch on Saturday, Mrs Hillary,' Dora graciously informed the proprietress.

'Will it be the ten-forty-five?' enquired Mrs Hillary briskly.

'We're being picked up by a friend. Remember, Dotty, to ask for a rebate on our railway tickets.'

'I should think you're not sorry to see the back of that pair,' Mrs Anstruther remarked, when the doctor's noble Daimler had driven away. 'It wouldn't surprise me to know someone's been trying to track them down ever since their arrival here. It's perfectly clear that Miss Garth's a mental case. I only hope you won't find their cheque bounces.'

'I've got the number of the car, haven't I?' said Mrs Hillary sweetly, 'and no one's going to abandon a practically new Daimler.'

But Mrs A had the last word. 'I notice they chose a Saturday to go,' she said. 'The one day you can't get in touch with a bank. By Monday goodness knows where they may be.'

CHAPTER ELEVEN

If she had had second sight Mrs Anstruther couldn't have pin-pointed the day more accurately, for it was on Monday that everything seemed to happen at once. Up till that time everything seemed to be going perfectly. After the doctor, having fed and wined them, had dropped them in Ditcham, Dora said, 'I'd like to make a suggestion. How would you like it if we set up house together here in the cottage?'

Imogen stared, incredulous. 'You mean, for good?'

'Well, for the present anyway. I mistrust people who try to look into the future and shape it the way they think it should be, it would take all the excitement out of life if you knew what was going to happen next week, but so long as it suits us both . . .'

'But you'll be getting married,' protested Imogen.

'I might just as well use the same argument with you. I had an Aunt Penelope, when she was past sixty she married a man fifteen years her junior. Everyone said he was hanging up his hat on a golden hook, but the marriage went like a bomb, till it was broken up by natural causes.'

'She died,' speculated Imogen, in reverent tones.

'He did. She's the sort that stumps along the bank of the Nile, when she's about eighty-five, poking at alligators with her umbrella.'

'Do they have alligators on the banks of the Nile?'

'Well, caymen or something. But I shall go on calling you Dotty. Who gave you your first name?'

'Mother played *The Winter's Tale* just before I was born, Uncle Terry, who died years ago, was the King. She had such silly lines to say, something about choosing an eagle and not a puttock, and nobody knew what a puttock was and of course a lot of people giggled. Flora said once she felt as if she'd married into a lunatic asylum, and Charles said he felt much the same about the House of Commons. Dora, are you certain?'

'I didn't suggest it before, I thought we'd wait and see if we were—what that awful Mrs Anstruther would call *sympatico*. The truth is, I feel it a bit lonely here all on my own. I did think at first the ghostly Mr P might turn up and give me a little company, but perhaps he was a woman-hater. No one's ever mentioned a wife.'

'You lived by yourself in London,' Imogen pointed out.

'That's different. You're never lonely in London. How can you be? It's like living in the heart of the world, there's always something going on. Here you only have your neighbours, and you have to like them whether you really do or not. In London you don't exactly have neighbours—or rather, the whole world's your neighbour.'

Imogen laughed delightedly. 'How amazed Flora will be. She's always secretly regarded me as her cross.'

'And now she's going to be done out of her crown!'

So there they were, everything as nice as pie, when suddenly—it was like a bomb exploding, or rain falling alike on the just and the unjust.

It started with a telephone call shortly before 10 a.m. at the Cottage, when a deep impersonal voice asked for Miss Chester.

'My name is Parsons,' said the voice. 'Mr Crook may have mentioned me. He's been away from town since Saturday, which is why he hasn't been able to get in touch with you since your return, but he'll be back this morning, and he'd like you to come to lunch with him, and discuss the situation.'

'You mean me and Miss Garland?' enquired Dora.

'No. He feels it might be safer for Miss Garland to

remain where she is, but he suggests that she might get someone—her sister-in-law, say—to come over to be with her during your absence. Mr Crook,' he continued a shade more severely, 'doesn't care to take unnecessary risks.'

'And he thinks she is in danger? No, don't answer that. Ask a silly question. Yes, I'm sure Lady Garland would come over, we'll contact her at once. She's pretty sure to be coming into Ditcham today, seeing it's Monday.'

'Monday?' repeated the voice, in rather troubled tones.

'Every Monday there's a sale on the Village Green, and most people—locals anyway—turn out, because you can get quite startling bargains and anyway it's a sort of meeting place, like a coffee morning. Flora—Lady Garland—usually goes to that—so she could come on. I could be at Mr Crook's office about twelve-thirty,' she added. 'Trains from here aren't very good, but I'll tell Miss Garland to stay indoors . . .'

'Tell her to put up the chain on the front door and not open it to anyone, even if he does look like a postman or a policeman, not until her sister-in-law arrives, that is. And if Lady Garland can't come, get someone else. Isn't there a curate or someone?'

'About a quarter of a rector,' said Dora demurely. 'Still, you can reassure Mr Crook we'll take good care of his client.'

'I should have thought I was as safe with you on the London train as anywhere,' said Imogen, when she got the news, but Dora said, 'I think we must have discovered something quite valuable, and even someone like the Little Man can't be in two places at once. If he's following me on the train, you'll be all right here, but if I've gone to London and you come, too . . . It's a compliment really,' she wound up. 'Like the Royal Family not all travelling by the same plane in case of a crash. I'd better see if I can get Parker's taxi. Then I could catch the eleven-one, and if I get a taxi at Victoria I should just make my appointment for half-past twelve. You know, Dotty, I dare say it's all frightful, but you must admit life can be very exciting.'

'I'd better ring Flora, I suppose,' Imogen conceded.

'Let's hope she's free.'

'Oh, Flora wouldn't be left out of a thing like this for anything. And she'd do practically anything to ensure my safety. Between ourselves, she's so grateful to you for taking me off her hands—well, you heard her yesterday at lunch, she was quite excited about the Little Man but she nearly fainted with relief when you told her we were setting up here together. She'd do anything to oblige you at the moment.'

'I liked your brother,' said Dora. 'He said living with you was like living in a detective story, you never knew what might turn up in the next chapter.'

'Flora doesn't read detective stories. She thinks they're frivolous.'

'She should tell that to the Bench of Bishops. I gather that thrillers and theological works are all they ever read. Now, Dotty, do be sensible until Lady G. appears. Faith may be one of the theological virtues, but like virtue, it can be overdone.'

'I might go as far as the churchyard,' suggested Dotty. 'It's practically on our back door step, and there's a right of way through, and even if you can break into a cottage breaking into a churchyard when mourners and visitors may appear at any moment, to say nothing of the sexton—he'd frighten half-a-dozen little men, he had to dig a grave and then the old man he dug it for didn't die, and he's got to fill it in or something. The postman told us. I'll get Flora now.' She began to dial. 'Oh, Flora . . .'

Charles came in from getting a breath of fresh air, as he put it, in time to see his wife hanging up the telephone.

'Was that someone for me?' he said. 'That old rascal, Ben Plowright, hasn't died, after all, and everybody seems pretty put out about it. This is about the fourth time he's cheated the undertaker. Who was that?'

'That was Dotty on the line. She wants me to go over. At least, Mr Crook wants me to go over. Miss Chester's going to London to meet him, and doesn't think your sister should be left on her own. I've said Yes, of course. I can drop those leaflets of yours at the Conservative office, I might even be able to see if old Mrs Scratchback has got those glasses she was trying to find for us. I gather Miss Chester will be back in the afternoon.'

'I can't imagine what you and Dotty will find to say to one another,' returned her husband frankly. 'Those two women talked the hindlegs off a whole flock of goats yesterday afternoon. I wonder why Crook doesn't want Dotty as well.'

'He sounds apprehensive, at least it was his partner, a man called Parsons who telephoned, very rigid about Dotty having someone with her and apparently she's going to lock the front door, so unless someone comes down the chimney . . .'

'It sounds to me,' remarked Charles, 'as though that precious couple really did unearth something at Postman's Bay. Grave-diggers aren't in it with that pair. If they joined an archaeological expedition they'd have uncovered a whole undreamed-of city by this time.' A city with no Houses of Parliament, moreover. 'Well, keep an eye on the old girl. I should miss Dotty. She may not be everybody's money, but she's a collector's piece just the same.'

'I suppose,' mused Flora, 'Dotty hasn't let something out to Miss Chester that she thinks Crook ought to know.'

'I thought you said Crook rang her.'

'Yes—it must have been that because it was a man called Parsons—oh well, I suppose we shall soon know. All the same, if it was that, it would complicate the situation, and explain why Crook wanted to see Miss Chester alone.'

'If you're right, Dotty's a better man than I am, Gunga Din,' returned Charles frankly. 'I'd sooner try to withhold information from the Recording Angel.'

Flora collected the pamphlets and drove off to Ditcham, leaving Charles to get on with his voluminous correspondence. At least a score of ladies in the neighbourhood would have donated their services free in this connection, but Charles felt he did enough for his country as it was. And if the work did get beyond him or he strained his wrist—well, what's a wife for?

The second letter he opened came from his son, Tim, explaining, with the enthusiasm of his years, that his next communication would probably come from gaol. He had participated in some form of demonstration, 'and really,' he wrote, 'the beaks here put such an absurdly high value on chaps like me that, even if I had the will to meet their demands, I wouldn't have the wherewithal. Sorry to blot your scutcheon and all that.'

'Not to worry,' Charles wrote back, 'they'll only say you're a chip off the old block. I've been protesting from the instant I came into this world, according to your grandmother, and it'll be good to know I'm getting something out of the rates. Believe it or not, old boy, at heart you're as much of a Tory as I am.'

That'll get his dander, thought Charles, with a grin, turning to his more official correspondence, practically all of it from the half-wits who had the privilege of being his constituents. He worked away, dealing with letters, answering telephone calls, too busy even to mix himself a drink until the phone rang for about the fortieth time, and this time it was Flora on the other end.

'Thank goodness!' she exclaimed. 'Who says women are the gossips of the human race? I began to think you must have taken off the receiver. Every time I tried the line was engaged.'

'I would if I dared,' said Charles, 'take off the receiver, I mean. But Miss Mitchum is as pig-headed as most of her sex, and she'd go on buzzing me till she did attract my attention. If you ask me, phone charges are much too low. If they had to pay five bob for the privilege of speaking to me, that bell would be virtually silenced. What is it, Flo? What's wrong?'

'I suppose,' Flora hesitated, 'don't think me crazy, Charles—but I suppose Dotty isn't with you?'

'With me? Well, of course not. You went to keep her company and she swore she wouldn't leave the cottage . . .'

'I know, but something must have happened, because I'm speaking from the cottage now, and there's neither hide nor hair of her.'

'You can't have looked in the right place,' urged Charles foolishly.

'Short of digging up the garden or exploring the chimney—there aren't any cellars here.'

'Don't tell me you've gone haywire, too.' Charles began to wonder how it would feel to be the one sane person in a lunatic world.

'I rang the front door bell and tapped on the letter-box to let her know I was there. I had to leave the car on the Church Green, you can't park it in the lane. She didn't answer and I looked through the living-room window—no one there, so I went round the back. It doesn't seem to have occurred to your dear sister that there's not much sense bolting a front door if you leave the back unlocked.'

'You mean, anyone could get in?'

'How do you think I'm using their telephone now? I wondered if she might have had an accident, slipped, knocked herself out somehow, but there isn't a trace of her, no message.'

'I suppose she couldn't have gone up to the Green, thinking there's safety in numbers?'

'I was there—no luck with the glasses by the way—I didn't see a sign of Dotty, and even though I wasn't looking out for her she'd have been watching for me. I even looked over the churchyard wall, but it's like that old proverb, empty as a graveyard. Charles, I'm worried.'

'You realize what the village is going to say, don't you? That old Mr Poppycock or whatever his name was has taken the opportunity to claim a belated bride. I suppose you're sure it was old Dotty on the phone?'

'I'm not such a bad amateur actress myself, but even I couldn't fake her voice, it's inimitable. Oh no, it was Dotty all right. And if at the eleventh hour she'd decided to go with Miss Chester—though I think that highly unlikely—she'd have put a note under that old Gruffanuff door-knocker they've got.'

'How about her clothes? Have you looked to see if that bag of hers is lying around? She never goes anywhere without it, and there can't be two like it in the whole world. And she'd take a coat or something. Or she might have remembered something in a hurry and gone down to the village shop.'

'I suppose you haven't been out since I left? If she'd tried to phone . . .'

'She'd have got the engaged signal practically non-stop. Sometimes I think what a peaceful world it must have been before Bell invented the telephone. I suppose she couldn't be having a bath?'

'If Dotty was having a bath you'd think you were standing on the edge of the Niagara Falls. Still, I'll take a look in her room, though why she should have departed with or without luggage defeats me. Don't hang up, Charles, or I'll never get through again. I won't be more than a minute or so.'

Charles balanced the instrument between his ear and his shoulder and continued to slit envelopes. It seemed to him that these days most of his correspondence came under the head of GIMME. Gimme higher wages, gimme a larger pension, gimme a lower tax evaluation—so it went all round the clock. Some of them virtually hinted—Gimme a more efficient Member of Parliament, someone who'll realize MY interests are paramount.

It seemed some time before Flora returned, but at least it meant some fretful constituent couldn't contact the Member. 'There's no sign of that awful tapestry bag,' she reported. 'I don't know about her clothes, I don't know quite what she had or how many pairs of shoes, but all her usual gear is on the dressing-table—and don't ask me if I'm sure I've looked in the right room, because there's only one room that could possibly be Dotty's. It makes me think of that Stanley Spencer picture, "Resurrection Morning" or some such name, people bursting up out of their graves, turning the churchyard into a positive rubbish-dump. I kept thinking she must be hidden somewhere among those monstrous possessions of hers, but, take my word for it, Charles, there's no living creature in the house.'

'Are you tying this up with Dotty's mysterious little stranger of Postman's Bay?' Charles demanded.

'I don't see how even Dotty can get mixed up with two mysteries simultaneously.'

'But have some sense, Flo. He's the last person she'd open the door to.'

'She might think he was the postman . . .'

'Everybody knows old Burke, and anyway he calls round about ten o'clock, and we know she was all right then.'

'It's Monday,' murmured Flora. 'I wonder if the laundryman called . . .'

'Having got possession of whatever van they use—how on earth would he know the company's name. I suppose there might have been a telegram—but that would have been phoned through. Might be worth asking if a wire has been received for Pieman's Cottage.'

'You know what Miss Mitchum is, besides being the postmistress, I mean. She'd never be able to keep a story like that to herself. Anyway, by this time everyone will know Miss Chester has gone to London.'

'You don't suppose Dotty thought she'd come over to us on the bus?'

'If she did, why isn't she here? And if she'd fallen down or had some accident we should have known long ago. Considering half the village thinks she's a witch, she's got a surprising number of friends.'

'Well, stay in, in case there's a telephone message and I'll hang about round here.'

After Flora had hung up Charles sat reflecting it was bad enough having to deal with constituents, most of whom couldn't spell the word REASON, without having an eccentric sister tacked on. Good thing old Flo had her head screwed on all right. His darling Edna, Tim's mother, whose name he never mentioned and of whom, in the course of years, he thought less and less, would have been completely flabbergasted.

The telephone rang again, and it was another idiot constituent on the line. He thought wistfully of the lake of fire and brimstone.

Flora came out of the empty cottage and walked up to the Green, but it seemed as deserted as the house. The world was calm, quiet, an epitome of peace, you'd have said, not at all the kind of jungle where a woman who'd been in the pink at ten-thirty could have vanished like a puff of dust a couple of hours later.

A voice said 'Good morning' and she turned and there was the rector, hurrying towards the church, carrying an armful of flowers that he seemed to be regarding with some suspicion.

'I came to see my sister-in-law,' explained Flora, who knew the rector in the way the Member's wife knows everyone, 'but she seems to have gone out. What lovely flowers. I suppose you didn't see her, Miss Garland, I mean?'

'I saw Miss Chester going off in Parker's taxi to catch the eleven-one to town,' Mr Bunyan said, 'but unless Miss Garland was under the seat . . . Perhaps she's gone up to see Willy Masters. Or the Market.'

'I don't think so. I looked in there for a minute, but there was no sign of her.'

'I didn't notice her there either,' the rector said. 'While you're waiting her return, Lady Garland, perhaps you could arrange these for me. I may be a Philistine, but I always think flowers look their best where the Lord intended them to grow. Still, these have been offered as a thanksgiving, so one shouldn't grudge them in His service.'

Flora said that while she waited for her sister-in-law she might as well give a hand, then fearing she might sound ungracious, added quickly, 'What's the occasion?'

'The village will tell you it's a miracle. Sometimes man's faith shames me, truly it does. A down-to-earth fellow like me would say the medical profession was responsible in the main. Either they blundered in the first place or they've shown uncommon skill at the eleventh hour. Old Ben Plowright . . .'

'Yes, of course,' exclaimed Flora. 'I heard about him. So he's not going to die, after all.'

'Never a very considerate fellow,' Mr Bunyan confirmed. 'Been teetering on the brink these four years, then at last he decides to launch away, notice prepared for the local *Argus*, service arranged, his favourite hymn—"Now the labourer's task is o'er"—though considering the quantitative nature of his labour you'd not think he'd notice much difference. Even his grave dug—he chose that plot over by the fig tree, my sexton didn't care for it at all, practically outside the churchyard, he says, and even an old rogue like Ben Plowright can ask for consecrated ground. But I can tell you this, Lady Garland, if it's not consecrated now, it will be by the time we heap the clods on old Ben's box—and then he uncurls like one of those creatures that hibernate for the winter. You know, Lady Garland, there are times when the animal creation can teach us a useful lesson. What's wrong with a nice warm sleep in the cold weather unless you can afford to migrate like the swallows, and the Lord's provided them with a natural media, as you might say. Anyway, old Ben's sitting up and cussing loud and strong and the village is calling it a miracle, and I've seen the piece that young fellow from the *Argus* has written about him—a modern Lazarus. But what I've often wondered is—what was Lazarus's reaction at being pulled back from the Heavenly Vision to the companionship of those two sisters of his, always at loggerheads, and him the buffer, I dare say. Still, if they've a mind to thank the Lord for a miracle, who am I to stop them? It's not often they bother Him, and they make a change from the saints.'

'Wasn't he—isn't he—your oldest inhabitant?'

'And attributes his great age to the quality of the local beer, and I have to admit, Lady Garland, Mr Crook was at one with him there. And that's a man whose judgment you'd respect.'

'The longevity of Penton and Ditcham old people is notorious,' acknowledged Flora. 'Still, even so, I dare say you'll soon find a use for the grave before long, and your sexton can stop feeling injured. Why, Mr Bunyan, what is it?'

'My dear Lady Garland, you cannot disinherit a man because he doesn't die to order. That grave is Ben's future residence, reserved for him, and it's not like a house, you can't let it out on lease till the owner's ready for occupation. I dare say it may stay empty a little while yet, but no one else will be given the key. Now—there's a tap in the churchyard here, where the ladies fill the vases.' He moved ahead to show where it was, but Flora had ceased to listen.

'Mr Bunyan!' she exclaimed. 'Look! See that.'

On a moss-grown Saxon memorial shaped like a cross a gaudy tapestry handbag was jauntily slung.

'That's Imogen's bag.' Flora moved forwards; the rector laid the flowers on a nearby stone. 'What on earth was she doing putting it there?'

'I think I can tell you that,' said Mr Bunyan. 'She comes in sometimes to clip the grass round the edges of the old graves.'

'But whose grave was this? It's much too old to have belonged to anyone we knew.'

'It doesn't have to be an acquaintance,' Mr Bunyan explained. 'The old lady who lies here was the village scold, they dipped her in Merrion's Lake, and she was contrary enough to catch pneumonia. It was February and snow on the hills, the record says. The ones responsible considered it an Act of God, but wishing to show sympathy for a fellow-sinner, one supposes, they clubbed together to give her a churchyard burial and a headstone.'

'I wonder what made them choose a cross,' murmured Flora.

'It's generally associated with a heavenly crown. I can tell you this, Lady Garland, that reticule must have been left there after ten-thirty, because that's when Thomas, my sexton, came to cover over the grave.'

'Oh, that's the tarpaulin, of course.'

'In a great state he was, talking of fellows who couldn't make up their minds and paid no heed to the trouble they caused others. Not even Miss Garland would dare start clipping while old Tom was around. He makes me think of those mighty voices in the Bible that made the seas turn back upon themselves.'

'But would he see Dotty if she was clipping here? The fig-tree's practically out of sight.'

'I wouldn't care to count on it, Lady Garland. The Eye of the Almighty's not more searching than my sexton's eye when he's seeking a grievance.'

'She couldn't have intended it—the bag, I mean—as a sort of message, I suppose—an S O S.'

'In that case, it's a pity she left no clue to the code. I'd say, Lady Garland, the fellow we should contact now is Mr Crook.'

'If he's taking Miss Chester out to lunch surely he'll have left his office by now. It's gone twelve-thirty.'

'I don't doubt he'll have left an address where he can be called, like the doctor. There's a man with a vocation, Lady Garland. That boy that wouldn't take No for an answer has nothing on him. We'll get Miss Mitchum to find his number—oh, I doubt we'll have much difficulty tracking the gentleman down.'

In which he was right, but even a far-sighted little nonentity like Mr Bunyan couldn't have guessed the result of the call.

'This is Parsons. Mr Crook's not expected back yet. Miss Chester . . .? Oh yes, there seems to have been some misunderstanding. She called here at twelve-thirty, expecting to meet Mr Crook, but he knew nothing of the appointment.'

'You mean, the whole thing was a plot to get Miss Chester out of the way and leave Miss Garland without defence?'

'It does seem like it,' Bill admitted.

Flora, who was listening over the rector's shoulder, snatched the receiver from him. 'This is absurd,' she cried. 'I mean, unflappability is all very well, but it has its limits. Do you appreciate that my sister-in-law may be in serious danger?'

'Mr Crook said, if you rang up, not to call the police, it would only make things worse.'

'When on earth did he say that?'

'He telephoned about a quarter of an hour after Miss Chester came in. He generally keeps in touch. Something else might have turned up in the neighbourhood. He's coming along to your part of the world right away. I fancy Miss Chester's coming back, too.'

'What does she suppose she can do now?'

'As much as she can do in London,' suggested Bill. 'Mr Crook has great faith in Miss Chester.'

And sounding as cool as any snowflake Bill Parsons rang off.

CHAPTER TWELVE

'WHAT CAN SHE DO NOW?' Flora had demanded, and Bill had replied that she could do as much at Ditcham as she could in London. But, as Crook was wont to observe, 'There's no accounting for dames, they're not only on the spot when a thing happens, sometimes they can exercise that mysterious feminine intuition that enables them to be there before the event actually takes place. Like the young lady called Bright, who travelled faster than light, so could return from a journey on the previous night. Yes, I dare say that's not quite what the poet said,' Crook would defend himself, 'but at my school it was thought cissy to quote poetry correctly.'

Dora came into Bloomsbury Street in a state of daze. It was a lovely morning; hot and golden, and every window shimmered with light. But she saw none of them.

'What good am I to her if I can't help her in a crisis?' she demanded, aloud.

A plump young woman, wearing the uniform of a Traffic Warden, with improbable golden curls escaping from her cap, stopped to ask if she was all right.

'I'm on the horns of a dilemma,' Dora confessed.

The Traffic Warden was more down to earth than an earthworm. 'Then you'd better get off them pretty quickly, hadn't you, dear? They don't like that kind of thing round here. This is a respectable part of London.'

'I don't know what to do,' Dora confessed.

'Haven't you got a friend?' asked the Traffic Warden, whose job was to book cars, not semi-hysterical young women.

A smile that challenged the sun broke over Dora's face.

'Do you know what you are?' she said. 'An angel. Just as much as if you came bursting through a cloud tootling a long trumpet.'

A taxi came trundling by and she hailed it. 'I'll say a good word for you on Judgment Day,' she promised through the window and told the driver—'240 Harley Street.'

In Harley Street, Dr Ambrose Martin was wondering how it is that some mornings seem longer than a week. He'd just contrived to rid himself of a woman who was, he told his super-efficient secretary, born to be a Black Widow, and was preparing to go out to lunch when the bell of his outer office shrilled. He shared the Harley Street house with three other consultants and a common receptionist who sorted the arrivals.

'Surely you haven't made another appointment for me at this hour?' cried the scandalized Martin. 'I've got my clinic at St Roger's at two o'clock. I can't see anyone now, not if it's Royalty bringing crown and sceptre.'

'I certainly made no appointment for you,' said frigid Miss Keir (Martin used to say that when computers took over there'd be more errors in his records than there'd ever been when she held sway.)

She went into the outer office, and he heard voices, hers even cooler than Bill's had been, and a woman's voice, warm and insistent.

'I will give him your message,' he heard Miss Keir say, and gasped inwardly. It was the first time a patient without an appointment had ever got past the door.

'It's no one we know,' Miss Keir reported. 'Not even a patient, but she asked me to give you this.'

She held out a used envelope addressed to Miss Dora Chester, Pieman's Cottage, Ditcham. Across the top six words were scrawled. 'A matter of life and death.'

'Naturally,' said Miss Keir, 'they all say that.'

And then she had the surprise of her life, because Dr

Martin swooped past, practically flattening her against the wall.

'Ring Dr Bennet and ask him if he can take my clinic this afternoon,' he said, as he shot past. 'I might come in later. And you can go to lunch now, if you like. Leave the answering service on, and deal with anything urgent when you get back.'

In the outer office Dora was admiring the neat lay-out of *Punches* and *Country Life*, each copy carefully overlapping the previous one.

'They make me think of elephants,' she said, 'when they walk in a line, each one holding the tail of the one in front.'

'One's always learning something new. Tell me—whose life, whose death?'

'Well, not mine, of course, seeing I'm here with you. It's Dotty—I was lured up to London by a false message to meet Mr Crook but when I got to his office he didn't know anything about it. Mr Parsons, I mean. Mr Crook wasn't there.'

'Have you been in touch with the cottage?' Martin enquired.

Dora looked at him in absolute amazement. 'Why didn't I think of that? I suppose because I realized it would be too late. I wondered who I could ask to help us—Mr Crook does so dislike the police—and I thought of you.'

'Speaking for myself,' said the doctor, 'I find my intelligence functions better when I've got some food inside me. We might go along to the Ring o' Bells for a sandwich—if we see Jorrocks there—yes, I know about Mr Crook disliking the police, but it never does to antagonize them . . .'

'Is it really his name?'

'It's not the poor chap's fault. It was his father's first.'

'What worries me,' said Dora, 'is I'm sure they'll all try and make out that somehow, whatever's happened, it's Dotty's fault. They do tend to treat her like a zany, and actually, even though her conclusions sometimes sound very odd, they're just as likely to be right as anyone else's.'

From the Ring o' Bells, where Jorrocks was conspicuous by his absence, Dora rang Pieman's Cottage. She didn't mention the doctor, just said she was on her way, and in return was told Mr Crook had been informed and was doing likewise.

'I think, considering the local train service, my Daimler might do the journey quicker,' the doctor said, as they swallowed their coffee and put down their cups. 'It has all the charm of Sleepy Hollow but I gather it only runs about two trains a day, and then you need a taxi from the station.'

'I have always,' said Dora firmly, 'longed to arrive at Pieman's Cottage in a Daimler.'

In the village excitement reigned supreme. Imogen's disappearance was everybody's business. Two women had come forward, convinced they'd seen her on the 11.15 bus, but seeing they were what were locally known as strangers and that their descriptions differed in almost every detail, no one paid much attention to them. Willy Masters was a far more reliable witness. The local bus stopped practically outside his door, so that no one could have boarded it or dismounted without his seeing her. This particular morning he had gone out to collect a parcel the driver was bringing in and had seen everyone in the queue, and was dead certain Imogen hadn't been among them. As to why the missing woman's reticule should be found in the churchyard no one could say, though one woman, bolder than the rest, said it was well known the poor lady was a bit soft in the head.

A search of the churchyard discovered a large pair of scissors, too small to be described as shears, lying among some cut grass by one of the ancient graves. So it seemed likely that Dotty might have been at work there. Old

Thomas Potter, who lived in a hump-backed cottage just across the road (the whole village to Dora looked like something out of a Grimm's Fairy Tale) said, scowling, that there hadn't been no lady cutting no grass not when he was covering over the unwanted grave. Oh yes, he'd seen her at the job occasionally, and considered her action a dead liberty (a phrase he had picked up from his urbanized son). The graves were his department . . .

'But not your perquisite, Tom,' the Rector pointed out gently.

'It's blackleg labour,' old Tom insisted. 'If I was a Union man I'd get my shop steward to call a strike.'

'Oh, get along with you, Tom,' Mr Bunyan adjured him softly. 'You know you'd never pay Union dues.'

Asked again if he recalled the time when he finished his job with old Ben's grave, he said sullenly it could be 10.15 or a few minutes later—what were the odds? He belonged to a forgotten generation that couldn't be bothered with watches, and mostly told the time of day by the condition of the sky, the flight of birds and the lowing of cattle. (The fact that in this civilized age God's time and man's time are substantially different didn't bother him.)

'What puzzles me,' said Flora candidly, 'is why whoever fashioned this diabolical plot tried to drag me in.'

'Mr Crook 'ud not think it seemly to leave Miss Garland on her own,' offered Mr Bunyan. 'And you being, so to speak, her next of kin . . .'

'And, of course, by the time I arrived he didn't mean Dotty to be here. It's still very difficult to understand how he managed to trick her out of the house, though.'

They were still on this point when Dr Martin and Dora came dashing through the village, as noticeable as Boadicea in her chariot.

'She was perfectly all right at, say, twenty to eleven,' Dora declared. 'She stood on the doorstep watching me get into Parker's taxi, waving her hand and saying Give my love to Mr Crook.'

'And at some time she went into the churchyard and started to cut grass round one of the old graves. I got here about twelve, I suppose. Well, I had one or two jobs to do in Ditcham, and I couldn't see what harm could come to her if she kept the doors fastened and refused to answer any bells.'

'And she must have got tired of her own company and thought she'd do a bit of clipping.'

'Which would explain why the back door wasn't locked.'

'If there'd been a telephone call,' surmised Dora, 'she'd have come in then. I mean, it's only in films that a woman can resist a telephone call. I wonder if that could have been the way of it. Someone rang her, she went into the house, leaving her bag on the tombstone—if she didn't leave it there herself, it was someone who knew her well, she always left her bag on that stone, because of the arms of the cross, I mean it wouldn't fall off. Then, while she was answering the phone, X, who's been waiting for this minute, follows her in . . .'

'Knocks her out and puts her where?'

'The graveyard looks more like a jungle to me,' offered the doctor frankly. 'I should have thought you might have hidden half a dozen bodies there . . .'

'My sister-in-law's no lightweight,' said Flora with family candour. 'Oh!' She jumped as the telephone rang.

'It's for you,' said Dora an instant later. 'I think it's your husband.'

They all watched Flora pick up the receiver, as though in some mysterious way attentiveness could reveal both sides of the conversation.

'Well, whatever you think, of course,' they heard her say. 'You know Dotty, though. She has the most extraordinary ideas of practical jokes, and we should look so foolish . . .'

A sound as of a furious macaw chattered over the line. 'You don't have to break my ear-drums,' complained Flora. 'And if you think we should tell the police—only what are we going to tell them? Well—why not? We've already got the Church and medicine, and Mr Crook's coming like a flash of light. Why not the politicians and the police as well? Let it hail . . .' She stopped abruptly.

As though some unseen influence had been awaiting its clue, rain suddenly began to fall, without warning, without so much as a whisper, gallons and gallons of it, plunging down from the sky, as though someone had removed a celestial stopcock. And with the storm came the onslaught of thunder and the lightning splintering across the sky.

'When I was little,' Dora confided to the doctor, 'I used to think it was a sign that God was angry and was scolding the angels. Oh poor Dotty, if she's out in this! And she hasn't even taken her umbrella. It's the one with the duck's head in the hall.'

'What's going on?' demanded Charles's irritable voice at the end of the line.

'It's just started coming down cats and dogs.'

'It's fine enough here.'

'Only because it hasn't caught up with you yet.'

'Have you tried the local hospital?'

Flora seemed visibly startled. 'No. I didn't think of it. But everybody knows Dotty by sight, if there'd been an accident you'd have been informed right away. But I'll ring them if you like. Yes, yes, I said Come Over. We shall be like the League of Nations before we're through.'

'She was only wearing her gardening clothes,' insisted Dora, 'she wouldn't have gone further than the churchyard in them.'

'It's like going round in a maze,' added Flora. 'You keep coming back to where you started. Arrow pointing nowhere.'

Charles arrived a few minutes later. He was the sort of

man who can look distinguished even in a Burberry. 'Any-chance she went to the Market?' he enquired.

'I just looked in,' acknowledged Flora doubtfully, 'but I didn't see her. Mr Bunyan—no, you said not—but I don't see how anyone could have overlooked Dotty.'

'Suppose,' Dora suggested, 'someone came in disguise, like a Salvation Army lass—Dotty's very soft about the Sally Army . . .'

'If there'd been a Salvationist in Ditcham this morning everyone would know,' said the Rector. 'They're about the most selective religious community I've ever served.'

There was another sound as of Boanerges ramping through the village and Crook drove up in the Superb.

'This little chap they were talking about,' he suggested, addressing himself to the doctor, as being the most reasonable person present. 'How would anyone notice him if he came strolling down the street?'

'You'd notice a strange fly walking on the ceiling,' said Dora rashly. 'All this talk about country people being slow and daft is so much poppycock. I believe they can even distinguish between one blackbird and another.'

'All the same, he fits into the picture somewhere. Just exactly what did Sugar tell him?'

'She said she was a special investigator looking into the history of a man called Sumner who used to run an hotel at Postman's Bay, because his wife didn't know whether she was a wife or a widow and she found it very confusing.'

'But no one could think of Dotty as a source of danger,' Flora protested.

'Never safe to go by appearances,' Crook warned them. 'One of my recent cases—as nice a roly-poly little dame as you could look for, passion cats and minding her own business—but it ain't her fault she ain't underground this very minute.'

'And, of course, he was interested in her. She noticed him long before I did—she really would be rather a good private eye. To me he was just a rather dull little man, probably convalescing at one of the cheaper private hotels, but Dotty was convinced he spelt trouble.'

'But—' Flora sounded incredulous—'would he take her seriously?'

'That 'ud depend on whether he had something to hide,' said Crook. 'If he hadn't he'd probably think her a regular scream. If he had—well, his obvious reaction 'ud be to make sure she couldn't talk.'

'And Dotty is certain he meant to harm her, if that girl hadn't come along,' urged Dora. 'And even if people do think she's sometimes a bit odd they don't notice how often she's right. Besides, what was the point of following her up the cliff, and snatching her book from her to make sure she'd go with him to get it back?'

'You're preaching to the converted,' Martin told her. 'From what I've heard he sounds the spitting image of the fellow who was out to put the black on Ponting. As to who he actually is doesn't seem to me important—let the police solve that mystery.'

'And it all fits together so well,' Dora pursued. 'He gets me out of the way to London—no one tried to follow me or even travelled in the same carriage—he makes sure that Lady Garland will be coming over—he might even have rung up and said there'd been an accident to the cab and—no, in that case Dotty would have brought her bag with her—but somehow he cajoled her into the house . . .'

'It all sounds fine,' Charles acknowledged, 'the only thing against it is Dotty herself. I happen to know my sister—she mightn't take any A levels or whatever they are, but she's intelligent enough. It's just that the original nature of her intelligence is apt to elude the common man.'

'Oh, darling,' pleaded his wife, 'you're not on the floor of the House now.'

'Point I'm trying to make is that if I was the little man and had the sense I was born with, and had a choice between an attack by my sister or ditto a wild cow, I'd choose the wild cow. They do have a certain logic. You mark my words, if anyone's lying in a strange grave it's just as likely to be this little chap you're all on about—more, in fact, than—Good God, padre, what bee have you got in your bonnet now?'

For Mr Bunyan had suddenly turned a dirty-white colour and was looking about him as though the room had suddenly turned into a cabin on an ocean-going liner when the wind was getting up.

'Oh no!' he whispered, but not as though he were addressing anyone present—his God, perhaps, thought Crook, watching intently. 'Not that. There must be a limit to human wickedness.'

'There must be some place where the rim of the world goes down into eternity,' Crook reminded him, 'but you'd be hard put to find it. Come on, padre, tell us what's on your mind.'

'It's fantastic—grotesque—perhaps I am losing mine—my mind, I mean. It was Sir Charles saying the unknown grave. I remembered . . .'

This time it was Flora who intervened, crying, 'No, of course it isn't possible. It isn't, is it? I mean, all this time and us speculating and perhaps . . .'

'Where's this grave you're talking about?' asked Crook. It was difficult for a man of his complexion to change colour, but Dora, watching him, thought she detected an unnatural pallor under the mahogany of his cheeks. 'In the graveyard?'

There's a chap we could do with in the House, Charles thought. Blow through the stuffiness like a wind, I shouldn't wonder. A cleansing wind. He switched off his thoughts to listen to the rest of the conversation.

'Old Ben Plowright—we were expecting to bury him today.'

'And you think someone thought it would be a fine joke to bury my client instead?'

'Well, not a joke. A—a security measure, perhaps.'

'Has everyone gone crazy?' Flora asked, staring from face to face and seeing the same dread in each. 'How would anyone know about the grave in the first place, let alone the funeral being postponed?'

'It's the first thing you'd hear if you walked round the Green,' the rector told her. 'The village is humming with the story. Well, we don't get a miracle in Ditcham, and that's what people are calling it, every day of the week.'

'What lies beyond the churchyard?' asked Dr Martin in the harshest voice Dora had ever heard him use.

'The marshes.'

'So, even if he didn't know about the grave, they'd provide hiding-places.' He stopped. 'Where is this hole in the ground?'

The rector turned like an automaton. 'I could show you.'

'But if Dotty was clipping the old grave at this end of the churchyard,' protested Flora. 'I mean, she's not exactly a sylph.'

'Point taken,' said Crook. 'Then perhaps X lured her . . .'

'She's not a donkey to follow any carrot,' Dora assured him.

'Maybe if she gets a message, accident to her pal's car or . . .'

'She wouldn't walk through the marshes to get to the station.'

'I'd like to have you testifying on my side,' Crook told her, which was the highest compliment he could pay anyone. 'There are wheelbarrows,' he added, looking round as if he expected one to materialize under his eyes.

'If you saw someone wheeling a body in a wheelbarrow,' exploded Charles.

'It don't have to look like a body.'

'And, come to think of it, if the body was Dotty probably no one would think twice about it. If it were me—or my wife—'

'But the grave's covered over with a tarpaulin, I saw it this morning—you can't believe that then . . .'

'Well, I don't think anything happened to her *after* you arrived, Lady G.'

'If only I hadn't gone to the Market I'd have been here earlier.'

'Any boards a lazy old man like my sexton put down could be shifted by a child.'

'You're all talking as if it were a game . . .'

The sentences rose and fell like stones flung through the mephitic air. When they turned to the window they saw the rain was still falling.

'Why are we waiting?' Dora cried, and it was almost a shout. She turned blindly towards the door. The doctor's hand fell on her arm.

'Operation MALE,' he said. 'If there's anything in our supposition you'll have your hands full in due course.'

'Imogen is my husband's sister,' Flora protested.

'And your husband will be there.'

'Now show some sense, Flo,' urged Charles impatiently. 'You couldn't leave Miss Chester alone in any case.'

Dora ran into the hall and pulled down a rough blue reefer jacket of the type worn by roadmen. 'No winds can penetrate it and even rain comes a poor second. And there's this,' she continued, pulling up the lid of a rug-chest. She pushed a most superior type of ground-sheet into Crook's surprised arms. 'Tartan one side, macintosh the other,' she panted. Crook had looked like a large red bear before, now he looked like a bear from an Icelandic Christmas-tree. Charles buttoned his Burberry to the throat, the doctor was equally well-equipped, only the rector had no protection, but he presumably relied on the armour of righteousness to preserve him through thick and thin. Dora and Lady Garland stood at the window a minute later watching the four men stride through the dazzling rain. The soil in these parts was clay.

'Make them take their boots off when they come in,' said Flora automatically. 'Otherwise you'll never get the floors clean.'

'How can you talk like that?' Dora cried, and her companion coloured.

'Can you really believe this is happening?' she asked. She pulled out a wheel-backed chair and sat down. 'It's like a nightmare.'

'Things happen so fast,' Dora protested. 'Do you remember your reaction when you heard about the bomb on Hiroshima?'

'You can't possibly remember that,' protested Flora. 'You can't have been more than three or four years old.'

'I remember the day, in a sense it's the first day I ever do remember. The war didn't seem strange, because I'd never known any other environment, but I heard the wireless, heard it without listening to it, and it was as though a wall of silence had suddenly been erected round us. Nobody spoke. I remember saying "What happened? Is it the King?" I couldn't think of anything worse. They talked a lot about the King and someone called Winnie. I thought Winnie must be the King's consort. They said, "No, it's not the King." And I said, "Who's dead then?" and someone said, "Half a nation." It wasn't true, of course, but I had in some degree the same feeling I have now, as though I'd walked out of reality into a nightmare. There's no true comparison, of course, but it seemed too bad to be fact, just as this seems too bad. I keep seeing Dotty standing on the step in those truly remarkable garden clothes of hers, waving and calling, 'Give my love to Mr Crook.' Restlessly she moved about the room. 'They'll be like sponges when they do come back,' she said. 'Be glad of a cup of tea, I should think.' She went into the kitchen, filled the gay blue kettle and put it on the stove. 'Whichever way it goes they'll want that.'

'Why do you say whichever way?'

'Whether they find anyone—anything—or whether they don't. I don't myself believe they will. Mr Crook's so impulsive . . .'

'I'd have thought that doctor of yours had his head screwed on all right,' Flora told her, 'and I didn't see him hesitating much.'

'No. I suppose they see so many horrors it becomes rather run-of-the-mill to them.'

'If they find what Mr Crook seems to think they possibly may, I don't see how that could appear run-of-the-mill to anyone.'

'I can't get over the idea, all the time we were talking . . .' Dora snapped open a cupboard and started putting cups and saucers on a tray. The china clattered, and she opened another cupboard and said, 'At least we needn't wait for them to give ourselves a bit of a heartener.' She produced a brandy bottle and poured two generous dollops into tall glasses.

'I could do with that,' Flora acknowledged.

The rain began to clear as rapidly as it had started, a faint blue fold appeared in the leaden sky. Flora drained off the brandy and set down her glass.

'They've been gone a long time,' she said.

'Too long to have found nothing,' Dora agreed. 'Unless they are going further afield.'

She shivered and went to stand at the window. 'I keep trying to think—why would she go that way? If she'd gone past the rectory someone would have seen her.' Flora had nothing to say and after a moment the younger woman flung up the window-pane so that a shower of raindrops fell on her face and hands.

'Here they come!' she cried, suddenly. 'Something has happened, they're running.'

Flora came quickly to her side. 'It's Charles and—who? Oh, Mr Crook.'

Charles raced through the churchyard and burst into the cottage.

'Telephone?' he said, and snatched up the instrument. Dora poured a little brandy and put the glass in his hand. They heard him give his name and the address of the cottage.

'Send an ambulance instantly,' he commanded. 'Tell the driver to go round by the back of the churchyard, it can stop on the footpath, if that's what they call it. I might give it a different name myself, and so might a coroner. No, not to worry. We've got a doctor and we've got a priest. I dare say you'll send one of your chaps along,' he added.

'You must tell us,' cried Flora, as he seemed prepared to rush off without another word. 'Did you find . . .?'

'It's not an empty grave any longer, that's about all I can tell you at the moment. The doctor's gone for his bag of instruments, and Crook's fetching a tow-rope out of his car, says he carries one these days because some chap tried to overturn him in a ditch about a year ago, and you never know when history won't repeat itself. Wouldn't surprise me to learn he carries a spare pair of angels' wings in a suit-case against the Day of Judgment. No, Flo, stay here with Miss Chester. There's nothing you can do except re-direct that fool driver if he comes to the front door.'

He said he hadn't time to stay for tea, but he swallowed the brandy before he tore away.

'It's Dotty,' said Dora in a choked sort of voice, 'of course it's Dotty. It would be too much of a coincidence for two people to vanish on the same day.'

'He didn't actually say . . .'

'He said the grave wasn't empty, didn't he? Of course, they're six feet deep, though I'd be surprised to know that lazy old man ever got down that far. They won't do anything till the ambulance comes, I suppose.'

'I don't see why two ambulance men can help her more than a doctor and her own brother.'

'To say nothing of the rector and Mr Crook.' Dora moved to where her companion sat and took her hand. It burned as though with fever. 'They'll tell us as soon as they know.'

'If I could pinch myself, wake up, find none of it's true,' she went on. 'I remember saying once how terrible it is to be so deep in a nightmare it seems the reality, so that even when you wake you can't believe you're in your own place. And she said—this friend—it was worse when you woke from your nightmare and found *that* was the reality. I know now what she meant.' She couldn't keep silent.

'It started when Miss Plum went through the window, that was like something out of *Alice-Through-The-Looking-Glass*, and nothing that's happened since then has seemed quite true. Even this cottage, Dotty coming to live with me, making new friends . . . Hallo, there goes the ambulance. They haven't wasted much time.'

In the mysterious way in which such things happen, news of something untoward had already spread through the tiny community, and a few people had collected, like anticipatory vultures, and were clustering round the gate. Dora suddenly rushed to the front door and flung it open.

'Shoo! Shoo!' she cried, waving her arms, as though they were hens or invading cats.

'It's no good,' said Flora's weary voice. 'They've seen the ambulance, it's better than a tom-tom. And they're only following a human instinct.'

'Like a hyena is human,' stuttered Dora. She boiled an extra kettle, more for something to do than for any other reason. Then she found some more glasses and grouped them round the brandy-bottle.

It wasn't so long as it seemed before they could see Mr Crook and the rector picking their way among the graves.

They weren't hurrying this time, they could afford to take it easy now.

'They're *crawling*!' accused Dora. 'Do you suppose that means . . .' She looked at Flora, but Flora sat like a creature carved from stone.

CHAPTER THIRTEEN

'Sir Charles took his car and followed the ambulance,' Mr Bunyan said, pausing to scrape the clay from his boots on the scraper Dora had thoughtfully provided. 'The doctor went in the ambulance with Miss Garland.'

'Couldn't have prised him off with a pair of tweezers,' added Crook frankly, marching in and leaving clay prints everywhere. 'I will say that chap's got his wits about him.'

'So it was Dotty,' Dora said. 'You don't say how she is.'

'She's dead, isn't she?' stated Flora in a dull voice. 'Well of course, or they'd have told us.'

'She's breathing,' said Crook, with so much gravity both women were startled. 'I wouldn't like to go in and bat on more than that. But then a few hours in a new-made grave in this weather . . .'

'Don't,' whispered Flora. 'And all of us here.'

'I've heard you say you can survive everything but death,' observed Dora. 'And Dotty's very resilient—wouldn't you say?' She addressed her question to Crook.

'More than that, she's my client. I've only once lost a client, through foul play that is, and that was to my eternal shame. A nice old lady, too. All I can tell you,' he continued, answering Dora's question, 'is she ain't broke her neck in the fall, which is what the doc feared. Other injuries—' He shook his big head, shrugged his great shoulders. 'You can't do much of an examination *in situ* in those circumstances. So let's concentrate on the fact that she's still wobblin' on her perch, not lyin' on her back on the bottom of the cage.'

'It couldn't have been an accident,' whispered Flora, and Crook simply stared.

It was Mr Bunyan who answered. 'In Dr Martin's opinion, the lady had been drugged.'

'Drugged?' Both women stared at the rector as though they thought he'd taken leave of his senses. But Crook said, 'It 'ud explain a whole lot, everything, in fact, except the most important point of all—why would Sugar take food or drink from a stranger, specially after she'd been warned.'

'She certainly wouldn't have taken anything herself,' insisted Dora roundly. 'For one thing, there's nothing stronger than aspirin on the premises, and for another, she wouldn't even take them. I've heard her say that nobody should try to evade any experience and pain's one of them.'

'I must say she seems to have developed a remarkable philosophy since her acquaintance with you, Miss Chester,' Flora exclaimed.

'No one's suggesting she took 'em of her own free will,' Crook pointed out.

'But who—unless it's this mysterious Little Man. But though my sister-in-law was, to put it mildly, eccentric in some ways, she wouldn't have let that creature bamboozle her into opening the door to him. She only had to look out of one of the upper windows to see who was on the step.'

'Well, of course she wouldn't let him in,' cried Dora impatiently.

'Then how do you suggest . . .?'

'Didn't you say the back door was open? Well, if Dotty was working in the churchyard she wouldn't squeeze through a window or anything and suppose someone telephoned—there's that box on the Green, and from there you could see if anybody was among the graves—there may be some men who can resist a shrilling phone, but I never heard of a woman who could. And if she left the window open you couldn't miss hearing it. And while she was answering it and wondering why no one answered someone could come up behind her . . .'

'If I ever want a lady assistant,' offered Crook handsomely, 'I'll give you first refusal. All the same, wouldn't she keep her eye on the back door?'

'You can't think of everything,' protested Dora, 'and even if she did see him come in, what could she do? The front door was locked, she couldn't try and make a getaway through that, if she shouted no one would hear . . .'

'The rector might have been coming through the churchyard,' Flora suggested.

'Even so, he could hardly see into our living-room, even if he was trying,' Dora protested.

'Only forgettin' one thing,' murmured Crook, 'how did X persuade Sugar to take the drugged whatever-it-was?'

'Dr Martin thought it was probably coffee,' the rector said. 'It disguises almost any taste.'

'Dotty may be an eccentric, as you say,' retorted Dora hotly, 'but she wouldn't take a cup of coffee from someone who'd already given every impression of trying to push her off a cliff.'

'She might be playing for time,' offered Flora doubtfully, 'and she might even have drugged one of the cups, and he exchanged them . . .'

'While she was admirin' the view? You don't do Sugar justice, Lady G, honest you don't.'

'I'm only trying to find some conceivable explanation, no matter how far-fetched. The whole situation's so bizarre . . .'

'I'll tell you one thing,' said Dora, 'she never made any coffee. We only have the filter kind, and there's no sign of a used filter paper in the kitchen, let alone any cups.'

'Cups can be washed.' That was Mr Bunyan.

'If Imogen washed them it must be the first time in living memory she's ever put anything away as soon as she's finished with it,' observed Flora candidly.

'And if she had made the coffee she wouldn't turn her back on a stranger, even if he was six foot tall and looked like Gregory Peck.'

'It don't have to be a stranger,' Crook said slowly.

'But why should anyone . . . ? I tell you, there was no sign of her when I arrived.'

'A little man, you said,' murmured Crook.

'That's right.'

'Any little man could wear his collar back to front, and the hippies ain't the only ones who've adopted a more informal dress, ain't that so, Rector?'

Mr Bunyan stared. 'But however much of a hurry she was in Miss Garland wouldn't mistake a stranger for me, whatever he was wearing,' he protested. 'And you can't mean that I—I like to think we were friends.'

'I was wondering about that, too,' Crook agreed. 'Only—we keep coming back to the coffee, don't we? Now she wouldn't turn her back on someone she didn't know, but if it was a friend . . .'

'Charles always says Dotty's the most trusting creature living,' muttered Flora.

'You're not making any sense,' announced Dora, 'not if you're trying to implicate the rector. And if you think the Little Man could have tried to pass himself off as Mr Bunyan, well, the kindest thing I can say is that you never met him. Besides, drugs don't grow on trees. What drug did Dr Martin think it could be?'

'Probably pheno-barbitone.'

Flora gave a start. 'There was some of that at the Manor—I don't know if it's there now—the doctor prescribed it for Charles, but the only prescription Charles would accept would be one containing whisky. The perfectly good draughts and pills I've seen him pour down the loo—good riddance to bad rubbish, he says—but it still doesn't make sense. Even if Dotty had taken a handful—not that she'd know much about their properties, why was she only drugged and not poisoned outright?'

'Perhaps there weren't enough pheno-barbitone,' Dora suggested.

'Oh, Martin thinks it wasn't intended she should die of

drug poisoning,' Crook told them in what appeared even to Dora to be a remarkably heartless manner. 'Only—it's much easier to tote an unconscious body to the destination you've chosen for it than someone capable of fighting tooth and nail all along the line. And Sugar could fight like a tigress, take my word for that. I suppose—' he looked direct at Mr Bunyan—'it might have been quite a while before old Ben took possession of his tomb?'

'One of the shilly-shallying kind,' the rector agreed, 'blowing neither hot nor cold.'

'But would an outsider have known about the grave?' Flora said.

'He wouldn't have had to hang about the village for long without hearing. When old Tom has a grievance he makes sure the whole world knows it. Well, of course he had a grievance. It's the accepted thing that after a funeral the sexton gets his cut, so to speak. Fair enough. The incumbent gets his fee, if it's choral the choir get paid, the undertaker doesn't loan his hearse, why should old Tom be the only loser?'

'We seem to be going round and round and getting precisely nowhere,' said Flora, who was looking sheet-white. 'The only person who can enlighten us would be Dotty, if and when she comes round and if she remembers. There doesn't seem to be much point my stopping on here. Charles has his own car, he'll go straight back from the hospital, he's probably on his way now, and he'll expect to find a meal ready, the crisis hasn't yet been imagined that would stop my husband expecting his food on time.'

'Wouldn't he come back for you here?' asked Dora.

'He probably wouldn't expect me to stay. Well, what would be the sense? Everyone knows where I can be found. And he won't want to go on talking about it. In his own way, he's absurdly devoted to Imogen—I asked him once if he thought the Ancient Mariner ever got attached to his dead albatross, and he said . . .'

She was interrupted by the ringing of the telephone. 'You better wait a minute, Lady Garland,' Dora advised. 'It could be for you.'

But as it happened it was for Mr Crook.

'I'll tell 'em,' they heard him say. 'Yes, we'll all be here. What? Well, what do you expect? Thick on the ground as fleas on a hedgehog, I should think, having a whale of a time. Like the rector says, you don't get an attempted murder on your doorstep every day of the week. This ain't London or Chicago.' He hung up the receiver. 'Dr Martin calling,' he reported. 'Him and Sir Charles are on their way. Likewise the police. Everyone to stay put.'

'What more do they suppose we can tell them?' asked Flora, and her voice betrayed her exhaustion.

'They'll let us know, you can be sure of that,' Crook assured her. 'Well, not wasting much time, are they?' For a police car was drawing up outside the cottage.

'Perhaps there is news,' whispered Dora.

But the police had nothing fresh to tell them. Only, when they saw Mr Crook, the senior of the officers said, 'I wondered if we should find you here.'

'Lady's my client, ain't she?' Crook enquired.

'Does everybody in the police force know Mr Crook?' Dora wondered, and the second police officer murmured that the only coppers who didn't know Mr Crook were dead coppers.

'My husband should be here at any moment,' Flora was explaining. 'He accompanied his sister to the hospital. But you won't find he can tell you anything.'

'I understand he was present when Miss Garland was found,' said the inspector.

'I should have thought the person you wanted was the one who was present when she was put where she was found.'

Dora suddenly began to shake. 'Now then,' admonished Crook, sharply, 'no falling at the last fence. Your mate's as safe where she is now as she'd be tirling at Heaven's pin, and I dare say a whole lot safer. Always a wolf or two going around looking like an angel,' he added, for authority's benefit. 'We were trying to sift the chaff from the wheat,' he went on, 'but now you're here you can take over.'

'Very gracious,' said the inspector.

'Only Miss Chester's out—as a suspect, I mean—and the doctor's out, so unless you're trying to nominate the rector for the hot seat . . .' He broke off, as Charles came in, followed by the doctor. 'No sense asking for anything more at the moment,' he said. 'That stuff she took 'ull put her out for quite a while, and when she does come round . . .'

'She'll find a dirty great policeman sitting beside her bed, armed with a notebook and pencil,' broke in the irrepressible Mr Crook. 'Enough to put her out again, I shouldn't wonder.'

'I knew it was a mistake, her going down to Postman's Bay,' Flora said. 'I tried to dissuade her, but you might as well try to make water run uphill. Oh, I know she had Miss Chester for her bodyguard, but, without wishing to sound offensive, it hasn't eventually helped her very much.'

'Steady on, Flo!' said her husband. 'If you get a call from someone who says he's speaking for Mr Crook, and you know Mr Crook's waiting for your report, you've got to have a lot more than feminine intuition, you've got to have second sight to realize you're being taken for a ride.'

'In another minute, it'll be my fault because I wasn't here when Miss Chester left. Oh, I can see what you're all thinking. And in a way, you're right. But—to be honest—I didn't really take this story about the Little Man too seriously.'

The police inspector said, 'I thought you told us you tried to dissuade your sister-in-law from going to Postman's Bay.'

'Because Dotty—Miss Garland—must be the champion Turner-Up-Of-Flat-Stones. The fact that there could be an adder under one of them would never deter her. And I knew that Miss Styles had had this hotel at Postman's Bay. She told me that much and that her partner had proved dishonest. I didn't realize the partner was a man. But Miss Styles did fall out of a window, and I don't think her worst enemy could suggest it was suicide. So—if someone was so anxious to shut her mouth that he'd risk murder—why should he hesitate a second time?'

'You mean, you knew there was something about this hotel . . .?'

'I knew just what Miss Styles had told me, but if you'd known her you'd realize she wouldn't have suggested coming to live at the Manor in what, after all, can only be described as a dependent capacity, without some very good reason. And I saw no sense whatsoever in letting my sister in-law become involved. Because—and my husband will bear me out—Miss Garland never did anything by halves, she worked on what she called instinct.'

'But why should this man know that Miss Garland was going to Postman's Bay?'

Flora fired up suddenly. 'If your people had identified Miss Styles's murderer there would have been no need,' she declared. 'But with whoever it was still at large, and Imogen still to some degree under suspicion . . .'

For the second time Charles intervened, 'Take it easy, Flo. They're doing their best.'

'Only the lady's in the right of it,' intervened Crook. 'The police hadn't winkled out the criminal and dames are notoriously impatient. Me, I like a bit of spirit,' he added.

The police inspector recalled the phrase about looks that can kill, and wished he knew what sort they were.

'If Imogen hadn't been so crazy, telling the creature she was a private detective or whatever—I'm sure no one could have looked less like one . . .'

'You're forgetting Miss Marple and Miss Silver and the dame with the brolly,' Crook rebuked her.

'And in a way it was a kind of game for her,' added Dora

eagerly. 'Don't they say that people who live in the dark have to make their own sun? Dotty was like that. She hadn't had a very eventful life to date, so she had to make her own fun.'

For one of the few times in his life Crook felt a stab of compassion for the authorities. Dotty on her own was enough, but coupled with Dora it was sufficient to make a chap think of applying for his pension.

The rector said rather unexpectedly, 'I had a word with Willy Masters. There's not much escapes him; he didn't see anyone resembling Miss Chester's description of the Little Man, and he said there was no strange car parked on Church Green. The market crowd would park up the other end, of course,' he explained. Crook's sympathy for the police began to swell. They must have thought they'd walked straight into Cloud Cuckoo Land.

'So where does that land us?' the inspector demanded, and Crook said, 'When we've solved the problem of the doped coffee we ought to be within sight of the tape.'

'It wasn't made on the premises,' insisted Dora decidedly.

'So—X brought it with him.'

'I've told you till I'm tired that in present circumstances anyway Dotty wouldn't accept coffee from a stranger.'

'Like I said,' Crook reminded them, 'it don't have to be a stranger.'

'If you're making definite accusations,' the inspector began, but Crook said, somewhat less sunnily than usual, that he hoped he knew his duty as a citizen, which was to give the police all possible assistance. 'Law of elimination,' he continued. 'If it wasn't the Little Man, and we've no proof so far that he was even in Ditcham today, who else came to the house after Miss Chester left?'

'Well, I came, of course,' Flora agreed, 'but she wasn't here, and I didn't even find her bag in the churchyard till I came to get some water to do the rector's flowers. At that time,' she explained, 'I thought she must have dashed up to the village, arguing that no harm could come to her between here and the stores, particularly on a Monday when there are always people about.'

'Just to clear the air,' suggested Crook, 'I suppose you didn't happen to bring a Thermos of coffee with you.'

'Mind what you're saying,' exclaimed Charles. 'Even if you're a nut-case . . .'

'Lady Garland's only got to say Yes or No,' Crook pointed out.

'You're under no obligation to answer any questions Mr Crook may put to you,' said the inspector stiffly.

'I've nothing to hide. Everyone knows I take coffee with me in a Thermos if I'm likely to be out all morning. I can't face these coffee-shops, partly because half of them don't know how the stuff should be made, but mainly because I'm my husband's wife, and before I'm half-way through my first cup someone's sure to come and sit at my table and suggest I should tell Charles something . . . No one seems to think an MP's wife has any right to a private existence at all.'

'So you brought it today as usual?'

'Naturally I brought it. I thought my sister-in-law and I could share it . . .'

'Only she wasn't there.'

'That's what I said.'

'So . . .'

'I hung round for a bit, but coffee's like a drug to me, I'm absolutely addicted and when it seemed obvious that Imogen wasn't going to turn up I drank it myself. And seeing I'm in my right mind, I imagine it's obvious to everyone it hadn't been doctored.'

'Shared it with the rector, maybe?'

'It was rather late for coffee when I met Lady Garland,' interposed Mr Bunyan. 'It must have been about twelve-thirty.'

'And by that time I'd put the Thermos back in the boot of the car . . .'

'Havin' washed it under the tap?'

'Naturally.'

'So we're back at Square One. Oh, one more thing . . .'

The inspector intervened once more.

'I repeat, Lady Garland, you're under no obligation to answer any questions Mr Crook may put to you, or to make any statements, but—and this applies to everyone present—anything from now on that anyone may say, can be taken down and used in evidence.'

Dora drew an awed breath. 'I never expected to hear a policeman say that.'

'Just for the record, Lady Garland, you would have no objection to showing us the Thermos that contained the coffee.'

'She's just told you she washed it,' objected Charles.

'We like to do everything in an orderly way, Sir Charles. In the car, I think you said.'

'I don't understand what all this is about,' said Flora, 'but I'll fetch it, if you think it'll help you.'

'We'll accompany you to the car,' said the inspector easily. 'Sir Charles can come with us, if he wishes.'

'I should bloody hope so,' exploded Charles, who looked as though it would give him extreme delight to pitch a petrol bomb into the company.

The law and the Garlands departed. Dora had started to shake. The doctor caught her elbow. Mr Bunyan was staring out of the window, like Lot's wife, immobilized, as though contemplating a civilization that had started to crumble under his unbelieving eyes.

Crook oiled unobtrusively out of the room. 'Don't want to make a procession of it,' he murmured.

No one paid him the least attention.

The Thermos was in a small basket in the boot. As Flora

reached for it the inspector, now wearing gloves, she noticed, shouldered her gently aside. He removed the Thermos, shook it gently, to prove that it was indeed empty, and picked up the other contents of the basket. These were two paper cups, fitted one inside the other, and a cardboard phial marked Sweetaneesies.

'They're a form of saccharine,' Flora explained. 'I carry them everywhere.'

The inspector nodded and put the phial into an envelope. Then he separated the two beakers. There was a moment's silence, when even breathing was almost inaudible. Then the inspector said:

'Lady Garland—and you don't have to answer this if you don't wish—but *who drank out of the second cup?*'

CHAPTER FOURTEEN

'IT STILL DOESN'T make any sense.'

Dora looked from one to another of the three men remaining when the police and the two Garlands had driven away. 'How on earth could Dotty have been a danger to Lady G?'

'She did throw her weight around a bit,' said Crook frankly. 'Well, consider, good cow, consider. She'd been Miss Plum's constant companion for about two years, and whatever virtues Sugar may have I wouldn't say discretion was one of them. She was with Miss Plum the day she fell out of the window like some mysterious bird, it was just possible that above the rush of the water she had heard a word or two or even a tone or two, and sooner or later something might happen to turn her thoughts backwards. Now where did I hear that voice? that expression?—before? That sort of thing. Mind you, if she hadn't gone on her wild goose chase to Postman's Bay the odds are she'd have been safe. But she didn't only have to start askin' a lot of awkward questions, she had to confide in the little chap who'd taken over where Miss Plum left off.' He saw Dora's puzzled face. The doctor was watching Dora, Mr Bunyan was looking out of the window, watching no one. 'You didn't know Lady G. had been paying Miss Plum blackmail for years?'

'Did Dotty tell you? I mean, how would anyone dare? And anyway what did Miss Plum know? That the first Lady Garland wasn't really dead, after all, and she was living in sin with Charles? I didn't know anyone bothered about that sort of thing nowadays.'

'Not anything like that,' Crook assured her soberly. 'Somerset House has a record of her death, all square and above-board. No, where Miss Plum had Lady G over a barrel was on account of her first husband, Ernie Sinclair.'

'But he died in the war—Dotty told me.'

'Was killed in the war,' Crook corrected her, 'and not necessarily by an enemy bullet.'

'I wish you'd stop talking in riddles.' cried the doctor irritably, 'and come to the point. How did the fellow die?'

'I can only give you his widow's version, so here it is. And if you spot anything out of true, don't hesitate to mention it.'

He repeated the story that Flora had told her husband and the lawyer from London about Ernie Sinclair's death.

The rector was the first to break the silence. 'The poor woman!' he said gently.

'Poor Ernie Sinclair!' suggested Crook.

'To carry that burden for twenty years!' amplified the rector. 'To know your husband was a traitor . . .'

'I don't think, if Ernie Sinclair was a traitor, he'd have been the one to get the bullet,' offered Crook simply.

'But someone—oh no, you don't mean *Flora* shot him?'

'According to her, there was no one else there. No witness to the deathly clinch that ended in the gun going off and putting an end to poor Ernie.'

'That's a lot of bally-hoo,' said the doctor bluntly. 'If it was a hand-to-hand fight she'd have been saturated in blood, his blood. And don't tell me no one would have noticed.'

'No one did notice, because she wasn't. But someone noticed the converse.'

'You mean,' said Dora, 'that she wasn't covered with blood?'

'Precisely.'

'And that was Miss Plum?'

'She was a bit late answering the summons of the siren or the bomb or whatever, and dear Flora had gone to join the others in the shelter. I don't know if Miss Plum had heard the shot—like I said, I've only been told Lady G's version—

but she peeped into the hut or whatever and there he was —his troubles were over. She picked up the gun—and it wouldn't surprise me to know that Major Sinclair had been shot the width of the hut away. You see, I think when the lady told us her story she turned it round, so it was like seeing it in a looking-glass.'

'And Flora was the traitor?'

'I'm told being a double agent was a very paying proposition if you had the know-how and I'd say the lady had that. Mind you, none of this can be dragged up after twenty-five years, and it don't, in fact, matter to me which way it was. I'm only here to represent my client. Well, there it is. And then the luck turns in Lady G's direction again. The whole mob's dispersed on different assignments and the news comes through that Miss Plum was aboard a transport that blew up at sea. I'll bet Lady G never said her prayers more fervently than she did that night.'

'And then Miss Plum turned up again? But she hadn't any proof either. Why didn't Flora tell her to publish and be damned? She wouldn't have dared to start a story with no proof at all. Because she'd be asked why she hadn't said anything before.'

'Miss Plum had all her wits about her nearly all the time. She knew Lady G wasn't going to take a chance, even a whisper could start the ball rolling,' said Crook earnestly. He never minded mixing his metaphors. 'Lady G has come back, she's got old Miss Sinclair's money as Ernie's widow, she had the wherewithal to establish herself, and I wouldn't say lack of ambition was ever one of her faults.'

'And Miss Plum threatened all that.'

'She'd married into the County, she was Lady Himuckamuck, Sir Charles may be a wonder at the Talking Shop, but a woman like Lady G can run rings round him any hour of the day or night. I dare say he didn't know what hit him till he heard himself saying I will, and found his best man handing him the ring.'

'And she paid Miss Plum—but Miss Plum went to live at the Manor. Wasn't that crazy?'

'I don't doubt Miss Plum had her reasons. In my experience no blackmailer stops short at one victim and most of them over-reach themselves in the end. That's when they get careless. Blackmail may be money for old rope, but even old rope can be twisted into a noose. Remember the story of the cockroach and the tortoise? A cockroach was being threatened by a tortoise, so it sought refuge in the only place where it could hope for immunity, under the tortoise's armpit. That must be one of the occupational hazards of bein' a tortoise, you can't scratch under your own armpit.'

'And Lady Garland was Miss Plum's tortoise. And Dotty . . .'

'She was her bodyguard. Remember the hymn—"gird thy heavenly armour on, wear it ever night and day"—Sugar was Miss Plum's armour. She'd argue no one would risk a capital crime on the Manor property or with a witness like Sugar who had eyes like the beasts in the Revelation, before and behind.'

'So why did Miss Plum come to grief?'

'She's like a lot of the sorority, she became careless, and when the sisters become careless they start to push their luck. And that's when they catch a crab.'

'Dotty always said it couldn't be very interesting for Miss Plum at the Manor, she seems to have worked very hard.'

'I dare say the cockroach didn't specially like the tortoise's armpit, armpits being what they are. But there must have been others besides Lady G who wouldn't have gone into mourning if Miss P had been run over by a bus. And that's what Miss P didn't remember.'

'But what could she have done after so long?' Dora's voice was still full of bewilderment.

Crook shrugged. 'Stepped up her demands, maybe. Or started to make her power felt to a degree that Lady G found beyond bearing. It's not always the money the blackmailer wants, though he won't say No to it, it's the power. I dare say she hadn't had much authority before, it 'ud be the breath of life to her.'

'Or, of course, Dotty may have had the right idea when she said perhaps Miss Plum pushed Sumner off the cliff. Oh, I know it could never be proved, but no one can be logical all the time. And she couldn't prove Ernie Sinclair's death either. Mr Crook, do you think Lady Garland pushed Miss Plum out of the window?'

'We know someone did, and it 'ud be someone Miss Plum wouldn't think she'd cause to fear. I'd say she was expected at the Montblanc, and Miss Plum arranged for Miss G to be in the bath, a place you can't suddenly burst out of, not if you hear voices. No doubt she thought she held all the aces in the pack, and I dare say she did, but what she didn't remember was the fifth ace the other chap has up his sleeve, along of his arm.'

'And if Flora moved towards the window Miss Plum could have gone with her—is that what you mean?'

'That cockroach,' said Crook impressively, 'was only safe so long as he stayed tight in the tortoise's armpit. Let him come out for even half a minute for a breath of air, and he's done, finished, kaput. She was accustomed to making snap decisions—my guess is that Ernie came back unexpected and caught her red-handed and she didn't stop to argue, maybe he was a patriot who really would have handed her over, I think she pulled out her little gun—these MI characters were often armed in their own interest, I'm told —one thing, she didn't have time to think. And she could move like a flash. One push, Miss P topples, Lady G's out of the room like a shaft of light, down the stairs—safer than the lift, no one recognizes a stranger on stairs, then into the street where a demented female is staring at what's left of Miss Plum—shock for her, too, and shock slows up the mental processes—over the road and into the phone-box. She must have worked it all out. Fact that the line was dead wouldn't make any difference. She handed it to me on a plate, you know,' he added, almost reverently. 'I could have done it, she said. And, of course, I've no alibi. Told the usual story, went to a teashop on her owney-oh, safer really than a cinema, might get asked awkward questions, but a teashop—no!'

'Have you a grain of proof of any of this?' Martin asked. 'Or are you merely postulating a theory?'

'If I had any proof I'd have handed it to the fuzz long ago, so I must be whatever-you-said-it-was a theory.'

'But would she take the risk?'

'There was a picture in a boys' paper when I was a kid, showing two crocs, one either side of a little piccaninny, and they're both opening their smiling jaws and saying, "Of two evils choose the least," and the little Black Sambo is saying, "But which is the least?" I guess that was Lady Garland's problem, too. Miss Plum was getting greedy, there was no knowing what she might demand next. And then Lady G had been there before, so to speak, once anyway.'

'You mean, her husband?'

'Well, I don't have much doubt about him, do you? And it wouldn't surprise me when the books are opened on the Last Day to know she knew more about Auntie's death than she ever let on.'

'Auntie?'

'Ernie's Auntie Sinclair. A wealthy old lady—I took the trouble to check at Somerset House. Old lady, living on her own except for Nursie, who'd been in attendance for fifteen years, and I dare say hoped to reap her whirlwind when the old lady handed in her dinner-pail. Nursie went out every Thursday afternoon, and it was on a Thursday that the old lady did her Jack-and-Jill act and came tumbling down. Thursday was the day Lady G—who wasn't Lady G then, of course—used to go over and keep dear departed Ernie's auntie company, and oh why, why had she chosen that particular afternoon to go to a French cinema show?'

'If she was in a cinema she couldn't have been with Miss Sinclair,' offered Dora sensibly.

'Meaning no one saw her go there. But I dare say no one saw her go into the cinema either. But old ladies have a way of falling downstairs if they get a sharp push in the back. Or if someone ties a bit of string across the head of the stairs, nips down and rings the front-door bell, knowing Auntie's all alone in the house. So—wham, down she comes, sight not being what it was, I dare say . . .'

'Your imagination does you credit,' the doctor told him. 'But there's no certainty that a fall downstairs will break your neck.'

'In which case she'd no doubt have died of shock,' offered Crook comfortably.

'Did Flora get the money?' Dora asked.

'Go to the top of the class,' Crook congratulated her. 'She knew Auntie had left her the bulk of the boodle in her will, but there was always Nursie hovering on the touch line, and Nursie was *in situ* seven days a week. Maybe the old lady dropped a hint—Nursie not so young as she used to be, the faithful servant . . .'

'But suppose Flora couldn't have proved she'd been to the pictures—if questions were asked, I mean?' Dora urged.

'You bet your sweet life she'd be able to prove it. She'd keep her half of her ticket that afternoon if she'd never kept a ticket before. It was Nursie found the old lady, Nursie coming back at seven, a bit earlier than usual, rang the doctor, rang Ernie's widow, and got a dusty answer. And for why? Because Flora Sinclair was sitting out the second house—she wouldn't dare not go, questions might be asked, she had to commit that film to memory. No,' he added, answering the doctor's unspoken question, 'I haven't got any proof of that either. But I don't need it, I ain't the police.'

'Could Dotty have found out about them?' wondered Dora. 'But even if she did, and didn't tell me because it was a family matter, she wouldn't have involved her own people. And Flora Garland must have known I wouldn't just take it as a visitation from Heaven if something happened to Dotty. I'm like the burying beetle—you know, the kind that goes on scooping out the earth till it's dug a hole big enough to hide its victim.'

'Ah,' said Crook gravely, 'but don't it occur to you you mightn't have been given the time?'

'You mean—' Dora sounded scandalized—'I might have been in danger?'

'Oh, come on, Crook,' the doctor exclaimed, 'you're making her sound like Lucrezia Borgia.'

'Which one was she?' asked Crook guilelessly.

'So—who was it who rang up pretending to be Parsons?'

'Who do you suppose?' Crook asked.

Dora's face was expressive of such self-contempt that Martin caught her by the arm.

'You can't surely blame yourself for that?'

'If I'd realized it wasn't a London call I'd have known there was something fishy.'

'Not any more,' said the doctor. 'You can get through direct from London without calling the operator. I don't say it works from your end—didn't I hear that Lady G ran a sort of amateur ENSA during the war—had rather a mannish voice anyway. Naturally she wouldn't assume Crook's personality—the Archangel Gabriel could hardly copy *him*—but if a chap calling himself Parsons and identifying himself as your legal adviser's right-hand man gives you a message—well, I'd be sorry for any man who married a woman who could be that suspicious.'

'Must have seemed as if fitted like a glove,' Crook acknowledged. 'You and Sugar had handed Lady G the situation on a plate the day before, you hadn't had a chance of opening your grief to yours truly, there was this mysterious little man who'd been seen by the doctor and by Ponting, if that was the fellow's name, and probably there are half-a-dozen other chaps who could identify him—you couldn't have a more hopeful suspect—Lady G wasn't going to take any chances of getting herself identified with that lot at Postman's Bay, though, come to think of it, I don't suppose most of them used names their mums and dads would have recognized. The trouble with honest people,' he added with candour, 'is they spike you in the belly much more often than your out-and-out villain. Having nothing to hide, it don't occur to them to use any finesse. But it's true, they'll say, why shouldn't I tell it? Oh yes, Lady G thought she had it made. Trouble with these Clever Dicks is it never seems to occur to them the other chap may have brains, too.'

'Seeing you know all the answers,' said the doctor (and I'd as lief have him on my side as agin me, Crook decided), 'maybe you can explain how Lady G could have got a full-grown woman like Miss Garland from the tombstone she was trimming to a new-made grave half across the churchyard. I know about the old cave-dwellers who dragged their victims around by the hair of their heads, but you can't do that with a lady like Miss Garland whose hair's about as long as a well-shorn poodle.'

'She wouldn't have to drag her,' explained Crook. 'Lady had the use of her legs.'

'You mean, she meekly walked over to the grave?'

'How would she know there was a grave there?' Dora demanded.

'She knew when I met her,' put in the rector, and they all looked as if one of the ancient church statues, for the most part noseless and nameless, had spoken. 'She spoke of the tarpaulin.'

'They were talking about it in the village,' put in Dora. 'The postman told us.'

'But why was she coming from that direction?' Dora asked

in perplexed tones. 'She wouldn't approach the cottage from that side, and you can't really see the grave unless you came in from the far lane.'

'That was the main reason old Ben picked the site. "I don't want a lot of Nosey Parkers staring at me when I can't defend myself," that's what he said. "A dead man's got a right to a bit of privacy." '

'You can work it out for yourself,' said Crook thoughtfully. For once his natural ebullience seemed to be blown away like chaff on the wind. 'She waits till she's sure Miss Chester's out of the way, then along she comes, maybe she did put in an appearance at the Market, though she'd be about as difficult to overlook as a shire horse—still, now everyone gets these free spectacles their sight seems a lot worse than it was when they had to depend on good sense as well as their own eyesight—down she comes, finds Sugar working in the churchyard. Hobby of hers?' he added to the rector.

But it was Dora who answered. The rector had gone into another meditative coma. 'She always says that under the Welfare State people think no end about the living, but they've no time to consider the dead. And she did say she fancied being out of doors while I was in London, more than being mewed up in four walls. Who wrote that story about the snake that suddenly came through the ceiling? But I'm interrupting you, Mr Crook.'

'Too easy,' Crook said. 'Lady G comes round the side of the house, finds her sister-in-law in the pink. "What's all this about Miss Chester going to London and leaving you on your owney-oh?" ' His audience started. It was uncanny how his voice changed, he might have been an amateur ventriloquist. (Well, where's the sense of mixing with some of the shocking bad hats that have come my way if I haven't learned a tip or two? Crook would have enquired.) ' "But I'm not on my owney-oh, you're here, Flora." "Good heavens, how can you stand the sun? In any case, it's time for elevenses, can't we find a bit of shade?"

'And she scans the horizon and sees the fig-tree and, knowing there's a conveniently close empty grave, she suggests why don't we sit over there. Out with the Thermos—Sugar got a sweet tooth?' he added in his normal voice.

'Dotty? Oh, she likes sugar in her coffee, if that's what you mean.'

'That's just what I mean. Lady G pours out the coffee—nice disposable cups, you see—she can't have guessed they were goin' to prove her undoing—and while Sugar's taking off her gardening gloves or whatever she puts in a pellet or two from the Sweetaneesie box, only, of course, they ain't Sweetaneesies. And a lady a lot less muscular than her ladyship could push back a tarpaulin and roll a body into the grave. Mind you, she wasn't to be poisoned, just doped, so she couldn't put up any fight. And it could be weeks, months even, before anybody thought of shifting the tarpaulin again. Of course, if old Ben Whosit changed his mind overnight, that 'ud have put the cat well and truly among the pigeons . . .'

'Oh, don't, Mr Crook,' pleaded Dora. 'I can't believe it. People don't behave like that—not to their own relations.'

'Losing your memory?' asked Crook kindly. 'She was an old hand at the game. There was Hubby Ernie Sinclair—no, don't ask me about proof, I never saw the Pyramids so I couldn't actually prove they're there but I never heard of anyone who doubted it. Then Miss Plum—I don't think a hotel like the Montblanc would take kindly to a gent visiting a lady in her bedroom, not with all those lounges and bars on the premises—and anyway, if our Mr Smyth wanted a word with Miss Plum, what was wrong with Madame Tussaud's, where they were due to meet the next day in any case? And, like I said, it wouldn't make me pass out with amazement if I heard the Recording Angel say she was responsible for old Miss Sinclair's demise.'

'But Flora?' Dora was very hard to convince.

'Well, but ask yourself—who had access to the drug? We know there was some at the Manor. Who drank out of the second cup? You mark my words, when the lab boys have done their job, you'll find there were traces of the phenobarbitone in one of those beakers. Can't wash a cardboard cup like you can a china one.'

'She must have been crazy to keep the cups at all,' Dora protested.

'I don't suppose she meant to. But she thought she had a clear field. If she'd left them around here they'd have attracted attention—I don't suppose you go in for that sort of labour-saving devices—no, my guess is she meant to add to the litter on the Green on the way back—always a deal of litter after an auction or market or whatever . . .'

'She wanted to go home while Sir Charles was still at the hospital,' Dora recalled slowly. 'That would have been her chance.'

'Poor Sir Charles!' said Dora.

'Spare Lady Garland a thought,' said the rector unexpectedly. 'There's a moral blindness as well as the physical kind, though it doesn't excite the same sympathy.'

'Still, you don't let blind folk go around on their own, walking under traffic or pushing old folk into the gutter. And your morally blind ones—only I call them opportunists—the sooner they're under lock and key where they can't do any more harm, the better for us all.'

'What's the charge going to be?' asked Martin. 'Miss Garland is going to recover, so it can't be murder; as for the other victims, oh, I admit you've cooked up a very pretty case against Lady G, but you've no proof, and I doubt if there's a lawyer living who'd take the thing into court.'

'It's nothing to me how many people the lady put underground,' Crook pointed out. 'I'm only here to defend Sugar's good name; after this I don't think anyone's goin' to suggest it was her pushed Miss Plum out of the window, because, if so, why was someone trying to give her a free ticket to a better world? Now when we've made our statements, I'm going straight back to the Smoke. Give you a lift, honey?' He turned invitingly to Dora.

'You're forgetting,' said Dora. 'I don't live in London any longer. My home is here.'

'That's what you think,' said Mr Worldly-Wise Crook, 'but it won't be your home much longer, not with the British Press being what it is. The Montblanc won't be in it.'

'If you imagine Dora will be any safer in that museum piece of yours—why, a helicopter couldn't miss it,' cried the doctor indignantly. 'Besides, she has to go somewhere, and it's going to be the same wherever she is.'

'No little sister or anyone?' suggested Crook wistfully.

'My only sister's in America with a brand-new husband.'

'Brothers?'

'A Dean in the North, who'd consider I'd brought discredit on the cloth getting mixed up in this sort of affair at all.'

'There's a bobby outside,' Crook suggested. 'If you was to knock off his helmet they could hold you for assault, and I can't think of any place where you'd be safer for the night than a prison-cell. Probably treat you like Grace Darling or someone,' he added hopefully, 'and they'd put a guard on the cottage. Otherwise everyone 'ud be stripping it for mementoes.'

When that plan found no favour he gave up. When they'd made the statements demanded of them by authority he caught Dora by the elbow and rushed her into The Superb. The reporters were gathering like vultures round a carcass. Crook shoved his great red head out of the car window.

'If you chaps don't clear the road pronto,' he threatened, 'I'll mow the lot of you down and swear it was self-defence.'

'He'd do it, what's more,' said one of the pressmen. 'We should get danger-money with chaps like him about.'

CHAPTER FIFTEEN

Crook had hoped to be present when, on the following day, a recovered Imogen gave her story to the police. But on this occasion authority had Ward Sister's backing, so Crook and Dora had to wait another twenty-four hours. In view of the publicity attendant on the case Imogen had been given a side-ward for one, about the size of a mouse-trap. Sister took one glance at Crook and said her first duty was to her patient. Miss Chester might pay a short visit . . .

'I'm her man of affairs,' explained Crook, with his engaging alligator grin. 'You try and keep me out and I'll turn myself into a rattle-snake and come oozing through the keyhole. This is a criminal case, remember. If you want to protect your patient against one, you should keep your eyes for the boys in blue.'

'You know all the first part,' Dotty assured him when a disapproving Sister had retired. 'Dora will have told you about the phone call from Mr Parsons and the message that Flora or someone should come in to stay with me till she got back. I thought it was being a bit—well, fussy—but Flora said of course she'd come as soon as she could, and till then to wait in the house and not admit anyone. Well, I waited a bit, but she didn't come right away so I went into the graveyard. It's very friendly there, you never feel you're alone. There's an old woman buried there, no one seems to have liked her—not that anything much is done in country churchyards these days. Once upon a time the long grass was scythed, but then the scythers wouldn't do it for fear of harming their tools. Some of the stones are very low in the grass, and a vigorous man could snap a blade. I was thinking about this one—she was supposed to have been a witch—

wondering if she'd like to know that anyone bothered still or if she'd think it a dead liberty—that's old Tom's expression if he sees you doing anything in the churchyard—when I heard someone calling and I looked up and there was Flora. There's a gate into the churchyard from the lane behind the cottage and she said, "What or earth are you doing out here? I've been knocking and ringing . . ." So I had to tell her I'd blocked the bell—it's quite easy, you just put a bit of paper between it and the clapper, so if anyone did ring I shouldn't hear.'

'How were you going to hear Lady G?'

'Oh, I knew she'd come round rapping on the windows till I let her in. You'd need to be the Archangel Gabriel to keep Flora out. "I thought you must have fainted," she said, and I told her, "You know I never faint except in church and that was only the once," so she came in and she asked about the grave and did I know why Mr Crook wanted to see you, Dora, and not me. So I said it was like the Charge of the Light Brigade, theirs not to reason why, and you'd tell me when you came back, and she said she couldn't think why I wanted to work outside in the burning sun—but I like the sun and she always said she did, too. We used to say sometimes we must have been salamanders in an earlier incarnation, but she did look a bit—not exactly pale but not quite like herself. "It must be time for elevenses," she said. "How about a cup of coffee?" I knew she's a coffee-addict if that's the word, but I said I was afraid we'd run out and you'd be bringing some back from London, but I had some iced lemonade in the fridge and wouldn't that be cooler?'

Crook had a vision of them, the one so full of sinister purpose, the other equally resolute but not in the least aware of the issue at stake.

'So?' he said.

'I might have guessed Flora would have the last word. "You know I'm a travelling café," she said. "When you rang I thought I'd bring the Thermos over, and we could have a cup apiece in the cottage, but if you'd rather stay out here—only can't we find a patch of shade? How about that tree over there?" '

'Meaning old Ben Plowright's tree?'

'Of course, there was a shady place nearer, where that big flat gravestone—the Murdocks—is. It's the size of a table, and I'm sure picnickers have often used it for one, and I don't suppose the dead mind, why should they, a bit of company for them, but Flora has a thing about sitting on graves—she *says* it's because they're so old and moss-grown they make marks on your dress and you often can't get them out, not even with this new wonder detergent. Anyway, we trailed over to the tree, and it was lovely and cool there. I didn't draw Flora's attention to the grave just behind us, because she didn't seem to have noticed it, and that might have upset her, so we settled down and she poured out the coffee into two of those horrid hygienic cardboard cups—I never think coffee tastes the same out of them, but she says they're economical, only where's the sense in being economical if it costs you pleasure? Still, she gave me one and then said, "I haven't sugared it, but these are just as good and less fattening," and she produced a little bottle of things like aspirins, to look at, I mean, and she said, "They're every bit as good as sugar, I take them everywhere." She shook about four into my cup, which she said would be the equivalent of two lumps of sugar, but, as Dora knows, I always take three. I said, "I don't think they do their job very well," so Flora said, "You probably haven't got enough," and put two more into my hand. Only—I know they say you can't taste anything through coffee, but I did think they had a funny taste, and I certainly didn't want any more, so I said, "Oh, look out, Flora! That spider!" She's terrified of spiders—so while she drew up her legs and hunted about and slapped away with a handkerchief I slid the two extra tablets into the pocket of my gardening apron.'

'Tell the police that?' asked Crook.

Dotty looked amazed. 'Of course. I thought you had to tell them everything.'

'I hope they were grateful,' said Crook. 'That is, if the tablets were still there.'

'Oh, I'm sure they were. They're deep pockets and I put them under my gardening gloves.' Her brow furrowed. 'I still don't understand, did they have something to do with me fainting? Flora's so careful about things, if she had a name like they do in Indian tribes hers would be Law-and-Order. I do remember feeling suddenly rather dizzy and Flora said, "No wonder, how long had you been cutting in that blazing sun without a hat?" And something about hoping Dora knew what she was taking on. Then she said, "Why not have forty winks?" and I was a bit surprised, because that's not her sort of expression, and then she went on, "I'll keep watch in case the rector appears, and wake you in good time." But I didn't see why Mr Bunyan should mind me dropping off in his graveyard—he calls it God's Acre, and I dare say it doesn't make so much difference whether you sleep above or below ground. It's not like going to sleep during one of Mr Bunyan's sermons, though actually they're so unexpected you have to stay awake.'

'So you had forty winks?' suggested Crook.

'More than that, I should think. Because the policeman said I must have rolled over and fallen into old Ben's grave. I thought how furious he'd be if he knew. He lived with a sister for years, and she did absolutely everything for him, but he was the only one allowed to sit in the big armchair. Once let a woman share your kingdom, he'd say . . . And then I remembered seeing a tarpaulin over the grave, and there wasn't any wind, so it couldn't have been shifted, and anyway I thought it was against the Law to leave a grave open—and dangerous, too. It's like leaving your bed unmade all day, you can be sure that's the one afternoon someone—a window-cleaner, say—will call and want to go into your room. And another thing I don't understand—why didn't Flora stop me rolling into the grave? She was supposed to be there till Dora came back.' Suddenly her eyes darkened, her cheeks paled. 'Is that why no one will tell me anything about her? Because something happened to her, too? Did the Little Man . . .?' She stopped dead.

'What's the last thing you remember telling your sister-in-law?'

'I said I had a great surprise for her, it was going to be a surprise to the whole neighbourhood. They could never complain again nothing ever happens. She said was it something to do with mysterious Mr Smyth, and I said well, in a way, he did come into it, in fact, he was a pretty important participator.' She brought the word out proudly.

'What were you going to tell her?' Dora demanded.

Imogen's eyes widened. 'About you and Dr Martin, of course. Oh, I know everybody thinks I'm a bit—you know—' she touched her forehead—'but I have eyes for more than reading inscriptions on gravestones. I expect he fell in love with you that first afternoon at Penton,' she went on. 'I mean, he certainly didn't get mixed up in this just for me, and doctors are like Members of Parliament, they can't afford a lot of publicity, not unless it's worth while.'

'I think you must have a temperature,' said Dora firmly.

'If anyone's got a temperature it's you. You should just *see* the colour of your face. Anyway, think how useful it'll be having a doctor in the family.' She drew a deep breath. 'I do think it's interesting the things that happen to the people I know. Oh!' Her brow clouded again. 'You didn't tell me about Flora.'

'Leave this to me,' Crook murmured, and he told her.

Ward Sister was furious. 'It's a good thing they don't issue tomahawks to nursing staff,' observed Crook piously, 'or there'd have been a scalpless ghost haunting the hospital for the next thousand years.'

'My patient,' stormed Sister, 'is Far Too Weak—'

'Weak?' howled Mr Crook. 'Take a gander at this, Sister. She gets followed by a thug who tries to push her off a cliff—don't make any error about that, she shouldn't be tucked up nice and cosy in your bed at this moment but be tossing to and fro among the crags till you wouldn't know if she was fish or flesh or good red herring; she's then doped, pushed into a grave, hauled up by a couple of chaps who're lost to the winching profession, rushed here in a kind of a hearse and incarcerated in a cell, and in forty-eight hours she's as chirpy as a sparrow.'

'Only if the sparrows wore mourning,' Sister snapped.

'That was a nice come-back,' approved Crook. 'I have to be on my way now, but Miss Chester could stay a bit—friend that sticketh closer than a Sister.' He laughed uproariously at his own idiotic joke.

Imogen put out her hand and grasped Dora's. Sister, that Iron Duchess, actually relented.

'Twenty minutes, not a second more.'

She followed Crook firmly down the corridor. 'You can take that worried frown off your face, Sister,' Crook assured her. 'If ever I saw a dame all set to get the Queen's telegram on achieving her century, that one is it.'

Flora, remanded in custody on a charge of attempted murder, bail being refused in the circumstances (and lucky for her, reflected Crook, at least this way she wouldn't be the victim of a road accident or be found in one of the wayside ponds after dark—the feeling for Imogen when the story broke astounded everyone, even Dora) faced her lawyer, who was more afraid of her than he'd be of the Lord Chief Justice.

'This charge,' she said scornfully, 'who's going to substantiate it?'

'Your sister-in-law . . .'

'You shouldn't have much difficulty in persuading Counsel she was in no condition to remember anything clearly.'

'You might have some difficulty in persuading a jury (a) that Miss Garland drugged herself and (b) uncovered a grave for the express purpose of rolling into it.'

'The grave was never covered, I should have noticed it.'

'There is a witness who recalls your mentioning the tarpaulin.'

'Then it's your job to prove he's mistaken.'

'And how do you propose to explain your leaving Miss Garland when you had come for the express purpose of remaining with her until her friend returned?'

'She was fast asleep . . .'

'You're not forgetting you told your husband you hadn't set eyes on her.'

'Whose side are you supposed to be on?' Flora demanded.

'There is, moreover, the laboratory evidence of the phenobarbitone traces in one of the cups, and a number of phenobarbitone tablets in the phial.'

'I don't know why you worry me with all these problems,' exclaimed Flora grandly. 'I'm employing you to get me a verdict of Not Guilty. How you do it is your concern, not mine. And I can assure you of this,' she added maliciously, 'if your name was Arthur Crook you'd do it.'

'Now that Lady Dracula is unlikely to be released to the world for a good many years, how about our considering our own plans?' Dr Martin suggested to Dora, not long after the last recorded conversation.

'I have been thinking,' Dora assured him. 'I wondered if it would be a good idea to take Dotty away for a little, right out of the country, I mean. She said something once about Venice.'

'I always intended to spend my honeymoon in Venice.'

'Do you know,' Dora's voice became dreamy, 'if you're buried in Venice they take your coffin on a gondola or something to a special island—I can't remember its name—and the mourners follow in smaller gondolas, and wreaths are thrown upon the water.'

'I wasn't for the moment associating Venice with funerals,' said the doctor drily.

'I wonder what happened to the Little Man,' brooded Dora. 'Of course, his name wasn't Smyth with or without a Y—I expect he's overseas somewhere by this time . . .'

'And if he's got any sense he won't come back. I don't mean just because of the law, but personally I wouldn't care to be on Lady Garland's list of rejects.'

'But she's in prison.'

'A little thing like that wouldn't stop her. Still, never mind about her. How soon will you marry me, Dora, my darling?'

'But you hardly know me,' Dora cried, 'only as the other half of Dotty.'

'You forget,' said Ambrose Martin solemnly, 'I am a member of a magical profession.'

'Yes, of course. You have phosphorescent eyes, or something. Then you ought to see I can't marry you out of the blue and leave Dotty stranded like a whale.'

'What's wrong with her going back to keep house for her brother? She may not have the hostess qualities of Lady Garland, but at least he needn't fear arsenic in his soup.'

'She can't do that, because Sir Charles is going on this special mission—it was in *The Times* a few days ago—they said they meant to appoint him before all the troubles started, and perhaps they did, but of course, it's very convenient for them now. Though I should think Charles was pretty inconvenient for them most of the time. He will ask the most awkward questions in the House, Dotty says, and it's so embarrassing when the Minister concerned doesn't know the answer.'

'It's your turn to make a suggestion,' Ambrose told her.

Dora thought. Then she said, 'I know. We'll ask Mr Crook. He's certain to know the answer.'

'In Victorian times,' said Mr Crook briskly, when the question was posed to him, 'a lady often took a bosom friend with her on her honeymoon, just for the company.'

'I can give Dora all the company she needs on her honeymoon,' Ambrose assured him.

'How about Dotty making a match of it with the rector? I dare say he'd love the idea if someone was to put it into his head. And, mind you, they'd get on like a house on fire. She don't give me the impression of the cat that walks alone, not from choice. And they've got a lot in common, both live on the other side of the moon and don't even notice the difference. All that's wanted is someone to drop a penny in the slot to start the machine working.'

'I knew he'd think of something,' said Dora happily after Crook had left them. 'Don't you think that's a wonderful idea? Then we could keep Pieman's Cottage for week-ends, if you ever get any, and I shan't lose touch with Dotty . . .'

'There's the small matter of getting the rector to propose,' Ambrose murmured.

'I've heard him say what a warren that old Rectory is, and no one will come as housekeeper for what the church can afford to pay, and I'm sure Dotty isn't mercenary-minded, and if he thought she had nowhere to go . . .'

'I see you've got the poor devil hamstrung already,' the doctor said.

'Once he gets used to the idea he'll love it. Oh, and did you remember to ask Mr Crook about being our best man?'

'He said it was against his principles to attend bang-up weddings in West London churches, and you can't make a silk purse out of a sow's ear.'

'We don't have to have a bang-up wedding,' said Dora simply, 'and I hope you assured him we'd sooner have this sow's ear than all the silk purses in Bond Street.'

'How does he do it?' the doctor wondered, as others had wondered before him. 'Personal magnetism? It beats me. He's as good an example of the Darwinian theory as ever I've come across; if I saw him chittering at me out of a tree I wouldn't be a mite surprised, he wears the most awful clothes, come to think of it an ape 'ud dress better—and yet you all go in to bat for him.'

'It's you that's the ape,' cried his beloved warmly. 'You've missed the whole point. He's—oh, don't you see, it's just that he's a good man.'

After which, as Holy Writ hath it, there was silence in Heaven for the space of half-an-hour.

››› If you've enjoyed this book and would like to discover more great vintage crime and thriller titles, as well as the most exciting crime and thriller authors writing today, visit: ›››

www.ingramcontent.com/pod-product-compliance
Ingram Content Group UK Ltd.
Pitfield, Milton Keynes, MK11 3LW, UK
UKHW022317280225
455674UK00004B/345

9 781471 910388